OVEREMOTIONAL

DAVID FENNE

INK ROAD

First published in the UK in 2023 by Ink Road

INK ROAD is an imprint and trade mark of
Black & White Publishing Ltd
Nautical House, 104 Commercial Street, Edinburgh EH6 6NF

A division of Bonnier Books UK
4th Floor, Victoria House, Bloomsbury Square, London, WC1B 4DA
Owned by Bonnier Books
Sveavägen 56, Stockholm, Sweden

A CIP catalogue record for this book is available from the British Library.

ISBN: 978 1 78530 472 9

1 3 5 7 9 10 8 6 4 2

Typeset by Data Connection
Printed and bound in Great Britain by Clays Ltd, Elcograf S.p.A.

MIX
Paper from
responsible sources
FSC® C018072

www.ink-road.com

For John,
My doofus, my butthead, my everything.
book boop

Author's Note

OVEREMOTIONAL is a story about friendship, love, and lone-liness. It's about finding who you are and where you fit in the world. There are depictions of violence, drugging, and references to medical experimentation conducted on pregnant women in the past. While it is my hope this book is for everyone, I am including this note so that those sensitive to these issues can make an informed decision from the very beginning. After all, emotions have power, even if they aren't magic.

1

Steven

The first time I kissed another boy was probably the worst day of my life. One moment I'm waiting for the upstairs loo at a yay-we-did-our-first-week-of-mock-exams party, the next, I'm being led into a bedroom, and I'm making out with a total stranger.

And then his head exploded.

Like, actually exploded. I was dressed like a zombie at the time, which basically meant I'd ripped some old clothes and let Freya squirt me with fake blood. Unoriginal, but at least it disguised the *real* blood.

Oh god. The real blood.

Just what the hell was I supposed to do? I couldn't exactly explain to the police that I'd snogged someone's head out of existence. I had been careless. My powers had been getting stronger, but I thought one party would be fine. That I could keep my emotions in check. And now they've . . . killed someone. *I've* killed someone. So, I did what any seventeen-year-old walking atom bomb would do.

I ran.

Ran home, packed a bag and kept on running. Okay, there were some buses in there too, but I think it's safe to say no one will find me here. Grunsby-on-Sea: the official arse end of nowhere.

I need to stop thinking about it. I can't let myself get overemotional. Whenever I do, things ... happen. It's weird. Whatever I feel seems to manifest in some strange and horrific way. I can't be happy without inflicting misery. It's like the universe is conspiring against me – constantly playing cruel tricks. I try not to indulge it. I try not to feel anything.

That's why I'm alone.

No one around to hurt. It's safer for everyone else if I just stay here by myself and keep my emotions (and these damn manifestations) under control.

It's 11 a.m., but I just woke up. I say "woke," but I don't think I actually slept. My body was exhausted from lugging boxes around, but my mind just doesn't want to stop. Every night, I replay that party – that popping noise – over and over. Can't remember the last time I got eight hours.

I throw on some clothes and head into the kitchen: bread in the toaster, kettle on. It's a revolting kitchen, but not because it's dirty; it isn't. The moment I feel even a whiff of disgust, I draw all the dirt and dust in the flat toward me like a human vacuum. I guess I attract what disgusts me. Handy, but showering it all off is a pain. No, the kitchen is revolting because it hasn't been redecorated since 1954. Busy floral wallpaper is peeling from the walls, and the pink paint that once coated the cupboards is chipped and flaky. I wouldn't be surprised if the whole flat were made of asbestos.

I've been considering calling myself an emomancer. Makes sense. Pyromancers control fire and necromancers bring back the dead – at least in Dungeons and Dragons or whatever. So, emomancers have emotion powers. I mean, it sounds like I should dye my hair black and wear a trench coat, but what else can I call it? I don't think there are emos anymore anyway – a casualty of the noughties. I was too young to be one, but I do remember Freya's older brother straightening his hair within an inch of its life at the time.

The kettle boils, and I scoop some instant coffee (the supermarket own-brand kind that tastes like someone blended up topsoil) into a mug. I don't trust myself to have anything nicer. Two weeks ago, I tried a pumpkin spice latte and shattered every window in the high street. It was delicious, though. The memory of the spicy-sweet drink rushes to my lips, and my toast catches fire, yellow light fizzing around my hand.

Great.

At least burned toast might mean sunshine today. But sunshine might make me happy and cause a sinkhole in Grunsby town centre ...

I stop myself thinking. It's something I learned from one of those meditation apps. Not sure super-powered teenagers were their target demographic, but it works. I just picture white and nothing else, and usually everything balances out. No thoughts, no emotions, no *tricks*. I call them that because they are rarely treats.

I try to scrape the burned bits from the toast, but it's completely charred. My tricks seem to be getting stronger and more frequent lately. Used to be, I'd only cause a trick if there was a particularly strong emotion, and even then, there were long periods between them. Now I run out of fingers counting all the ones before lunch.

I thought a job might take my mind off things and keep my tricks under control. Plus I could use the cash. When I came to

3

Grunsby-on-Sea, a week or so ago, I tried to be a bartender in a run-down pub called the Lazy Cough. I was keeping everything together until some middle-aged hag demanded I make her a Porn Star Martini. What even is that? She kept shouting that Millennials were "entitled slackers" despite the fact I was born after the millennium, so I haven't touched a pair of skinny jeans in my life. She just kept going on. I could feel the tricks bubbling up inside me, feeding off my anger until I just couldn't take it and told her to shut up.

That was when I realised my anger manifests as fear in other people. Everyone fled the pub in terror like I'd brought an emotional support lion with me. I was banned from the premises and told I was lucky they didn't call the police.

Since then, I've been unloading cargo at the wharf when the ships come in. It's hard, manual work, but at least I don't have to think. Or worry about feeling. There are surprisingly few emotional reactions one can have to stacking crates and lugging boxes.

Thus far, no tricks.

As I pull on my boots, my triceps burn, and back muscles I didn't know I had grind like rusted gears. If the tricks don't kill me, then my sheer unfitness in the face of manual labour will. Why couldn't I have gone to the gym more often? The one at school was free for all sixth formers, but I felt too embarrassed to go. What if everyone laughed at me for standing on the elliptical the wrong way round? Someone might film me, and I could end up on TikTok. Freya loves watching videos of people hurting themselves. How I would love to laugh at someone else's misfortune for a change. But any rogue laughs could cause a thunderstorm or an old woman to slip and break her hip.

I don't know if there are any others like me. And if there are, would they make good things happen when they are happy, or would they be broken like me? I wonder if they can ... relieve their "teenage urges" without causing a hurricane.

I did that.

I finished, then looked out the window to see next door's shed flying around like it was about to drop on the Wicked Witch of the West. At first, I didn't connect the dots. My powers were still developing, and my hands weren't glowing different colours yet. It wasn't until puberty really had its claws around my hormones that I began to see the trail of devastation. Earthquakes, lightning strikes – I'm pretty sure I even caused a foot-and-mouth outbreak across the county when I bunked off school.

I was probably the most sexually frustrated teenager to ever walk the planet. I learned to stop thinking about it. And it works. It *was* working until a guy I had just met kissed me, and I made his head pop like an angry spot.

But it's not just sex stuff. Other tricks happen depending on how I feel. Things often go in pairs and opposites, and the stronger the emotion, the stronger the trick. I keep a little chart in my pocket to keep track: my cheat sheet. I've left some empty boxes because I seem to develop a new trick every couple of months. Just the other day, I pushed a convertible into a wall by admiring it.

I used to live my life and ignore whatever occasionally manifested. Now I don't have that luxury. All I can do is try not to feel – go about my day with mechanical efficiency, like a passenger in my own body. But it's so hard. Every time I slip up, something terrible happens.

At this point, all I want is to feel nothing.

Jacketed and booted, I step out of my gross time capsule of a rental flat, and the November sea breeze bashes my face. There's something particularly cruel about the seaside in winter. The wind is extra cold, and it carries salt that licks your face like a cat's tongue.

Grunsby-on-Sea is a dump. That's partly why I chose to come here: some vague sense of altruism. If I torture myself, then maybe nothing bad would happen to anyone else. This place topped every BuzzFeed listicle for worst places to live and was even voted "Most depressing town in the UK". Not that the Grunsbians have noticed. It probably wasn't always like this, though. Back in the forties, this was probably a lucrative holiday destination. People would take their kids to play at the seaside with jam sandwiches and ginger beer like something out of an Enid Blyton novel. Now the only visitors are film crews looking for the saddest looking place in England and emomancers hiding from the law, I guess.

At some point, some optimistic soul tried to liven the seafront up with a pastel-pink coat of paint over everything: railings, buildings, the old, ruined pier. Obviously, they didn't maintain it as everything in town is cracked and flaking from the sea air. Even the town's crown jewel, the Grand Regalia Hotel, which now offers "colour TV in every room", looks like it has a bad case of eczema. The hotel, situated just next to a rickety old Ferris wheel, overlooks the sunken pier like a post-apocalyptic art deco monstrosity. No one ever seems to be staying there, but I can hardly blame them. Any parent who willingly brought their child here today would have social services round faster than a seagull on chips.

One good thing about Grunsby-on-Sea is that no one bats an eyelid at you. It's the perfect place to hide away and have zero questions asked. You can walk to the corner shop without anyone sparing you a second glance.

Speaking of which, I pull my coat up over my mouth and head down the hill.

*

The shopkeeper grunts at me as the beeping door heralds my arrival. I'm the only one who seems to come in here, but it's not hard to see why. Plastered to every inch of the glass door are scraps of paper saying "no children", "no loud talking", "no browsing", "no old people" and "no phones".

I flash him an awkward no-lip smile and pick up a basket. Much like the rest of the town, the corner shop is frozen in time. Worn boxes of Jaffa cakes sit limply on the shelves; their sell-by date seemingly older than I am. I pick up a bottle of what I assume is Pepsi – the label is coated in so much dust, it is hard to see. My thumb streaks across it, and a handsome man with way too much gel in his hair looks back at me. Apparently, he's a football player from the 1998 World Cup – not that I have any clue about football despite my dad's repeated attempts to teach me.

I wonder what Mum and Dad are doing right now. They've been visiting my uncle in Madrid for the month – supposedly to "give me room to revise" for my mock A Levels, but I'm pretty sure they just wanted to sunbathe for the whole of November. By now, they're probably the colour of tanned leather and haven't worried about me once. I'm sure Freya's worrying, though. We've been best friends since we were six. She saw my *Ben 10* lunch box from across the playground, marched straight up to me, and demanded we play together. We pretended to turn into aliens and fight baddies together almost every lunchtime. Since then, she's always been in my life, except for that brief few months in Year Seven when we decided we hated each other. She's in my form but we don't have any subjects together. I tell her everything ... Well, almost everything.

Recently – well, before I went AWOL – she'd been boring me with every intimate detail of her new boyfriend, Marcus.

Prick.

I've never felt such an instant dislike for someone. He always insinuates that he's a lot smarter than me, just because he's already got uni offers for engineering. He can basically fix anything; it's super annoying. "Stevie, you're doing this wrong ..." "Stevie, I passed my driving test first time ..." "Stevie, I'm a prick who has biceps and a car ..."

Some people assume that I'm jealous, but I'm honestly not. Freya is like my sister – I imagine. I don't have any siblings. But I can safely say our relationship has only ever been platonic. I guess certain things bind you to someone for life. And, apparently, running around the playground pretending to be alien butterflies with freezing breath is one of them. God, I miss her so much ...

I catch myself, but it might have been too late. I stare at my fingers, hoping that nothing happens, but of course, it does. A faint yellow aura crackles around my hand. I'm manifesting happiness. The sky outside darkens, thunder crashing overhead. Long, spear-like rain plummets to the ground, and a powerful wind rips open the door to the shop.

I grab some milk and pay for it quickly, the shopkeeper too distracted by the sudden downpour to notice my glowing hands. Wrestling the door shut, I turn my face against the storm and trudge back up the hill.

By the time I am at the foot of the rusted metal steps to my flat, the worst of it has passed, but I am entirely saturated. Why couldn't I have packed a jacket with a hood? I didn't have much time to think. I just had to shove everything I could into a bag and leave before anyone noticed. Before anyone could stop me, and by anyone, I mean—

"Freya!"

Stood outside my little shabby door, almost completely dry under an obnoxious frog umbrella, is a copper-headed young woman. Her outfit is a coordinated event of oversized woollen things and bright-pink wellies, and her hair is piled up on her head in a messy bun.

"Alright, Percy? What does a girl have to do to get a cuppa around here?"

2

"You look like crap," I say.

And I definitely mean it. Steven Percival has always been built like a racing snake, but today he looks like a miner who got trapped underground. Skin and bone with eyes dark like a murderer. His wet, brown hair is unkempt and starting to curl at the edges.

"Nice umbrella," he says with a sneer. "Steal it from a primary school?"

"Marcus got it for me, actually."

Nothing. That's weird. I usually can't mention Marcus without Steven pretending to retch.

"Are you going to let me in? Because I don't fancy pneumonia, to be honest."

He mutters something under his breath, probably about the wellies, and fetches the keys from his coat.

His flat is probably the worst thing that I've ever seen. Wallpaper! Actual wallpaper ... in a house. Ew. I'm all for retro stuff – my earrings were my mum's in the nineties – but this is just way too old and way too ugly. No one wants to live in a place that was decorated when they were still doing rations.

While Steven busies about in the kitchen making tea, I perch on the vinyl-wrapped sofa in front of the deepest TV ever known to man. I check my phone out of habit, but it's been dead for the past three hours. Troy still has my charger. Lucky I wrote down everything before I left.

"Three sugars and strong enough to stand the spoon up," says Steven as he plonks a bone china cup on the coffee table in front of me. No bourbon biscuits, which is strange; we always have a packet with tea. He sits down on a worn armchair and eyes me suspiciously. He opens his mouth, but I hold up my hand. We aren't even going to consider talking until I have finished my tea. He stares at the floor, avoiding my gaze. His eyes seem hollow, like they've been drained of life. Creepy.

"Right. We are out of the cold, and tea has been drunk. First things first: have you gone full Norman Bates? Should I be checking this flat for dead old ladies?"

A flicker across his face. So, he is still there somewhere.

"The only old lady here is the one on the sofa." His voice is as dry as ever, but his face is stern and impassive.

"Great, now I guess my follow-up question is – what the actual hell, Steven Percival?"

He stares at me. He knows I am serious because I didn't call him Percy. Nothing passes his stony expression. Eventually, he shrugs and looks down at the tea gripped in his hands.

"That's it? Nothing to say? You disappear completely for over a week and don't have anything to say? I have been beside myself with worry, you tit. That little cover story you told school about a family emergency was a load of rubbish. I texted your mum, asking if everything was okay, but she didn't have a clue what I was on about."

Steven blanches at that. I can see a hundred panicked thoughts behind his eyes as his breath catches in his chest.

"Y-you texted—"

"Don't worry, I just pretended I was talking about their holiday," I say, rolling my eyes. Honestly, what kind of best friend would I be if I didn't lie to his parents? "I figured it was the pressure of A Levels or something. Mock exams or too many books to read or something – I don't know what you do in English Lit. I assumed you would text me eventually, and I would come over with a pack of bourbons, and we would talk everything through. But no. You ignore my texts, reject my calls, and pretend I don't exist. Even when we hated each other at the end of Year Seven, you never ignored me."

"That's because you kept telling people I cried during *Inside Out*."

"Percy, you did cry during *Inside Out*. A lot."

"You didn't have to tell everyone. Liam Stalworth thought I was such a loser."

"Oh, what a shame, the kid with a criminal record before he was ten thought you were a loser for crying at a Pixar movie."

"He made fun of me for months!"

"Whatever. The point is, you dropped off the face of the Earth, and I want to know why."

Steven pauses, a muscle flaring in his jaw. He mutters, "It's complicated," gets up and takes his empty cup out to the kitchen.

Ugh, I hate when he does this. If Steven Percival can do one thing, it's sweep out of a room when he wants to be dramatic.

∗

Steven

I take my cup to the kitchen because I don't know what to say. Freya will probably say I swept off dramatically. She's always saying I do that. What the hell is she doing here? No one was supposed to find me. I had been so careful. I took all the cash I could out of an ATM and left no paper trail. I bet she asked her dad to help. He's a police officer: probably got access to facial recognition software or some other equally unsettling tool for privacy invasion.

As I wash up my cup, I can feel Freya's eyes boring into me from the doorframe. She isn't going to let this go.

"I'm not going to let this go," she says.

Knew it.

"I can understand running away if exams got too much, but why here?" she asks, trying a different tack.

I consider the wool-clad figure by the threshold. Fierce hazel eyes scanning every inch of the revolting kitchen. Good thing Freya isn't an emomancer: she's so disgusted by the decor the whole flat would probably implode. I give her a bit. Mainly to just shut her up.

"Didn't think anyone would think to find me here."

"You've got that right. I've been in this town for half an hour, and already I want to throw myself into the sea."

"I think there's already a pretty long queue," I say, smiling weakly. "You might have to take a ticket and come back."

I probably shouldn't be cracking jokes, no matter how small. They lead to joy, and joy is *very* dangerous. Hopefully, the storm I just caused will mean no tricks for a little bit. My batteries have to recharge – at least that's the theory. But almost every time I think I understand this emomancy, it throws another curveball at me.

Freya smiles but then peers at me like she can't really see me.

"What is it?" I ask.

"Nothing, you just seem . . . muted."

I feel muted. But if I want to keep Freya and everyone else safe, then that's the price I have to pay. I have to be a diet version of myself: less emotional, less engaged, less sugar.

I shrug noncommittally, which just annoys her.

"Okay, if you won't tell me what you are running from or why you are here, then at least tell me when you are coming back?" she says, hopping up on the counter. Her legs idly kick the paint-chipped cupboards.

"I'm not coming back, Freya. I can't."

She rolls her eyes again and says, "You always have to be so bloody dramatic."

"No, you don't understand—"

"Then make me understand. Tell me. Talk to me. Say something!"

"FREYA, I CAN'T!"

I shouldn't have shouted. I try to stop it, but it's too late: a red shimmer is curling around my fingers, the temperature plummets, and Freya's face grows fearful. She jumps to her feet, backing out of the kitchen. I've never seen her so afraid in my life.

"Freya, I'm sorry. I didn't mean . . ." I trail away, not sure what to say. I close my eyes and think desperately of nothing but white. Pure white. No anger, no colour, just white. Breathe in for four and out for four. My heart slows down from its furious pounding.

"N-no, it's o-okay," she stutters, lingering at the doorframe. "Gave me a fright, is all."

"I shouldn't have got angry."

"It's fine. My fault. I shouldn't have come. Obviously, you are going through something and want to be left alone," Freya says as she heads toward the front door.

"Freya, wait."

It's true. I wanted to be left alone – that's why I came to this awful town. But I don't want to be lonely. And I don't want her to go. Not just yet.

Freya looks me up and down and frowns. Without saying a word, she puts down her frog umbrella and sits back down on the couch. I sit next to her, my bum squeaking on the vinyl wrapping.

"How did you even find me, McCormac?"

"Ah, if I told you, I'd have to kill you," she says quietly.

"Use your dad's police equipment?"

"Err, no. Your phone has been sharing its location with me since we went to that music festival."

I laugh – the first proper laugh in a month. My attempt to go off the grid foiled by my fear of being lost in a crowd. God, that's pathetic. Freya loves live music and had been trying to drag me to see something for ages. I only agreed to go if we shared our location at all times and didn't split up except for runs to the loo.

I hastily glance at my fingers, but no yellow, so I must be safe from tricks for a few minutes at least.

"Shouldn't you be in classes right now?" I ask.

"Could say the same to you."

"You know what I mean."

"Mocks are done, so no one's really doing anything till the end of term except talking about how they went. Which means I can follow my best friend to the arse end of nowhere to rescue him from crippling loneliness."

I laugh again. I am really pushing my luck. If my tricks come back, I might set her hair on fire. Joy is the most dangerous thing to feel.

"How were they then? Bet you aced everything," I ask, hoping to keep the subject off me for a bit.

"Biology was easy but boring. General Studies was a doss. Missed the whole back page of Maths because I'm an idiot. Chemistry: I think I had an aneurism on the second question but whatever. And just before my Psychology, your mum replied to me. I was so distracted I'm pretty sure I failed. But I was in good company; Troy had a nosebleed midway through. Got blood all over his test, bless him."

Ah, Troy Anderson: the new American guy in our year. Apparently, he did his AS levels over the summer and our school allowed him to come finish his A2s here. I've chatted with him a few times while waiting for Freya to get out of class. He seemed nice. An ethnically ambiguous All-American type with impossibly white teeth, a handsome face, and hair effortlessly parted at the side. I mean, he's a bit intense. Stares a lot and looks like he might ask you to join a cult. Then again, Americans can be a bit full-on. And tall. Probably all the corn syrup.

"Things have been a bit weird since you left. I haven't really seen Marcus much – he's fine, thanks for asking—"

"Didn't ask. Don't care."

She ignores me.

"Did you hear about what happened to a guy at his school? Harry Foxton? He died at that house party we went to after you'd left. Marcus says the whole school is freaked out."

I freeze. Someone has just reached down my throat and twisted my stomach. My mouth goes dry. How can all my saliva vanish so quickly? Harry. His name was Harry. My powers ... no, *I* killed Harry Foxton.

I glance at Freya, but she hasn't noticed the tremor spreading up my body. She's picking off the chipped nail varnish from her hand.

"Oh, really? What happened?" I ask, hopefully sounding nonchalant but definitely not.

"They reckon an appliance blew up or something. Faulty wiring, who knows. He was all burned when they found his body at the end of the night."

My body is shaking like mad. This is what you get for letting Freya drag you to a party. At least they don't know it was me yet. But bloody hell, I killed someone. By accident, of course. But someone ... Harry ... is dead, and it's all my fault. I screw up my eyes, and when I open them, Freya is staring right at me, mouth agog and her huge eyes even wider.

"What? What is it?"

"Percy ... you're ... glowing."

I look down. A black aura is dancing around my hands, but the rest of my body is giving off an intense light. The same light that followed me all the way to Grunsby-on-Sea. But I can't hide from this emotion. Just distract myself until I remember again. I don't need to look at my cheat sheet; I know what black means.

Guilt.

3

Freya

What the actual hell.

Steven Percival is glowing. Not like when he got sunburnt when our families went to Menorca or when you say pregnant women glow when they are actually just sweaty. He is a solar flare, and I can't take my eyes off him no matter how much I want to.

"I can explain," he says. Just like Steven to talk in dramatic clichés like this is some nineties sitcom.

But I can't say anything back.

I want to, but all I can do is stare like a goldfish that swam too hard into the wall of its tank.

Steven closes his eyes and breathes deeply. When he opens them again, there's a kind of blankness behind them. A calm tranquillity like he turned off his turmoil with the flick of a switch. The glow fades, and I can finally drop my gaze. Picked the wrong day to forget eyedrops: my contacts feel dry and scratchy and are threatening to murder my poor eyes. I blink furiously like I'm sending Morse code.

Steven is watching me but not saying anything. He's not even joking that I should have worn my granny glasses. Who even is this Steven-shaped lump on the sofa next to me?

"Sorry," he mumbles.

"What the bloody hell was that, Steven Percival?"

"It's hard to explain."

"Try."

"You weren't supposed to ... I didn't want ... It's ... I only came here ... And ..."

"Oh my god. Finish a bloody sentence."

He sighs, and I catch him glance at the door.

"Don't think you can get past me, Percy. Even with twelve stone of knitwear, I'm still faster than you."

It's true, and he knows it. Percy runs like a noodle at the best of times. I give him my best death stare, and his resolve breaks.

"I have these powers," he says, choosing his words very carefully.

"Like glowing?"

"That's one of them. I can do things – they depend on what emotion I'm feeling. But they come out all wrong. If I feel happy, then something terrible seems to happen; if I feel sad, something good happens."

We sit in silence for a while as this all sinks in. To be honest, I don't know what to think. If it were anyone else, I would say they were pulling my leg, but I know Percy. I've known him almost my entire life, and I know when he's lying or trying to be smart with me. Besides, he gave me a demonstration a few moments ago.

But how can this possibly be true? Superpowers don't exist. Even if they did, how did Steven hide it from me all these years? It makes absolutely no sense. No, it must be a trick of the light or something. Right?

"I can't control it," he mumbles. "I feel things, and stuff just happens." He looks weary and ... haunted. What happened to him?

"So you have emotion superpowers. You manifest whatever you're feeling like you're, I don't know . . . *Feeling Man*?"

"I prefer emomancer," he says with the barest hint of a chuckle.

"Emomancer?" I scoff.

"Yeah, like emotion and 'mancer' as in pyromancer, necrom—"

"Yeah, I got that, Percy. It's just a hilarious thing to call yourself. Bloody hell, you'll be getting snakebite piercings and wearing guyliner soon."

"So I should go by *Feeling Man* instead?"

"On second thoughts, no, it makes you sound like a sex offender. *Emotional Magician*? No, that's like you saw a woman in half then cry about it. *Captain Feels-a-Lot*? Nah. Wow, the Avengers make superhero branding look so easy. We can keep workshopping the name. What else can you do – other than sad-good, happy-bad?"

He hands me a crumpled slip of paper with a poorly drawn table on. Percy really has shocking handwriting. I can make out, "Steven's Emomancy Cheat Sheet" at the top.

"I've been keeping this cheat sheet with everything I've noticed. Like, when I'm angry, I make others frightened."

"How long?"

"Usually just a few minutes, I guess."

"No, you tit. I mean, how long have you been doing this? Being emotional litmus paper?"

"Oh. I guess it started when I was like twelve, but it was only occasionally. Now it's all the time, and they're getting worse. You can't tell anyone, Freya. Not until I get it back under control again."

I roll my eyes involuntarily. "Who am I going to tell, Percy? 'Hey, did you hear? Steven Percival is a low-budget superhero who might kill you if he laughs too hard.'"

"I'm *not* a superhero."

"No, you definitely don't have that Hemsworth body."

"Freya, I mean it," he says with just a hint of desperation, snatching back his cheat sheet. "This is serious."

Another eye roll. I know it's serious, but that has never stopped us from having a joke before. Even when Nanny died, Steven was making jokes about her catheter whilst I cried on his shoulder in the hospital. The foundation of our entire relationship is sarcasm and bourbon biscuits. Right now, there is a distinct lack of either.

"Fine. I swear to you I will not tell another soul, living or dead, that you are . . . *the Magnificent Moody-man*?" He cocks an eyebrow at me. "No, you're right. That was terrible. I thought the alliteration might help."

He sits back on the vinyl-wrapped sofa and sighs.

"Thanks," he mumbles, and we sit quietly for a moment. Out of the window, I can see a flat, grey sea washing over a sunken pier. Whatever happens, Steven needs to get out of this hellhole.

"I knew you'd been keeping secrets from me, Percy, but I never expected this. I just assumed you were gay or something."

I glance at him out the side of my vision. Nothing. Not even a twitch. Damn. Either he's really good at hiding how he feels, or he isn't gay (which I still refuse to accept.)

"Do you want another cuppa?" he asks, his face completely impassive.

Classic Percy. Every time I bring up his sexuality, he changes the subject. Let's review the evidence:

One: he has never had a girlfriend nor shown any interest in a girl.

Two: he is very well put together . . . well, usually.

Three: over the years, I have watched him get attached to one pretty boy after another and follow them around like a shadow until they turn out to be pricks.

And four: he's always Princess Peach in *Mario Kart*. That might've been so I had to be a short Italian plumber, but it's pretty damning evidence to me.

If he can come out of the closet about his powers, you'd think he could come out of the actual closet too.

*

Steven

I ignore Freya's attempt to pry for the umpteenth time. Does she really think that one day she'll catch me off guard? Trust me, if I can hide my stupid powers for six years, then I can hide anything. Well, unless I start to glow again and rainbows shoot out of my hands.

"Why don't we go for a walk on the beach?" Freya suggests as she redistributes the four metric tonnes of wool engulfing her.

"It's November, you freak."

"Perfect beach-walking weather."

"Fine," I say. "We can walk along the seafront for a bit. And then you really need to go back to Dorset."

"Percy, I didn't take four trains and two buses just to have a cup of tea and leave empty-handed."

"I don't want you getting hurt. I can't . . . I can't control it like I used to."

She doesn't say anything, just rolls her dinner-plate eyes in her round face for the four billionth time. I try a different approach.

"Won't your parents be expecting you back?"

"Dad's working nights, and I told Mum I was staying with you for a few days because of your 'family emergency'. You know, emotional support."

"What about Marcus?"

She looks away. Freya might not manifest her emotions like I do, but she telegraphs them like huge neon signs.

"You did tell him where you were going, right?"

"He has been really busy with his exams, and I didn't want to bother him. He wouldn't have come anyway. And I figured if you'd had some sort of mental breakdown, the last person you'd want to see is Marcus."

She has a point. Stupid Marcus with his stupid face and stupid muscles.

Prick.

"So, no one knows you've come halfway across the country?" I ask as I wrestle my feet into my trainers.

"I left a note in my room in case I got murdered on the journey. I also saw Troy on the way to school while I waited for the bus. I just told him I was checking in on you and your family emergency, and he seemed to buy it."

"Just like you bought my family emergency?"

"That's different. Troy believes anything anyone says," she says as she stands up like a mountain of wool rising from the sofa. She lumbers forward and knocks over the pile of DVDs at her feet. "Sorry, couldn't see over the scarves ... Percy, do you have the entire back catalogue of Pixar movies?"

I feel my ears flush scarlet.

"Y-yeah. I mean, all except *Cars 2*. I started watching the first ten minutes of *Up*, so I would, you know, feel ... sad."

"Bawl like a baby, you mean?"

I ignore her. "And it worked for a bit. It'd stop me blowing anything up for about an hour and make the weather nice."

"Jesus, that's masochistic. Did you punch yourself in the groin too?"

Freya stacks them again but spots that *Inside Out* is the only one still in its plastic wrapping. She picks it up and cocks one of her perfectly groomed eyebrows. I shrug and head for the door before she brings up my uncontrollable sobs when Bing Bong dies for the second time today.

*

Ten minutes later and Freya and I are walking arm in arm down the seafront. There isn't a lot to see or do. The amusement park and most of the seaside shops are closed for the winter, and Grunsby doesn't have any museums. It does have a charred, sunken pier and four pie shops on the high street.

I feel a small seed of happiness plant itself in the bottom of my stomach, and my fingers glow yellow. Guess the trickless window has closed. A storm whips up the sea like a grey beast thrashing wildly in a cage. Spears of rain hurtle down, and flashes of lightning strike the sea. Freya screams as thunder rumbles overhead, and her eyes bug out like a *Looney Tunes* character when they fall off a cliff – I forgot how jumpy she is. I breathe, let the happiness go, and think of nothing.

I feel nothing.

The thunderstorm dies down, but the rain doesn't, so we seek shelter under the roof of a hut that once sold seafood. A paint-chipped sign next to it still shows the prices of cockles and mussels in shillings and old pence. Is everything in this town stuck in 1956? The sign has also become the victim of graffiti, with such hits as "Gemma smellz", "DEMA BNBR6", and "TJ has a big willy" – truly this town is a work of art.

We should probably find a more sheltered spot. Freya points to an awning between a row of shops and the Grand Regalia Hotel. Below it, lights are flashing in a very large room. It's only when we are halfway towards it that I realise it's an amusement arcade.

The sign above it was clearly supposed to say "STARSHINE ARCADE", but the letters have either been blown out to sea or stolen years ago, so now it just says "__ARS___E ARCADE".

The inside is warm and, most importantly, dry. The carpets are burgundy with migraine-inducing swirly patterns that have been worn down by years of sand and salt. Two rows of penny falls machines flank the entrance, their coins tantalisingly close to the edge. When we were younger, Freya heard that if you stomp next to them, the coins fall without activating the alarm. Weeks of my life were lost to jumping around the arcade, and not once did anything ever fall.

I'm about to remind her of her stomping theory when I realise she's made a beeline for the shooting game at the back. The machine sits underneath a blacklight, which makes the neon trim pop but unfortunately reveals some dodgy-looking splatter on the screen. Freya fishes around inside her knitted cocoon, pulls out her purse, and starts loading up the machine.

"Come on, Percival," she goads. "Let's see if you're still a terrible shot."

I pick up the pink plastic handgun next to her, and we shoot terribly animated werewolves for three minutes. She wins as per usual. My accuracy is thirteen per cent, which honestly seems higher than I was anticipating. Freya jumps every time a were-wolf appears but somehow always manages a headshot. It's times like these when I am glad she isn't following her dad into the police force. The last thing a quiet, rural town needs is a jumpy, trigger-happy bobby with ninety-seven per cent accuracy.

I holster the gun, leaving Freya to her monster hunting, and look around this sad arcade. In the corner, behind a plastic screen, is a bored-looking attendant flicking through a tabloid magazine. Knockoff toys and sad-looking plushies are pinned to the wall behind her. I can see a Pikachu, who might have had a stroke, dangling from his foot for five hundred tickets, and a half-melted Power Ranger for three hundred. It doesn't look like any prizes have been claimed in a while. The only thing not covered in dust is an A5 poster stuck to the plexiglass – apparently, some missing girl from the local high school.

I decide I must get Freya that deformed Pikachu – it's sort of a tradition that we buy each other horrific gifts. As I put 50p into a Whack-a-Mole that appears to be missing several moles, I get the feeling I'm being watched. I casually glance over my shoulder. Under the awning is a young woman in a slightly-too-big business suit. Her auburn hair is cropped short around her small pixie-like features. An iPhone is pressed to her ear, but she is doing a terrible job at pretending to talk to someone. In fact, she is trying to scan the room nonchalantly, but her eyes keep focusing on Freya and me.

I'm being stupid. No one is following me. No one could have followed me . . . well, apart from Freya.

Piss biscuits, the Pixie is definitely staring. Okay, just keep calm and act natural.

I press the start button on the machine, and the moles begin to move. Veeeeerrryyyy slooooooowly. It's like shooting fish in a barrel – or like beating drugged-up rodents with a foam hammer. A string of tickets spits out then the machine dies. Stupid thing. As I duck down to pull them out, I steal another glance to see if the Business Pixie is still staring.

She is.

My heart is hammering. Keep calm, Percival. Now is not the time to panic and cause a trick. She looks official. Maybe she's the police or the FBI or something. No, the FBI are American. MI5? MI6? What is the difference? James Bond is MI6, I think – why did I have to fall asleep during *Skyfall*? Oh god, my brain needs to calm down. For all I know, Business Tinkerbell is just a woman on her lunch break. A woman on her lunch break who just took a photo of me on her phone.

I try to breathe slowly, but fear is bubbling through. Don't feel. Don't feel anything.

"Got you a present," says Freya in my ear. Before I know what's happening, she has slipped a strange silver ring with a multicoloured band on my ring finger. "And I didn't even ask your father's permission first, how very twenty-first century. Do you like it? It's a mood ring. Cost me 50 tickets. These were all the rage in the seventies, I think. It changes colour depending on what emotion you are feeling."

"Freya, I—"

"Yes, I know, you're probably *very* aware of what emotion you are feeling, but it's just a bit of fun. I think it just changes colour with heat, and your finger will probably turn green, but oh well. Let's see what mood you are in now," she says as she checks a little folded piece of paper. "Well, it turned blue, so that means fear.

Oh, look, if it turns purple, it means you are horny. Wait, aren't these designed for, like, ten-year-olds? Jesus. You'd think they—"

"Freya!" I say before she rambles on again. She stops and looks at me, bewildered. I incline my head ever so slightly, and she follows with her eyes over my shoulder.

"She's been staring and taking photos."

Freya frowns and looks at the woman again before muttering, "Okay, let's leave."

I turn around to go, but the pixie-face woman has now moved between the rows of penny falls, blocking the exit. A lump rises in my throat. Oh god, not only have I let myself be caught, Freya will be arrested too. Aiding and abetting. This can't get any worse.

"OI!" screams the attendant from behind the plexiglass. "DID YOU BREAK MY WACK-A-MOLE! I'LL KILL YOU."

The foam mallet suddenly burns red hot, and I drop it. I'm confused for all of three seconds until I see blue sparks fizzing around my hands.

Fear.

We need to get out of here, *now*. I grab Freya's hand and pull her towards a door marked "Employees Only".

"COME BACK HERE!" bellows the attendant, and I think I can hear Agent Pixie making a dash, but we are through the door, and I quickly lock it from the other side.

Freya is already at the other end of the small, dirty corridor, pushing on the emergency exit bars that lead to an alleyway. We dash outside and almost make it back to the seafront when a figure blocks the path.

"Don't move!" yells Agent Pixie in a bouncy Newcastle accent, although she sounds a little unsure of herself. First day on the job, maybe? "Put your hands where I can see them."

There's no way through. I suppose I could tackle her, but she might have some fancy ninja MI6 training or something. Or a gun. She hasn't drawn anything. Yet.

"Ladder behind us," whispers Freya. Considering her dad is a police officer, she seems to have no qualms ignoring this woman's orders. At least we're on the same page – I am *not* about to turn myself over to this woman.

Sure enough, at the other end of the alley there's a ladder on the concrete wall to the street above. But we'd be caught the moment we tried to climb. There must be something we can do? Something we can use? But we are in a small alley with only old crisp packets and two large bins to keep us company.

The bins. Maybe I could push them towards her. When I feel disgust, things pull towards me, and when I pushed that car away from me, I had been admiring it. I wanted it. Maybe I need to . . . admire the bins?

I focus as hard as I can. The bins are green and grey and have plastic lids on hinges. That's about it. They stink of rotten food and are covered in suspicious brown muck. Nothing really to admire. This is impossible, and Pixie-face is advancing towards us.

Maybe I could admire something else and focus it on the bins? But what? It needs to be something I want really bad. Oh god, this is hard under pressure. What is the thing I want more than anything right now? I'm hungry, so I can only think of food.

And then it comes to me: Mum's bacon sandwiches, crispy and drowned in ketchup. Every Sunday morning since I can remember, she would make them, and we'd sit together and watch telly while we ate. I'd give anything to have one right now.

My hand glows pink, and I throw them out towards the bins like I'm a wizard casting a spell. I'm not sure if that's how this works but screw it, I'm doing it now.

There is a flash of pink light. The bins stay exactly where they are, but Agent Pixie is flung off her feet, performs five summer-saults and lands with a splash halfway out to sea.

4

Marcus

This is such a waste of time *and* petrol. I've been speeding the whole way, but the ETA on my phone isn't getting any shorter. This is, without a doubt, the worst road trip I have ever done. And the stupid thing is that it'll be fine. Freya's phone is probably just dead; she always forgets to charge it. She'll frolic around the seafront with Stevie for a few hours and be back before dinner. I don't know why Troy has his knickers in a twist about this. I glance over at him.

He's still talking.

Hasn't realised I zoned out forty miles back. Why do Americans always talk for the sake of talking? He's got no chat either. He's just saying anything that pops into his head.

It's my fault. I let him come along. Then again, he did offer to pay the petrol money.

*

Troy

Why doesn't he say anything? Please say something. Like anything. Words, please! I keep talking and talking, hoping that he'll eventually join in and help fill the quiet, but he never does.

He zoned out like thirty minutes back and burdened me with the silence. Oh my gosh, if he doesn't open his mouth soon, I might have to fake a heart attack or something.

I suppose this is my own fault. I did ask him to drive. Had to basically bribe him with gas money. But what else was I supposed to do? Jack a car and head out by myself? Even if I wanted to, Brits seem to only drive stick for some reason, and I have no clue how that all works. Don't they realise the car can do all that for you? I watch Marcus push the gearstick back and forth as he weaves down these terrifying country lanes, and I thank God I'm not doing it. I have honestly never seen a road so narrow or bendy in my life. Every ten seconds, we jolt suddenly or swerve dramatically, and whenever another car comes toward us, we basically have to drive half in the bushes. It's like no one told Great Britain that highways exist.

Marcus isn't helping the situation. He has two driving speeds: fast and breakneck. And the weirdest thing is he told me the speed limit down here is sixty. Not that he's sticking to it.

Sixty-gosh-darn-miles-per-hour down a road narrower than a parking spot at Walmart.

Marcus yanks the wheel suddenly, and my head slams against the side of the car. I can't tell if there was something there or if he just wanted me to shut up.

Marcus

Finally. He shuts up. And all it took was almost crashing the car. Now he's rubbing his necklace like some sort of nervous tick. So long as his mouth isn't moving, I'm happy.

We are twenty minutes away now, and suddenly sheets of rain batter the car. Looks like we are heading right into a storm. Why did Troy have to drag me into this? Now I look like the insecure boyfriend who can't trust his girlfriend to disappear without telling him.

I mean, she probably *should* have told me.

It's not that I don't trust her. Freya always does Freya: she goes where she wants, and I'll be damned if I could ever win an argument with her. But she does have a bad habit of finding trouble, especially with Stevie. Something is going on with them, that's for sure.

*

Troy

Something is going on here, that's for sure.

First, I see Freya getting on a bus at the crack of dawn, then some woman in a suit starts asking me questions. "Do I go to school with Freya McCormac and Steven Percival?" "Will they be in today?" "Where was the last place I saw them?" Something about her just freaked me out. Don't think she was a cop but still probably something official. She sounded Scottish, so she can't be CIA. Anyway, I haven't told Marcus about it yet. He probably wouldn't be too thrilled helping a fugitive if Steven really is on the run. Why couldn't Freya have answered her phone? We could've avoided all of this.

Who am I actually doing this for: Freya or Steven? Like I know it's none of my business, and I've only met him a handful of times, but Steven's cute. I had a crush on him the moment I saw him in the many photos stuck to the inside of Freya's locker. I remember one in particular: a Polaroid of the two of them pulling stupid faces at a party. Yes, even with a cross-eyed grimace, Steven Percival was hot. With his short chestnut curls and a face that's cheeky yet boyishly handsome.

Plus the accent. Oh my gosh, British guys really don't understand how much their accent makes Americans weak at the knees. When I finally met him in person, he looked at me with those vivid green eyes, gave me a smirk and said, "Alright, mate?" I thought I might die. I just sat there staring at him like a total idiot until Freya got out of class. He tried making a joke about Freya taking too long, but I totally didn't get that he was being sarcastic until after he left.

British sense of humour: 1

American homosexual mess: 0

Every time I open my mouth around him, I turn to Jell-O. And the stupid thing is, I don't even know if he's interested in guys like that. I could be wasting my time pining for a straight guy. Then again, most gay men get hung up on a straight guy or two. And it's not like I haven't had offers since coming here. A guy in my Chem class keeps DMing me on Instagram ever since he saw me in a tank top at the gym, but I'm not interested. Besides, I'm going halfway across the country to rescue my friend and her potentially straight best friend who might be on the lam, all because I have a major crush on him.

Gosh, I'm a mess.

If anything, I am surprised Marcus doesn't care as much as I do. His girlfriend's best friend up and vanishes, and he didn't seem to care. Then his girlfriend takes four trains and two buses to find him without telling anyone, and it's an inconvenience to go check she's okay. Do these Brits suppress their emotions so much that they forget to care about their loved ones?

I pull out my phone and stare at the dot on the map – the place I saw Freya frantically googling after our Psychology exam. I only remembered it because it sounded like the most British sounding place name I've heard. *Grunsby-on-Sea*. It wasn't till after I saw that agent lady that I put two and two together and realised Freya was taking the bus there this morning.

We finally turn off this godforsaken road (if you can even call it that) and are on a roundabout when Marcus's phone loses all signal and freaks out. He makes three full loops of it before he sees the dirty sign for Grunsby-on-Sea and swerves to take the exit.

I would throw up, but Marcus wouldn't stop for snacks, so nothing is in my stomach. However, four hours without a pee, and I am about ready to pop. I don't even marvel at the quaint stone bridge we cross as we head into the town because I'm fighting the urge to wet myself.

"Can we stop, please? We won't find them any quicker if I have kidney failure," I ask, but Marcus grunts and mutters about how we're basically there now.

The road takes us around the outside of the town and then runs parallel to the sea. I spot a public restroom on the seafront below, so Marcus reluctantly parks. I jump out the car and waddle down the zigzag path to the small grey hut, trying not to pee myself.

Five minutes later, I walk out of possibly the worst restroom I have ever seen, traumatised but looking decidedly less pregnant. I'm halfway up the path when I hear shouting from the seafront below.

I race to the top and lean over the railing just in time to see two very familiar faces climbing a ladder below.

"Jesus, Percy!"

"I know, I know. I was aiming for the bloody bins."

The car door opens behind me, and Marcus's head pops up over the roof and says, "What're you doing?"

But then he sees them too.

The woollen-wrapped figure of Freya suddenly hauls herself up, with Steven not long after. He's gaunt with dark circles under his eyes, but seeing his face still makes me smile. My hand instinctively goes to Dad's dog tags around my neck.

They stand up and are about to start running when they clock Marcus and me not two feet away.

"Hey babe," says Freya between breaths. "Couldn't give us a lift?"

5

Excerpt from the report of
Field Director Fareborn: DEMA Case 1569GOS
Priority Epsilon
MON 23/11/2020
1407 GMT

It's been three days of field operations, and we finally appear to have some EMT activity. The target location, Grunsby-on-Sea, is not the prettiest of places, but it's hardly the worst I've been to on assignment.

Irregular weather patterns have been noted in Grunsby-on-Sea for approximately three weeks now, and DEMA's World Monitoring Algorithm has highlighted the town as a potential area of EMT interference. Today, for example, has had rain, brilliant sunshine, and a thunderstorm all before 1400 hours. Yes, this can often simply be a result of temperamental British weather – something that often interferes with the World Monitoring Algorithm. However, HQ believes the speed of the changes indicates the presence of an un-controlled EMT.

DEMA HQ gave this case a priority rating of Epsilon; however, I do not believe this to be accurate. The strength of the weather anomalies indicates a stronger EMT than an Epsilon (probably a Delta or Gamma.)

The low priority rating, coupled with the disappearance of nine DEMA operatives in the past four years, has resulted in a smaller field op team than usual; for this assignment, I have only one person working with me, Junior Agent Wren. After her fourth attempt at passing training, Junior Agent Wren has taken to her first time in the field with ... *gusto*. Her unbridled enthusiasm has been noted several times since this operation started. We have split up to cover more ground. Wren has been on reconnaissance duty whilst I set up surveillance in key locations and investigated local records at the library.

Thus far, my investigations have been fruitless. The indifference of the town to their record-keeping is truly astounding. Either nothing of consequence happens in Grunsby, or there is a serious and inexcusable lack of administration. Even a missing teenager from three months ago appears to have been handled with a shrug and a footnote in the local paper. To find our target, we will need to rely more heavily on our own reconnaissance and data gathering – the Grunsbians certainly haven't made our job easy for us.

I have instructed Junior Agent Wren to keep a low profile and scout out the town. Her findings will be invaluable to the mission's success, and I am confident she will rise to the occasion.

- End of Log -

✳

I have SERIOUS misgivings about Junior Agent Wren.

In the *hour and twenty-two* minutes since my last report, she has broken cover, engaged a suspected EMT, and damaged DEMA property. Find below a transcript of our conversation:

> ## Transcript of phone call to Field Director Fareborn from Junior Agent Wren
> ## 23/11/2020 1500 GMT

FDF_   Hello?

JAW_   YES! Field Director Fareborn - I knew it was a three - it's Gabby.

FDF_   Junior Agent Wren, I have told you repeatedly. You are to only use your operative rank and surname whilst on assignment.

JAW_   Sorry, Field Director Fareborn, I forgot.

FDF_   Why are you calling from an unknown number?

JAW_   Oh yeah, my phone got a bit . . . damaged in the line of duty. Sorry, I am fixing it as we speak.

FDF_   So you are calling me from . . . ?

JAW_   I'm in the lobby of the hotel by the seafront. The reception desk let me

dry off and use their phone. Proper
dead in here, like. Haven't seen
anyone come in other than—

FDF_   So you are using an unencrypted line
to call your senior operative?

JAW_   Sorry. I didn't know what else to do.

FDF_   (Sigh)

JAW_   It's fine. We can . . . talk in code.

FDF_   We will discuss this later. How did
you remember my mobile number?

JAW_   I wrote it down on a post-it. It got
a bit wet, and I wasn't sure if it
was an eight or a three at the end,
so I took a guess.

FDF_   You wrote down my number on a post-
it? Did it ever occur to you that
something like that could blow our
cover and compromise the mission?

JAW_   I bet it also goes against GDPR . . .
just a joke. Sorry, once my phone is
working again, I will destroy the
post-it, I promise. Like I'll burn it
or something . . . actually it might
be too wet to burn. Then I'll just
tear it up and chuck it in the ocean.
Oh, but I don't like littering. Then
I'll—

FDF_   WREN. Please get to the point of your call.

JAW_   Sorry, Ma'am. Well, that's also why my phone broke. I was doing recon on the beachfront when the weather changed really quickly, and I got to thinking that maybe there was a . . . you-know-what around. I saw a young man and a young woman, both late-teens, in the amusement arcade, so I started to surveillance them—

FDF_   Surveil.

JAW_   What?

FDF_   The verb of surveillance is surveil.

JAW_   Oh right, is it? Yeah. So I started to surveil them proper like, and I guess they realised and ran away.

FDF_   Okay, that sounds promising, especially if they ran for no reason.

JAW_   Well, if I'm being proper honest, I did leave my flash on when I took a picture.

FDF_   (sigh) Jesus.

JAW_   So I tried to cut them off around the front.

FDF_   You engaged them?

JAW_   Well, I tried, but then it all went
        a bit wrong.

FDF_   Your orders were strictly reconnais-
        sance. You were not given the order
        to engage.

JAW_   I know, I know, but I didn't want
        them to get away.

FDF_   Confrontation is Phase Five of the
        Neutralisation Protocol. We have
        barely started Phase One. If they
        were our target, you would have
        alerted them to our presence and put
        yourself in extreme danger. And if
        it wasn't, you have just scared two
        innocent members of the public who
        would have most likely involved the
        local authorities. Either way, our
        mission is now compromised.

JAW_   I know. I'm so sorry. I wasn't thinking.

FDF_   Clearly!

JAW_   It was definitely the target, though,
        Ma'am.

FDF_   How can you be sure?

JAW_   Because they threw us in the ocean.

FDF_   What?

JAW_   Well, not physically - they didn't

touch me. But there was a glow, and I flew out into the ocean. Had to hitch a ride on a fisher boat back to land. I knew I should have got the water-proof case for my phone. Couldn't tell who did it, but one of them was definitely a you-know-what.

FDF_   Description?

JAW_   Quite choppy and very cold. Tide was in too, so—

FDF_   The targets!

JAW_   Oh, yes. Male, about 5'10", slim, Caucasian, brown hair wearing a coat and scuffed trainers. Travelling with a ginger female, a little shorter, Caucasian, wearing a beige jumper, pink wellies, and a large scarf, seen carrying a frog umbrella. I did get a photo, but my phone still won't turn on.

FDF_   Okay. I'll pass this onto HQ, and we can start accessing CCTV around town. See if anyone knows either of them, but DO NOT engage if you see them again. Targets can be extremely dangerous when cornered, espe-cially if they can't fully control their . . . abilities. You know the protocol. We never engage on a first sighting. I cannot believe how utterly stupid you have been today.

JAW_ Sorry, ma'am.

FDF_ We will discuss this later. I'm afraid I will have to inform HQ too.

JAW_ I - I understand.

FDF_ And stick your phone in rice, for goodness sake, woman.

JAW_ Oh, I went to the little Tesco on the high street. They only had the microwave kind, so I put it in that.

FDF_ Your phone is sitting in microwave rice?

JAW_ Yeah, spicy Mexican.

FDF_ (sigh) Jesus Christ.

JAW_ Oh, and I lost the company credit card in the sea too. Sorry.

FDF_ I am terminating the call now, Junior Agent Wren.

JAW_ Oh right, see you lat—

- End of Log -

6

Steven

The car stinks of polish. Every surface has been so meticu-
lously cleaned and buffed to a shine that you'd swear it was
brand new ... well, if Freya and I hadn't just tracked in a
bunch of sand. Don't think Marcus has noticed yet, but he
will soon enough, and out will come his stupid little hand
vacuum. Given how anal he is about the inside, you'd think
he'd be just as careful about the outside. He overtakes a car
doing the speed limit and cuts up a lorry as it turns down a
side road. If Secret Agent Pixie doesn't find us, traffic enforce-
ment officers probably will.

Prick.

"Where am I supposed to be going?" grumbles Marcus to
Freya.

"Just keep going for a little bit," she says as vaguely as possible,
to which Marcus frowns and mutters something under his
breath. She glances over her shoulder at me in the back and asks,
"Should we go to your fl—"

But I shake my head, and she gets it. What if we are being
followed? For all we know, there are more of them.

Them.

Jesus, when did we end up in a spy movie? We need to lie low; let Tinkerbell lose our scent. Besides, every thriller I've ever watched tells me it's a bad idea to lead your pursuers straight to your house.

"Let's just head back home," suggests Freya.

Marcus's short locs wiggle as he shakes his head. "It's four hours back. I need to eat."

"Forgot your picnic basket?" I mutter sarcastically.

"Why would I pack a picnic?" Marcus replies completely seriously.

"We could stop at a gas station? They do have food at gas stations here, right?" says Troy from the seat next to me.

Yeah, they have food, but they also have a bunch of CCTV. Whenever they are looking for people on the news, they always show grainy black and white footage from petrol stations. Probably shouldn't leave more evidence if we are on the run.

"There's a multi-storey. Let's park up and get some lunch at a café," Freya suggests.

"Are you going to tell me what's going on?" Marcus grunts.

"Of course, but let's just park up and get food first. You hungry, Troy?"

"Errr yeah, I could eat," says Troy as he pushes his hair to the side. He throws a smile my way, and I can't help notice how white his teeth are. It's not like I have bad teeth, but mine feel like browning tombstones by comparison.

Marcus pulls in the multi-storey and parks over two spaces so that no one will scratch his precious baby. Serious prick move.

We spill out of the car, and Freya catches my arm as Troy and Marcus head for the stairs out.

"Should we tell them?" she whispers.

"What, that I have magic powers and am being hunted by a woman who probably wants to dissect me in a lab? Let's lie low for a bit. We'll have some lunch, then you three can go back home, and I'll sneak off back to my flat."

"You're coming with us, Percy."

"It's me they want, not you. I'll just be putting everyone at risk."

"For all we know, it was a case of mistaken identity. Wrong place, wrong time. Regardless, we are going to have to tell those two something."

"We'll figure something out. Why are they here? Did you call them?"

"Phone's dead. I figured I'd be back before anyone noticed."

"Weird."

Troy is holding the door for us, so we stop muttering as we approach. He flashes that Hollywood smile as we head out onto the high street. Marcus, ever the gentleman, hasn't waited. He's being extra prickish today.

We make our way over the road to a café. I can't see any CCTV, so I guess we're safe for now. Freya catches up with Marcus and leaves me with Troy.

"So, Steven, what's up?"

I hate it when he asks me this. *What's up?* What am I supposed to say to that? I understand it's like the American way of saying *You alright?*, but I just don't know the appropriate response. Is he actually asking, or is it just a politeness thing? I want to say something non-committal, but everything sounds cheesy or wrong in my accent. I need to say something. He's looking at me with those light brown eyes – how does someone with that much jaw still look like a puppy? It's like talking to a golden retriever.

"Yeah ... you?"

Damn it.

He blinks a little bit, confused obviously. Maybe he thinks he misheard me and doesn't want to be rude.

"Good. Good, yeah. It's all gooooood."

I don't have time to really dwell on this weird interaction because we are at the café door now, and Troy is opening it for me. He's about four inches taller, so he reaches over me to do it. He smells like synthetic cherry – the kind you get in American sweets.

The inside of the Happy Smiles Café is precisely how I imagined a café in this town would be: a greasy health-code violation that was decorated fifty years ago. The laminate flooring was white in another life but now is a sickly rotten grey. At the far end is a counter with a hatch and a waitress sitting with her feet up on a table. There are a few old biddies lifelessly drinking tea, some builders shuffling eggs around their plates, and a young man with dark hair by himself reading the newspaper.

Freya and Marcus already have a table, so I sit down next to her, and Troy sits opposite. We take off our jackets (or in Freya's case, her mountains of wool), and Troy passes out the sticky laminated menus.

Sat next to each other, Marcus and Troy couldn't look more different if they tried. Marcus is lean and toned with dark skin and is wearing a mustard T-shirt he probably spent two seconds picking out this morning. Meanwhile, Troy is broad, has lighter brown skin, and I can see his pecs outlined in his carefully selected baby blue button-down shirt. Sat with the two of them, I feel like a skinny mess – pretty sure I'm the only one without muscles at the table (Freya included).

The waitress, who looks doped-up on cough syrup, shuffles to our table and takes our orders without her face moving more than a centimetre. A minute later, she basically throws our drinks at us, then sits down at another table, feet up, and files her nails.

"Right, first things first. What the actual hell is going on?" Marcus says, ignoring Troy's flinch at the word "hell".

"Nothing. Nothing," Freya blurts, not amazingly convincingly. She is honestly the worst liar: her saucepan eyes are darting around like she's drunk her bodyweight in espressos.

"Well, obviously something, Freya. You disappear without telling me to this . . . dump, and when we find you, you're treating me like a getaway driver."

"I just came to get Steven. I got him. We can go back home."

"I told you, I'm not going back," I say, trying to suppress my frustration. The last thing I need is a trick with Marcus around.

"Why not?" Troy asks earnestly. He's always so bloody earnest.

"Because I can't, okay. Just take Freya with you and leave me here."

"Fine with me," Marcus grumbles.

"No, we aren't doing that!" Freya says, her eyes bulging from me to Marcus. "We are all going back together, and that's not up for discussion."

"You still haven't explained why you just left without telling me," Marcus says, glaring at Freya over his chipped mug of tea.

"I'm not a house cat, Marcus. Believe it or not, I am allowed outside without your permission."

"I know, but you're hardly popping to Tesco, Freya. You took like a million buses to go halfway across the country."

"Still none of your business."

"I'm your boyfriend – of course it's my business. I was worried about your safety."

Freya snorts and gives him one of her patented eyerolls. "You haven't texted me in four days because you've been revising for your exams. Don't give me that crap about worrying for my safety."

Troy is suddenly very interested in the contents of his mug, and I take this opportunity to inspect the yellowed ceiling panels. Honestly, Sartre got it wrong – hell isn't other people, it's being stuck between an arguing couple.

"Just because I don't text you, it doesn't mean I don't care. *I* still have exams."

"That's why I didn't ask you to come."

"Still should've told me."

"Okay, fine. Whatever."

"Don't give me whatever, Freya! I've just driven for four hours to be here because I was worried about you."

"I've only been gone six hours!"

"Troy said you might be in trouble."

This I am not expecting. Freya looks confused too; I know she is friends with Troy, but I didn't realise he cared this much about her. He fiddles with his collar uncomfortably.

"Well, I ... I just thought something might be up," he says sheepishly. "Your phone was off."

"Yeah, it died again," Freya says.

"Speaking of which," Troy says as he fishes around in his jacket pocket and pulls out a beaten-up phone charger. The rubber has worn away from the end, revealing several strands of metal fibres. Without anyone saying anything, I know it's Freya's.

"Oh, you're a lifesaver," she says as she ducks under the table to plug in her fire hazard.

The grey-eyed waitress comes back and dumps four plates of greasy muck that are supposed to be full Englishes in front of us. Marcus doesn't seem to mind and wolfs down half his plate before Freya has even started. She checks the temperature of her baked beans with her pinky and scrapes them off her toast with a grimace (I know for a fact she will only eat them cold or luke-warm at a push). Troy is poking the black pudding and looks like that woman in *Indiana Jones* who was served the monkey brains. I chuckle but stop myself with a quick glance at my hands. No glowing just yet – pushing that woman into the sea must have used a lot of my powers. At least I can enjoy my lunch for a few more minutes without the threat of setting Marcus on fire.

Oh, what I wouldn't give to set Marcus on fire . . .

"So why were you worried about me?" Freya asks Troy in between mouthfuls of bacon.

Troy looks like he's got trapped wind. He shifts in his seat and looks around. Why is he acting so weird? He leans forward, and to my surprise, he addresses me.

"Someone was asking about you."

"Me?" I glance at Freya, whose immaculate eyebrows are furrowed, and her hand is frozen holding bacon to her mouth.

"Yeah, this woman in a suit. She was Scottish or Irish or some-thing – I can't tell the difference. Anyway, she came up to me on my way to class and asked if Freya was in today, and I'd just seen you at the bus stop, so I said no. Then she asked if I knew Steven, so I said that you were Freya's best friend and had a family emergency. She left her card and told me to call her if I saw either of you. She seemed official, so – well, I don't know – I got spooked. I tried calling you, but your phone was . . . Then I remembered you looking up this town after our Psych exam. So I got Marcus to drive me, but I didn't tell him about the woman in the suit because I didn't think it was my place, and I was worried, so . . . Yeah. Sorry."

My mouth is exceedingly dry all of a sudden. I wait for someone to say anything, but no one does. All three of them are looking at me like I'm Jason Bourne – well, a Jason Bourne who isn't as cool or good-looking as Matt Damon. All I can think about is the pixie-faced woman in the suit who by now is probably halfway out in the English Channel.

"What did she look like?" I ask, my voice weak and breaking like I've just woken up.

"Forties, dark curly hair."

Okay, so not the pixie. Freya catches my eye, and I can tell she's thinking the same thing.

"What was that?" Marcus says, noticing our look.

"Nothing!" Freya says a bit too quickly.

"You two are hiding something."

"It's nothing – it's just . . ." Freya looks at me as if she's about to explode. Her eyes are bugging out of her head like they are ready to pop. "We were just chased by this woman in a suit by the seafront. But it sounds like a different woman."

"Why was *this* woman chasing you?" asks Troy.

"We don't know. We had only just lost her when you showed up. Isn't that right, Steven?"

"Y-yeah." God, I don't sound terribly convincing. I wouldn't even believe me. My heart is beginning to flutter the way it does when a big trick is bubbling up. I'm trying to isolate what I'm feeling: Fear? Anger? Sadness? Guilt? Too soon to tell. Maybe all four, fighting it out to be the one to manifest like an emotional pay-per-view battle royale. Think of white. Think of nothing. Hold back the tide.

"What the hell, Stevie? Why are all these women after you?"

"Probably my dashing good looks," I say, trying to lighten the mood, but no one seems amused. "I don't know. Maybe it's just a coincidence or something."

"If you've got nothing to hide, why did you run?"

"Marcus, leave it!" Freya hisses, glancing at me. But he ignores her with a wave. Prick. Anger definitely has the other emotions on the ropes now.

"No. Something is going on that you're not telling us. What is it, Stevie? You on the run or something?"

The bottom falls away from my insides, and my stomach plunges to my feet. I try to keep my face as passive as possible. Oh god, anger just lost its footing and is now getting pinned by fear. Think of white. Nothing but white. Feel nothing.

"I honestly don't know," I lie. "But someone starts running towards you, and you run away from them." Marcus is like a pit bull with an old slipper, and it's all I can do to get him to drop it.

"No, you don't. You ask them what they want and put your hands in the air," he says adamantly.

"Marcus, it wasn't like that," Freya says hastily. "It was just a young woman in a suit. We don't know who she was or what she wanted. Let's finish our lunch, go back home, and forget anything ever happened."

"We need to know if he has done something. I don't want to be harbouring a fugitive."

"Steven's not a fugitive; he's a bloody English student."

Now guilt has performed a suplex on fear and has anger in a headlock. I feel like a pot about to boil over. Any second, a trick is going to burst out of me, and it's either going to make everyone explode with anger or fear, or it'll light me up like a bloody Christmas tree.

Breath in for four, out for four. Let everything go. Think of white. Feel nothing.

Then I do.

Total knockout. The fight ends in a four-way draw.

Something switches inside me, and I don't care. I don't care about Marcus or Agent Pixie or any of it. I don't give a single toss.

I zone out of Freya and Marcus bickering and shrug non-committally when she asks me something. She frowns at me like I'm getting a face tattoo that she disapproves of but goes back to her row. And I don't care. I am entirely apathetic to everything going on, and for the first time today, I am at peace.

Without warning, Marcus stands up and points at Freya.

"You never support me," he yells but sounding more hurt than angry.

"How could you even say a thing like that!" she retorts, also standing up. Tears streak down her face as she clutches her chest. I look around, but no one else in the café seems to have noticed this sudden outburst.

"It's true!" Marcus says dramatically as he stands on his chair.

"You're lying!" Freya declares as she stands on hers.

Troy looks at me, confused and bewildered, then slides down in embarrassment. What the hell are they playing at? Why are they overacting like they are in a Mexican telenovela? Then I notice the builders on the table nearby having similarly dramatic shouting matches and the old biddies by the window laughing hysterically to each other.

The waitress comes over, and to my surprise, she doesn't tell them to get down off the furniture. Instead, she does something equally unexpected. She smiles.

"Did anyone save room for pudding? Can I tempt you with the Happy Smiles Fudge Surprise?" she practically sings, as chipper as a cheerleader. Her eyes are bright and green, and she's smiling like a Stepford Wife. What the hell is happening?

"N-no, thank you," I mutter as Freya and Marcus are now too busy kissing over the table to notice, and Troy seems to be hiding behind a menu. The waitress skips away and starts polishing tables like a Disney Princess, and that's when I notice a colour dancing between my fingers I haven't seen before.

Grey.

7

Steven

"I'm going to the toilet!" I yell to deaf ears and run out the door by the service hatch. I can hear the cacophony all the way down the corridor, but I find peace in the grubby men's room. It has one of those communal urinal troughs that has probably not been cleaned since it was installed. Blue-green rust covers most of the exposed piping, and chewing gum blocks the drain. The fragrant aroma of stale urine smacks my nose. Delightful.

My hands are still glowing grey, so I wash them vigorously in the sink for some reason.

Out damned spot and all that.

What the hell am I doing? I know that won't do anything, but it's the only thing I can think of. Usually, I try to think of white and unfeel whatever I'm feeling, but that won't work. Somehow, I caused this by unfeeling. How do you unfeel unfeeling? Double negative. Feel something? I feel panicked right now, but that doesn't seem to be doing anything. I splash water on my face a few times. Nothing. The grey light still slinks between my fingers like smoke.

I look rough. I don't think I've looked in a mirror properly since I got here. My hair's doing that stupid thing where it curls on the top, but I've stopped caring about it. My eyes are dark, and I don't think I've ever been this skinny. In the face, I mean. My body is still the same runtish frame it's always been.

"Lost in an existential crisis?" says a crisp voice.

I jump out of my skin. It's the young man who was by himself reading the newspaper. Early twenties perhaps with black hair in a messy but styled tousle and well-groomed stubble that frames his gentle smile. Under his coat, he's wearing a black turtleneck which looks like a pedestal holding up his handsome face. I wish I could wear turtlenecks, but I'm probably not cool enough to pull them off. This guy definitely is. Tall and tanned, he's standing in the doorway, hand tucked into the pocket of his fitted black trousers, looking like he just stepped off a runway in Milan.

"Oh no, I was just … washing my hands," I say, trying to seem nonchalant by giving a little laugh. Piss biscuits, I've drawn attention to my hands. I hide them behind my back and go to leave, but the stranger hasn't moved out of the way. He is just smiling at me.

"Had an accident, have we? Don't worry. It happens to all of us when we start," he says, rearranging the thick black glasses on the bridge of his nose. He is very well-spoken.

I don't know what to say. I don't know how to react. What does he mean? I give a polite non-committal laugh and go for the door, but he still doesn't budge.

"Let me see your hands?" he murmurs softly. It's a command, but he says it like a very intimate question. I open my mouth, but nothing comes out, so he leans in and whispers, "Don't worry. I know what you are."

Well, that can mean a few things.

"Sorry, I don't know what you're talking about."

"Yes, you do," he says calmly. "I saw what happened to your friends – what you did. I can help."

"Can you?"

"I'm like you."

Before my brain catches up and tells me not to, I raise my hands up to the stranger, and a smirk of curiosity bursts across his face.

"Grey?" he muses as he takes my hands in his own. They are cool and smooth and make mine feel like they are made of burlap. On his right index finger is a long silver ring, almost like a talon, that he taps gently on my palm. The trick swirls around our hands then is sucked into the ring like grey water going down the plughole.

And just like that, it's gone.

"Better?" says the stranger, still holding my hands.

"Errrm y-yeah – thank you," I stammer like a tit. "How did you—?"

"Like I said, I'm like you. Except, I've learned how to control it."

"How? How do you control it?" I sound desperate, but *I am* desperate. Desperate for all this to stop, so I can stop hiding. Stop hurting people.

The handsome stranger chuckles to himself and pushes his hair back. "Practice. I'm afraid it'll take more than thirty seconds in the men's room to learn."

"I want it to stop," I mumble.

"It's scary, I know. When your powers start manifesting, it can feel like you have no control. Like you're a bomb waiting to explode and hurt the people closest to you. And even if you can stop yourself feeling things, to live without sadness or anger or fear is to not really be human, is it? And it's near impossible.

58

I would be doing so well until I saw those bloody abandoned dog adverts. Then it would be storms and floods and who knows what. But there are ways to control, direct, and stop it. You won't find them unless someone teaches you, and it's not like there's a school for what we can do."

"I always hoped I'd be found by Professor X and taken to his school for emomancers," I say, which makes him laugh.

"Emomancers? I like that. Much grander than EMT. It makes us sound like we should be wearing robes and dancing around crypts."

"Are you telling me you don't? Now I feel silly sacrificing all those virgins."

He laughs again, and I grin like an idiot. But I can't help it – it's nice to have someone laugh at my stupid jokes. Marcus wouldn't know humour if it beat him to death with a whoopee cushion.

"I'm no Professor X, but I could teach you what I know if you like?"

My face flushes. I'm suddenly very aware of my hands. Have they always been so awkward? Like lumps of ham at the end of my spindly arms. I'm waving them too much or maybe not enough – I don't know. I stuff my hands into my pockets. There, problem solved. Now, why am I sweating so much?

"That would be amazing. Thank you . . ." Did he say his name? No, I don't think he did. Better say it again, so it doesn't look like I forgot. "Thank you."

"Zachary," he says, holding out his hand.

"Steven," I reply, shaking it and hoping mine aren't too sweaty.

"A pleasure to meet you, Steven," Zachary says. His eyes are vivid blue, like when someone oversaturates their pictures on Instagram. "I'm glad we met so serendipitously, although

I probably would have preferred a cleaner setting. What are you doing tonight?"

I was supposed to be working at the docks again, and if Freya had her way, I'd be back in Dorset by dinnertime.

"Nothing."

"Excellent. Come to mine any time after eight. I live in room 113 of the Grand Regalia Hotel on the seafront. Just head up to the eleventh floor."

"You live in a hotel room?"

"I know. I'm full of surprises," he says, giving me a wink. "Well, Steven, I best be going. Need to get my sewing machine fixed if I'm going to make a pair of emomancer's robes before tonight. Any preference on colour?"

"I mean, if you don't go for black with red trim, can you even call yourself a cult?"

He laughs, and dear God, he's got a magnetic smile. "You're funny. Until tonight, little emomancer."

"See you then, Professor X."

And with one last smile and a flick of his hair, Zachary is gone.

8

Freya

Why the hell am I snogging Marcus on top of the table? Like, full-on tongue down the throat, nails in his scalp snogging? Oh god, my shirt is undone. Marcus's hands are frozen around the clasps of my bra. That was close: we were just thirty seconds away from total boobage in the middle of a diner. What the actual hell is happening? More importantly, why is no one else bothered that this is happening? Well, apart from Troy, who's hiding behind a fort of menus. The lads arguing the next table over have stopped screaming like threatened primates, and the old ladies have either stopped laughing or gone into cardiac arrest – both equally likely scenarios.

Marcus pulls away in horror, wearing the same look he gave me when I said the guacamole he bought was too spicy. In fairness, my face is burning like it did when I ate the spicy guac. We clamber off the table, avoiding eye contact like one of us farted during sex. Using couple's telepathy, we agree to never talk of this again. I put the girls away and pick up the jumper I discarded in a pornographic daze.

Did someone slip hallucinogenics into our food or something? LSD in the tea? How else do you explain the recreation of Woodstock '69 that just took place in this disgusting café in Grunsby-on-Sea?

Urgh, my tea's gone cold, but it's giving me something to do, so I drink it anyway. Marcus is intently rearranging the condiments, and Troy looks shellshocked like he's just watched *The Human Centipede* – I hate that that's a point of reference for me now; I am never letting Marcus pick during movie night again.

It's soooooo quiet.

No one is talking, just the occasional slurp of cold tea to punctuate the silence.

I suddenly realise that Percy is missing. Guess he slipped away in all the insanity. Was this another of his powers manifesting? What emotion makes other people act like this?

After five minutes, which feel like five hours, Percy struts back from the loo, a stupid grin plastered all over his face. Once again, completely oblivious.

"What?" he asks. "What is it?"

✱

No one has said anything in seventeen minutes.

Not a single word since Percy came back to the table. The waitress threw the bill at the table, we paid and then left. Well, Marcus paid. The entire thing. Usually, he's the type of guy who works out how much he owes down to the penny. He even once calculated and paid for the exact percentage of nachos he had eaten. But nope, Marcus paid for the lot. I think he just wanted to leave as soon as possible. And given the speed at which he is now marching down Grunsby high street, I think he still does.

Steven tries a few times to say something but keeps bottling it. Probably because Troy is hanging off my sleeve like a lost puppy. Oh god, he probably thinks he was privy to some weird European sex ritual or something.

My phone buzzes. Somehow, Steven has managed to text me without anyone noticing.

Steven: Ned top rally.

I scowl at the notification on my lock screen. Obviously, he tried to do it without looking. I unlock my phone, drop it down to my side, and text him back while pretending to look at the architecture.

Me: "Ned top rally"? What does that mean? Jeez, Percy, you honestly are the worst texter. Just pretend you are looking at Instagram or something for a little bit, then text me properly.

His phone buzzes in his hand, and he tilts it up to his face. Subtle as a brick, Percy. He pantomimes a three-act opera of checking his Insta before bringing the phone closer to his chest and spends at least thirty seconds composing a three-word text.

Steven: Need to talk.

I roll my eyes at the stupid message. Of course, we do. Does he think I'll cease all communication until we get back to Dorset? I love him to pieces, but sometimes he can be the stupidest person I know.

63

Me: Well, I'm all ears – figuratively speaking. Is it about your you-know-what? I assume so, or you would have just said it out loud. Just text me whatever it is. We can talk properly when I get Marcus to pull over at the services.

By the time Steven has finished his reply, we are back at the multi-storey, Marcus has paid £6.50 at the ticket machine, and we're back in the car. I told Marcus I wanted to sleep, so I went in the back with Steven. Why can't that boy walk and text like a normal Gen Zer? While I wait for Steven to cross the T's and dot the I's, I shed my scarves and jumpers and leave a mannequin of wool in the middle seat. Finally, my phone buzzes.

Steven: So, I've decided not to go.

That's it? It taken him the best part of ten minutes to say that. I was expecting an essay, themes, subplots with side characters I'd grow to love. I look at him unimpressed, and he gives me that look like he doesn't know what he's done wrong. Before he gets a textual chastising, I give him an eye roll – one that says, "You're an idiot, Steven Percival."

Me: You're an idiot, Steven Percival. Is that it?!?! I was expecting *War and Peace*, and you cough out six words and a contraction?
Steven: Sorry! I just didn't know what to say.
Me: We've been over this about nine times today. You are coming back home with us. End of. I don't care if you think you are putting us in harm's way or whatever.

Steven: No, it's not that. I promise.

He pauses, then writes something out about six times before it finally pings over to me.

Steven: I met someone who can teach me to control it.
Me: Who?
 When?
 How?
Steven: Just some guy from the café.
 Tonight.
 I don't know yet, but he stopped whatever I caused back there, and he said I could learn to do it myself.

By now, we are out of the multi-storey, and Marcus is caning it up the high street. His face is set to an intense pout – God, he's hot when he's like this. I should embarrass him more often. Though he probably should slow down these narrow wibbly-wobbly streets, or he'll knock down a pensioner.

Me: You caused that?!
Steven: Yes.
Me: Jesus, Percy. What emotion causes others to stand on a table in their bra and snog their boyfriend?
Steven: Don't know. I can't really remember. It all happened so fast.
Me: Just want to reiterate I was ten seconds away from committing indecent exposure.
Steven: And I didn't think their Food Hygiene Rating could go any lower . . .

He finishes off that last text with a vomiting emoji. I send him four emojis of the middle finger.

A long beep of the horn makes me look up. We're near a school, and the car in front has stopped for a lollipop lady helping some children across the road, but Marcus doesn't seem too bothered about that bit of the Highway Code. The lollipop lady stops picking her nose and sticks her fingers up at us, but Marcus is away, hurtling down the road like we have the mob on our tail.

Steven: Jesus, is he trying to kill us?

Me: He's still embarrassed about what happened in the café.

His next text is just a rooster emoji, but I gather his meaning.

Me: Is this guy going to teach you here?

Steven: That was the plan. I was supposed to go to the hotel on the seafront tonight.

Me: And he'd help you control it?

Steven: Yeah.

"Marcus, change of plan," I say suddenly, which makes Troy jump. "We're going to head back in the morning."

"You what?" he grunts as he swerves around a pair of dustmen wheeling bins out to their lorry.

"It's getting on, and I don't want to get back super late. Besides, Steven still has to pack up his stuff."

"I don't care. We are going home now. I am not spending another minute in this town."

"Fine. Don't. Drop Steven and me at his flat, and you and Troy can go home now. We'll come up in the morning on public transport."

"Oh, I don't mind staying and helping you guys pack," says Troy, throwing a glance at Steven.

"I am not driving all the way back home without you. We are all going now. End of," Marcus decrees and punctuates with a sanctimonious gear change.

"Marcus, pull over right now, or I'll scream bloody murder out of the window."

"Like hell, you will."

Red rag to a bull, Marcus. I roll down the window, stick my head out and yell, "HELP! WE ARE BEING KIDNAPPED!"

"ALRIGHT, FINE!" Marcus takes a few deep breaths and pulls over into a lay-by. "I will drop Stevie off at his flat, then drive back to Dorset. Anyone who wants to stay in this insane asylum can stay. Anyone who wants to come with me back to normality can."

"Good," I say as passive-aggressively as I can. My phone buzzes.

Steven: Thanks.

Marcus and I don't speak for the rest of the journey to Steven's flat. We pull up on the hill just outside, and everyone but Marcus gets out. He keeps the motor running.

"Seriously?" he says, rolling down the window. "You're staying here?"

"Absolutely," I say. Troy is on one side of me, trying his best to smile as though nothing is wrong, and Steven is on the other, beaming like the cat that got the cream.

"Freya, I am your boyfriend. Not Stevie. At some point, you are going to have to put me first and stop pandering to him."

"If you are asking me to choose between you and my best friend, you are going to lose. Every. Single. Time. I am not that girl."

"I am not asking you to—"

But Marcus never finishes his sentence because his car suddenly rolls backwards down the hill. Troy runs after him, but the car is going too fast now. Marcus is trying to swerve out of the way, but he accidentally mounts the curb and smashes into a lamppost. The back windscreen explodes, and his boot crumples. Marcus jumps out of the driver's seat just in time for the lamppost to come crashing down on the roof, smashing the front windscreen and making a massive dent down the middle of the whole car.

Marcus can't say anything. He looks like he's just been kicked repeatedly in the balls. Troy is already checking him over for injuries, but he seems unhurt – thank God. I look behind me and see Steven is similarly dumbfounded. His hands are glowing yellow.

"Crap," he whispers under his breath.

9

Troy

I have never seen a grown man weep so much over a car before. Marcus is still sobbing on the sidewalk like he's just lost a child. Pretty sure if a streetlight fell on Freya, he'd just shrug. And I thought Americans were supposed to be obsessed with their cars. Mind you, most teenagers back home have huge pickup trucks that get half a mile to the gallon. Brits seem content to zip around in tiny pods no bigger than a chicken nugget: kinda hard to be obsessed with a nugget-mobile. Still, Marcus grieves his tiny car, completely ignoring the fact that he narrowly avoided being crushed to death along with it.

Straight men, ironically, really need to get their priorities straight.

*

Marcus

My car . . . My baby . . . This is the worst day of my entire life.

*

69

Troy

I pat Marcus on the shoulder, which is probably super patronising, but I don't know what else to do. How do you console a guy bawling over damaged property? Marcus is not usually the type of guy to show how he feels. Yet now, he is clinging on to me, getting tears on my button-down.

Oh man, why has girlfriend duty fallen to me? Sure, Freya rushed down to check he was okay, but for the last five minutes, she and Steven have been having a super-secret discussion just out of earshot. I keep looking over, but they avoid my gaze in that intentional-but-trying-to-look-unintentional way. Something is going on for sure, but all I can do for now be Marcus's human handkerchief.

Freya eventually comes over with a smile like nothing is wrong and suggests we leave Marcus to grieve.

"Do we need to do anything or call anyone?" I ask as we head up the rusted staircase to Steven's apartment.

"No, don't worry. Once Marcus snaps out of it, he'll call AA," she replies.

I laugh. I find British humour hard to pick up on, but sometimes it's really out there.

"Gotta check in with his sponsor?" I ask, trying to join in on the joke, but I just get blank stares back.

"Sponsor?" Steven asks. I can't tell if he is ribbing me.

"Yeah, like AA sponsor. Wait, what are you talking about?"

"The breakdown service," Freya says.

"Oh, like Triple A? Gotcha. In America, AA is like Alcoholics Anonymous."

"Yeah, we know. We have that here too," says Steven.

"Isn't that confusing? Both being called AA?"

"We usually get it through context," says Freya, which makes Steven chuckle. Whenever they are together, I can't help but feel left out. And insanely jealous. Jealous of Steven that he has a best friend to confide in. Jealous of Freya that she can talk to Steven freely without melting into a puddle of incomprehensible pudding.

Steven's apartment is on the third floor, which I remember is the British second floor. My first week here was spent forever in the wrong place until Freya explained the existence of the "ground floor" to me. It's like everyone got together before I arrived and thought up ways to confuse me. Like dates. Oh my gosh, dates. I almost caused an international incident when I put my date of birth Month/Day on all my forms. I get the small/bigger/biggest argument, but honestly, it makes looking through the calendar so much easier to start with the month.

Anyway.

I'm getting serious crack-den motel vibes from this place, even before he opens the door: the paint chipping off everything, dark brown stains seemingly everywhere, bars on windows, the general smell of pee.

The inside, though, is quaint and British as heck. The kind of place a grandma would live and keep cats. There's a shelf of novelty teapots in the living room for crying out loud.

Steven leads us through to the kitchen, and almost immediately, the electric kettle is on. Ah yes, sometimes stereotypes really are true. Brits cannot go anywhere without drinking hot tea. A pathological need for boiled leaf juice. Everyone has a kettle in their homes, regardless of whether they drink it or not. Freya shouted at me once because I told her I boil water in the microwave when I make hot tea back home – like I committed a cardinal sin or murdered a puppy. I do like tea, but Brits never have a selection. Just what they call "normal tea" with or without sugar and milk. That's it.

Steven passes me a cup, and our fingers brush against each other as I reach for it. He smiles at me too. My spine shivers. I feel like I'm in a Jane Austen novel where touching someone's arm is considered third base.

"Oh, that's so much better," Freya says with a little sigh as she gets lost in her tea trance. "Right, I'll bring Marcus down his. He'll need it."

Freya takes the fourth mug of tea down to Marcus, leaving me and Steven alone. Now's my chance. Just play it cool.

I sip my tea, but it hits the back of my throat, and I cough. Real cool. I am such a dingus. My eyes are streaming, and I can't stop. I try to suppress it, but nope – the universe is just that cruel. I turn to cough in the sink, and Steven is behind me, hitting me on the back.

"Th-thanks," I mutter when it finally stops.

"Blimey, I didn't realise tea was that toxic to Americans," he says with a smirk.

"Not enough corn syrup."

YES! He laughs at that. I think that might be the first time I've made Steven Percival laugh, and all it took was mild asphyxiation.

"Here," he says, handing me water in a green whisky glass that is straight out of the fifties. "Try not to choke on this one too."

"No promises, but I'll try. Thanks."

Steven checks his phone briefly, then hops up on the kitchen counter opposite me. I would do the same, but I'm by the stove, and the last thing I want is to set my pants on fire. I go for what I hope is a casual lean instead.

"I hope Marcus is okay," I say. Ugh, why is it so hard to start a conversation with someone you are attracted to?

"He'll be fine. He wasn't hurt."

"Try telling him that. He was howling so much I thought he'd left an arm in there. I can't believe how wrecked his car got. Guess he'll remember his parking brake in future."

"Y-yeah," Steven says, then quickly changes the subject. "So, how are you enjoying your stay in Britain's finest seaside town?"

"Like, I know it's supposed to be terrible, but I think it's pretty cute."

"Cute?" He laughs incredulously.

"Yeah. Everything here is so quaint and small and made of brick."

"What are things made of back home then?"

"Wood, I guess?"

He tsks and shakes his head, saying, "Did you learn nothing from the *Three Little Pigs*?"

"I've also never been to the beach before and—"

"You've never been to the beach before?"

"You realise Arizona is landlocked, right?"

He looks genuinely surprised by this. In fairness, I couldn't point to most places in Europe on a map.

"It's just nice to see more of England. There's so much here I want to see," I say.

"Trust me, there are far nicer places to visit than Grunsby-on-Sea."

A lull in conversation settles. And it was going so well. Okay, let's keep asking stuff – but what? I look around, but the kitchen

73

doesn't give me any lifelines. Just a very old-fashioned room with a cooker, cupboards, and . . . a washing machine! Gold. He liked the transatlantic cultural differences before – time to double down.

"So, I have to ask. What is with British people having washing machines in their kitchen?"

"Where else would you put them?" he says, his face lighting up.

"In the garage or utility room. Most apartment buildings have communal ones in the basement."

"I think some people do, but it's just more convenient, isn't it?"

"Yeah, but you're preparing food in the kitchen. Completely separate activity to washing your underwear."

"Ah, but what if you are using your underwear in the kitchen?"

"In what way?"

"Dunno. Ran out of tea towels to dry your hands?"

"What is it with you people and tea? You call your evening meals tea, and now you have towels for tea too."

"What do you call them then? Burger towels?"

"*Dish*towels. You know, because you dry your dishes with them."

"Ah, but what if you want to dry your teabags to use them again?"

"*Then* you'd need a tea towel."

We laugh again, and oh my gosh, it's working. Step one: have an actual conversation with him where I don't sound like an idiot – check. I just need to keep this up, and soon he'll . . . Well, I'm not actually sure what the end goal is here, but at least we're bonding. I think.

Steven frowns and tilts his head like a German shepherd who's heard a funny noise.

"Don't take this the wrong way, but why did you come here, Troy?"

"I guess I wanted a change of scenery, and I've always wanted to go to England. So I—"

"No, I mean, why did you come here? To Grunsby?"

Oh gosh. Why couldn't I have choked now? I can't lie this quickly, but I can't exactly tell him the truth – something in the middle.

"Well, I was . . . you know, worried. About Freya. And I guess about you too."

He doesn't look totally satisfied with that.

"I feel like I'm missing something. Some woman asks about me, and you persuade Marcus to drive halfway across the country?"

"I know. I can't really explain it. Looking back, it might seem a little rash, but at the time . . . I don't know. I just knew I had to do something. I thought you might be in trouble, and Marcus had a right to know what his girlfriend was doing. Plus, he's the only person I know who has a car. Well, *had* a car. I'm staying with my aunt, and she doesn't drive."

He doesn't say anything back, but I can tell he doesn't buy it. What else can I say? I wanted to make sure you're safe because I have a major crush on you that will probably be unrequited, and I thought this might be a good opportunity to get to know you or something, but also I was scared that you were wanted by the authorities and – oh gosh, I'm now aiding and abetting, and I didn't think this all the way through, but I still don't really care because I'm an idiot who is patting himself on the back for keeping you entertained in a conversation that has lasted less than ten minutes.

Breathe, Anderson.

"Well, I'm glad you came. You turned up in the nick of time."

He's glad I'm here! Technically he's glad I provided a getaway car, but still.

"What do you think that woman wanted? The one that chased you on the beachfront?"

"Err yeah, it's weird that. I don't know either."

I raise an eyebrow. Now it's his turn to be coy. He's hiding something too.

"I'm just glad you and Freya are safe. Has your family emergency resolved itself?"

He takes a few seconds to realise what I'm talking about.

"Oh y-yeah, I—"

But before he can concoct a cover story, he's interrupted by the front door opening. Freya stomps into the kitchen, crosses her arms, and rolls her eyes.

"Well, the car's a total write-off."

76

10

Steven

From the top of the metal stairs, we watch Marcus howling like an injured animal as he tries to prise the car door open. With all the crashing and banging, it's like an impromptu performance of *Stomp*, but with a lot more swearing.

I mean, it's my fault. Of course, it is. I felt so happy Freya stood by me that I lost control and caused the handbrake to fail. I nearly killed my best friend's boyfriend, and I know I should feel guilty ... but honestly, this is my favourite trick I've ever done. Not only is it absolutely hilarious to see that prick's pride and joy crushed into a pancake of crumpled metal, but it means I can stay in Grunsby a few more days – now that's something I never thought I'd be happy about. I'll just have to think of an excuse to sneak off tonight to meet Zachary. I really should stop smiling – I look like a psychopath. And I'll probably manifest a trick again – feels like my grace period should have run out by now. Okay, neutral face activated.

Eventually, the police come and take down his details with all the enthusiasm of a trip to the post office. Naturally, I hide up here the whole time – I still don't know who is in league with Agent Pixie, and there could be a warrant out for me. Unlikely, but better to be safe. Troy and Freya give statements, then leave Marcus to call his insurance. Ugh, he is going to be insufferable.

Half an hour later, Marcus is finally off the phone and comes up to the flat.

"Stupid insurance," Marcus grunts as he bangs open the front door with his usual air of decorum. Guess he's taking his production of *Stomp* on the road.

"What did they say?" asks Freya, now on her fourth cup of tea. How her teeth haven't eroded away to stumps with all the sugar is beyond me. She and Troy have been sitting on the vinyl-wrapped couch watching crappy game shows while I've been pottering around, making my flat somewhat presentable. I thought it best to stay busy to keep the tricks at bay so I don't set Freya on fire or cause Troy to be mauled by a tiger.

"What's the point of having insurance if they won't do anything when you need to use it," he says, storming into the living room and taking his anger out on my skirting board with his £300 trainers.

"What, they're not paying out? They can't do that, surely?" says Troy.

"No, they'll pay out. The woman says it's a write-off, so I'll get market value."

"Then what's the problem?" I ask.

"The problem, *Stevie*, is that they won't send out a courtesy car because the damage is irreparable."

"So what are you going to do?" asks Freya as she stands up and rubs his arm sympathetically.

"They put me through to a car hire place, but they say they can't get anything to me until Wednesday because this place seems to be in a different bloody time zone. There's only one bus in and one bus out a week, so public transport is a no-go. Can't exactly ask Mum to bunk off her shift at the hospital to pick me up, so I'm stuck here."

Piss biscuits.

That backfired.

"Will you miss any of your mocks?" Freya asks.

"General Studies is tomorrow, but who cares. My Physics one is on Friday, though."

As long as Marcus doesn't stay here, everything should be fine.

"I'm sure Steven won't mind if we all crash here till the hire car comes," says Freya.

I'm going to kill her.

I open my mouth but realise I can't protest without being a dick. Thankfully, it seems Marcus hates that idea just as much as I do.

"No, it's fine. We'll get a hotel."

Wow, he really must be desperate not to stay here if he is offering to pay for a hotel.

"There's one on the seafront. I'll google it," says Freya, unlocking her phone and typing away with lightning speed. "Here, the Grand Regalia. Oh god, their website is awful. Look at these fonts – it's like a fansite from the nineties. I can't even scroll down, this banner won't stop flashing, and it's still – you know what? I'll just call the number instead. Everyone shut up."

Annoying Freya habit number 74: she can text, watch telly, read a book, and do her ironing all at the same time, but *cannot* speak on the phone if anyone else is talking. We sit in silence whilst Freya puts on her snooty telephone voice that sounds like she's a sixty-five-year-old-widow who writes letters of complaint.

"Hello, yes, is this the Grand Regalia Hotel? Fabulous. I want to enquire about booking a room? Just two nights, from today until Wednesday afternoon if possible? ... Hello? Hello? Cow hung up on me!"

"Take it that's a no then," I say, trying to not sound disappointed.

"She said they were fully booked and put the phone down."

"Weird, I have literally never seen anyone go in or out of that hotel," I say.

"There must be another one, surely," says Marcus, not altogether successfully hiding his desperation. Hey, I am right there with you – if I had the money, I would buy you a car so you can go home. Kidneys fetch a good price on the black market, right?

"Next nearest one is twenty-four miles away," says Freya, shaking her head.

"B&B? Airbnb? Motel? Hostel? Campsite? Caravan? There must be somewhere?" he pleads.

"Sorry, babe. I think this is it. We'll all stay here till the hire car comes. It'll be like a holiday away together. We're going to have so much fun!"

And just like that, the universe plays another trick on me, but without the coloured sparkles.

Guess I'll go find that blow-up bed the landlady keeps in the wardrobe.

*

Two hours later, Marcus and Freya burst back into the flat, laden down with bags of shopping. He's been in an understandably foul mood, so Freya took him out for a walk to get supplies.

Judging by the thunderous look on his face, I'd say their escapade hasn't cheered him up in the slightest. They have dinner, which is a relief.

Troy and I have spent the time rearranging the furniture, so the air mattress can fit in the living room. Troy will take that tonight, and I'm on the sofa, so Freya and Marcus can have the bed. Troy's a nice guy – the time has flown by, and I haven't really noticed. We just chatted about school and how he likes the UK. The best part is that no tricks have manifested since the car crash. My battery must be low, or maybe I've reached a state of balance for the time being (with no Marcus around – coincidence, I don't think). Whatever the cause, I'm not looking a gift horse in the mouth. Explaining to Troy why it is raining indoors is something I can't even bear to think about. And nor do I want to clean it up . . . again.

With shopping unloaded, Freya bounces into the room, cup of tea already in hand.

"Right, we are here for two breakfasts and two dinners, so I reckon we each do one of them? I'll do dinner now if you like, and Marcus will do some chicken tomorrow. You boys fancy doing breakfasts?" Freya says, plonking down on the air mattress next to Troy.

"Oh, I . . . umm. I don't really know how to . . . you know . . ." Troy mumbles.

"What? Cook?" I ask, sitting up on the couch with a squeak. Troy nods sheepishly. "How are you alive? How do you eat? Photosynthesis?"

"I've lived mostly on takeout or microwave dinners."

"Not even scrambled eggs?" I ask.

"Nope. Never even cracked one."

"How about this? I'll do breakfast tomorrow and teach you how to cook eggs," I suggest. "Then you can do it Wednesday morning?"

Troy's face lights up. He's got very shiny eyes when he smiles. Like a Pixar character.

"That sounds perfect."

As Troy says this, the clouds shift, and a glorious sunset bursts through the window. I see why photographers call it the golden hour. Even my crappy flat looks beautiful in the warm amber glow.

11

Steven

We sit with our bowls of pasta watching *Brave*, Troy and I on
the air mattress and Freya and Marcus on the couch. I like *Brave*,
and thankfully there aren't any majorly happy or sad bits, so I
reckon I'll be safe.

I check my phone, and it's 7.15 p.m. – only 45 minutes before
I'm supposed to meet Zachary for my lesson. A bubble of excitement surges within me.

The power trips with a yellow spark, and everything goes dark.

"Dodgy wiring," I yell, getting up so quickly that Troy almost
spills his pasta on the air mattress. Marcus grunts and Troy seems
more confused than anything, but Freya whips her head around
and stares at me like a meerkat caught in a headlight. Do meerkats
do that? Whatever, she's looking at me all panicked. I nod and hold
my hands up to say it's fine, then head to the fuse box in the hallway.

None of the fuses have tripped. This is all on me. Okay,
think sad things. Maybe that will counter it. Bambi's mum
dying . . . Nope. Elsa's mum and dad dying . . . Nope. Mufasa
dying . . . What is with Disney and killing parents? Okay,
probably something more real and less animated is needed.
Something authentic.

But it's hard. I don't feel sad right now. Watching a movie with friends – it's nice. It's normal. But I suppose it can't last. I can't do this beyond these three days. I can't go with them. This was just a taste of honey – of a normality that I can't ever really own. Because I am one good day away from killing someone else, someone I care about. As soon as the hire car comes, they'll go, and I will go on living this half-life on my own.

Alone.

The lights come on.

"I have to pop out now," I shout through to the room. "I forgot I have a shift tonight. Don't wait up for me, and help yourselves to anything."

I go before I hear any of their protests or questions. I'm down the metal stairs before I know it, and not long after that, I pass the wreck of Marcus's car. I walk down the long hill until I hit the seafront. It's slightly longer to go this way than diagonally through the town, but I have some time to kill. There is no way in hell I am turning up early; I'd rather chop off my arm. That being said, I want to be there now and get started. But no, play it cool, Percival.

The sea is dark and foreboding, with not a single light from a boat or star from the cloudy sky. The gentle rock of the waves and the hum from the amber streetlamps are the only noises. I swear I could be the only thing in the world right now.

The Grand Regalia Hotel looms into view: a gaudy relic of the twenties opposite the half-sunken pier. Greek pillars flank the outside, where a weather-worn sign displays its name in giant gold letters. A column of windows stretches up the centre like a cylinder of glass, and the rest of the hotel spreads either side of it like bat wings.

It's huge! I can't understand why a seaside hotel this big in November is fully booked. Peeking out from behind is the Ferris wheel that I've never seen move. I can't really blame people for steering clear of it – the compartments have wire mesh around them like cages, and the peeling paint has revealed an alarming amount of rust. Hasn't Grunsby ever heard of health and safety?

I walk into the lobby, and it's giving me serious *Tower of Terror* vibes. It was probably once very glamorous, with its high ceilings and architectural flourishes, but clearly the cleaning staff aren't being paid enough. The gold trim that frames the walls, lift, and reception desk is tarnished and grubby, and the sad stack of leaflets by the entrance are crumpled and water damaged.

A grey-eyed young man in a mustard-stained shirt and tie looks up at me from the reception desk. Should I say something? Announce that I am meeting someone on the eleventh floor that I met in a toilet? Oh god, that sounds wrong! I keep running through ways to put it, but in every scenario, I seem like an escort who never took a class in subtlety. My mouth is open. I need to say words.

Thankfully, I don't have to; the receptionist loses interest in me and goes back to whatever he was doing. That was easy.

I puff my chest up and walk with purpose to the lift, praying that no one else spots me. The creaky gold doors slide open – this is definitely a death trap, right? Unless I want to climb eleven flights of stairs before I see Zachary, I'm going to have to chance it. Potential death or mild pit stains ... I'll take potential death right about now.

I get in, press the button, and the lift creaks up to the eleventh floor. Wonder if I'm about to see some creepy little girl ghosts? Nope. No deranged fathers wielding axes or rivers of blood. Just a long, thin corridor with red carpet and dark wood-panelled walls lit by cobwebbed chandeliers.

I'm going to be murdered, aren't I?

Slowly, I walk down the corridor and stop at the first door. They're all on the left-hand side, and this one is room 110. Weirdly, when I get to the next one, the tarnished metal numbers say 119. Then the next few are 112 and 116. Does anything make sense in this stupid town?

After five rooms, the corridor bends, and I'm in the central glass column I saw from the outside. From here, I can see all the lights of the town reflected in the dark sea, like an ocean of iridescent treacle. No time to enjoy the view, I need to find Zachary's room.

Round the corner is an identical corridor, although this wing doesn't have a lift – just a door leading to the stairs. The doors are still in a higgledy-piggledy order: 111, 117, 115, 118, and ... 113! Right at the end, just as innocuous as the rest.

I knock on the door. Was that too quiet? Maybe I should knock again but louder. But then he might think I'm impatient. Okay, I'll wait. If he doesn't come in a minute, I'll knock again. But what if he wonders where I am, opens the door, and sees I am standing like a lemon, like I don't understand how doors work. Ugh. SCREW IT. I knock again but loud and firm this time.

The door opens, and the handsome face of Zachary pops around it and says, "Steven! Sorry, I had music on. You weren't waiting out here too long, were you?"

"No, not at all," I reply, grinning like an idiot. He's ditched the turtleneck jumper and now has a smart silky shirt on. It's dark with a pattern like paisley but less headache-inducing. Without the jacket on, I can see he has a slimmer build, but it suits how tall he is. I never realised how tall he was earlier. At least six foot three.

He must be a fashion model – no one is that tall, handsome, and fashionable unless they get paid to be.

"Come in," he says, holding the door for me. As I brush past him, I smell his musty aftershave – it's strong and earthy and must have just been applied. I like it.

Bloody hell. His room is stunning. It's like something out of *The Great Gatsby*. Almost everything is a classy dark green and there are gold geometric shapes everywhere I look. There's a mahogany writing desk, a sofa shaped like a clamshell, and wall lights made up of glass rods like little chandeliers. A fancy fan-shaped window looks out across the sea, and a door leads off to what I assume is a separate bedroom. There are just lines and squares and flourishes in every direction, and by God, it's classy. I've died and gone to art deco heaven.

"What do you think?" he asks me, taking off his glasses with one hand and running his fingers effortlessly through his hair with the other.

"It's alright," I say with a smirk. "Could have tidied up before I arrived."

"My apologies. I was too busy getting the virgins on the altar. Stubborn little things. Drink?"

He picks up a crystal decanter with some brown stuff in it. Whisky? Brandy? Heroin? Could be anything, but right now, I couldn't give a toss. Whatever he is offering, I am sure it'll be classy and great. I nod, and he pours one for both of us.

"Cheers," Zachary says, passing me a fancy tumbler and chinking it with his own. He smiles at me. He is *really* good at smiling. He could be a professional smiler or compete in the Smiling Olympics. I'm pretty sure I grin back at him like I'm holding in a fart. I sip the drink quickly and hope he didn't notice.

Balls, it's whisky and not the sweet Tennessee kind. The chest-burning, breath-catching Scottish kind. I mean, I don't hate it, but my sixth-former palate is used to a £3.50 bottle of vodka and supermarket-value lemonade. This is probably the most expensive drink I have ever drunk, and it's definitely wasted on me. I sip it again out of politeness.

"Come, let's sit down," he says, guiding me to the sofa. I want to put my Scotch down on the coffee table, but it looks like it's worth more than my parents' house, and I don't want to make a ring. Why aren't there any coasters? Guess I'll have to finish it.

He sits at the other end but swivels to face me and stretches out his leg. His ankle ever so gently comes to rest on mine. He's talking, but my whole brain is currently redirecting its processing power to just above my foot. Is he doing it deliberately? Surely, it's just an accident? People touch other people without realising all the time. Like on the bus. But there is lots of room; he didn't need to rest it there. I can feel the heat and pressure from his body, and it's all I can think about. It's like I'm embracing the sun. I know he can't possibly be that warm, and it's just an ankle, but for some reason, it feels like everything. It feels right.

"You okay?" he says. What was he just talking about?

"Yeah, sorry, I was miles away. Must be the whisky."

"Wow, two sips and he's away with the fairies. You must be a cheap date."

I laugh nervously and sip my drink again. Why am I such a doofus?

"I was just asking if you are new in town? I haven't seen you around before?"

"Errr yeah, I've been here a few weeks now. I sort of ran away from sixth form because of my ... you know."

"Your crippling inability to drink spirits?" he says, pushing his black curls back.

"Obviously. What about you? Have you been here long?"

"My whole life, basically."

"Ouch. Sorry."

"Oh, it's not so bad. I enjoy being near the sea. I don't think I could ever live without seeing it."

"There are other seaside towns that aren't as . . ."

"Depressing? Yes, I know, but it's home. I'd miss my morning swim in the Grunsby seas, and I'd never get a place as nice as this again."

"Speaking of which, how come you live in a hotel in 1924?"

"Long and mostly boring story. My uncle used to own this hotel, and he gave me this room when I needed a place to stay. The new owners don't mind; I don't think they get many visitors anyway. Plus, I save money on a gym membership by doing the Charleston four times a day."

"And you save money on a television by getting blackout drunk on absinthe too."

"Aha, yes, though a Netflix subscription might be cheaper in the long run." He finishes his drink and gets up, taking his warm ankle with him.

"Do your parents live here too?" I ask, glancing around in case we're suddenly interrupted.

"Both dead, I'm afraid. Don't worry, happened a long time ago. So it's just me." He holds his glass up and says, "Another?"

"Still working my way through this one."

"Very cheap date by the looks of things. So, Steven, tell me about your powers."

12

Steven

Where to start? I'm hesitating, and he can tell. He sweeps back around the couch but doesn't sit down. Instead, he points his first two fingers, and his claw-shaped ring glows faintly pink. He flicks his fingers to the side, and a velvet armchair flies out from the corner, stopping in front of me. He sits down casually – like he hasn't just defied the laws of physics.

"Big question, and personal too – sorry. I just want to get an understanding of them, so I can figure out how best to help. Let's start small. When did you first realise you were different?"

Ooft, that's still pretty personal. But he's looking at me with those eyes that are so vivid I'd swear they were contact lenses if he weren't wearing glasses. I want to tell him everything.

"I guess when I was around thirteen? It started with just making bad things happen. I thought I was cursed or just super unlucky. Then the other emotions began manifesting and I started glowing whenever they happened."

"And what sort of things can you do?"

"A lot of natural disasters and weather changing. Making things fly towards and away from me. Making good or bad things happen, err … making myself glow … and making people angry or frightened. Oh, and whatever happened at the café earlier too." I want to tell him about my cheat sheet, but I feel a bit embarrassed to show him. My handwriting really isn't the neatest.

"I see. And when was the last time you manifested something?"

"About an hour ago. I accidentally blew the power in my flat. I managed to fix it, though."

"With your powers?"

"Yeah, I just sort of felt sad and focused on the lights."

"Wonderful!" he says, clapping his hands together. "So, you can be selective in how you focus them?"

"Errr, not exactly," I mumble, remembering a Geordie woman in a suit being flung out to sea. "That's probably the first time it's worked. I tried to do it earlier, but I sort of . . . missed."

"That's okay," he replies kindly. "They're hard to master, and there isn't a manual to study. But if you have done it once, then focusing will be easier the next time. It's like cutting wood: after the first cut, you have a groove for the rest to follow. Eventually, you'll be able to push or pull a single grain of rice out of a pile." He leans forward in his chair, and a lock of curls falls into his face. All I want to do right now is push it behind his ears, but he beats me to it. "I take it you still have very little control over when these manifestations occur?"

"Yeah. It used to be every now and again, but the last few months, I've been making stuff happen four or five times a day."

"And have they stayed the same or got stronger?"

"About the same. They've always been quite . . . destructive." Which is the understatement of the century. When I'm not causing natural disasters, I'm vaporising a guy's head. I stare at my lap, suddenly feeling a ball of undigested shame hanging in my insides. But then his hand is at my cheek, raising it back up again. I seriously need to find out what brand of moisturiser he uses because I've never felt hands so soft.

"Hey," he says gently, looking straight into my eyes, "whatever you've done, it's not your fault. Okay? You can't help the way you were made."

Jesus, I am melting like an Easter egg left in the sun.

"You are here now to get help," he continues, "so that you can control your powers. Not be controlled by them."

"I just feel like a mistake."

"You are a wonderful quirk of nature. There is nothing wrong with you."

"But don't you ever just want to be normal?" I ask.

"No. Not ever. We are extraordinary and different and a little bit magical. Why would I ever want to be normal? Trust me, Steven. I've been there. These powers are gifts. You are a gift."

He lets go of my face and sits back in his armchair. He's like a king on a velvet throne, and I feel so inadequate in his presence. So helpless, so naive, so young. But he doesn't seem to mind. He's talking to me with patience and understanding, and for the first time in a long while, I don't feel like I have to hide.

"Did you lose control before?" I ask – why do I feel like I'm about to cry?

"All the time. I caused accidents and hurt people and hated myself, but then I was taught how to harness and redirect it, and I've remained in control since. And by the time I am through with you, you'll be the same."

This makes me smile inside and out. My heart feels like it might soar straight up out of my chest and smack Zachary in the face. I'm blushing – I can tell because my stupid ears feel hot. My hands start to fizz with yellow light, and suddenly the beautiful coffee table cracks and splits in two.

"Oh my god. I am so sorry!" I say, getting to my feet.

"Hush. It's fine," says Zachary, also standing. "Accidents happen."

"But it looked expensive. I am so, so sorry . . ."

I trail off because Zachary has taken both my hands in his. He squeezes gently, and I can feel the cool metal of his ring in my palm. I look down, and the yellow fog is being sucked into his ring, just like in the café earlier. And then it's all gone. He is still holding my hands and looking intently into my eyes. Nothing else in the world matters or exists right now. His eyebrows furrow, and a question hangs on his lips. For a while, he says nothing, and we are frozen in this moment. Then he murmurs, "Yellow," and cocks his head at me like he can't quite see my edges. I don't want to lose the connection, but he gently lets my hands go and sinks back down.

Shakily, I take my seat and say thanks to no one in particular. I suddenly feel very embarrassed.

"Yellow," he repeats to himself. I don't really know what to do or say. He comes out of his pensive trance by sitting forward and surveying me. He's like a scientist looking over a chemical formula and trying to figure out the solution. Or the problem.

Without taking his eyes from me, Zachary flicks his first two fingers again. This time yellow crackles around them, and the broken table comes back together like it's never been apart.

Then it hits me. His powers are the other way around. Or maybe mine are the mismatched ones. His happiness fixed the table while mine broke it, and he's never seen it be the other way around.

93

"I felt happy," I offer.

"I know," he replies simply.

"That's what always happens when I feel happiness: something bad."

"And when you feel angry, what then?"

"I make others scared. It's like, whatever I feel, the opposite happens. Is that not normal for emomancers?"

He chuckles at the word, then says, "No, it's not normal. But just because it's not normal doesn't mean it's wrong."

*

We finish our drinks as I tell him the things my reversed powers have done over the years (with a few obvious omissions). He listens and offers sympathetic held tilts and knowing nods. Eventually, I finish (wow, I've been talking a long time), and he sits back in his chair pensively.

"I see," he says, selecting his next words carefully. "From the sounds of it, there is a straightforward inversion to your powers. Emotions come in pairs: opposites that contrast and complement each other. But this doesn't mean there is a strict binary. We don't flip a switch from happy to sad. It's more like a complicated system of sliders and buttons; sometimes two opposing things can be felt simultaneously, and other times neither. We might feel angry to disguise the fear trapped deep down."

"Does that mean I can manifest two at once?" I ask.

"Unfortunately, no – or at least in my own experience, no. What we do is we manifest emotions in their purest form. Whenever there is a conflict, one will win out over the others, and that is the power you'll tap into. It doesn't invalidate whatever else you might be feeling, but it just relegates it to the background. Your heart will always know what emotion it's feeling, even if your brain tries to deceive you. Tell me, how do you currently control your powers?"

"I try to think of nothing, like a blank piece of paper. Things calm down eventually."

"Sheer willpower? I'm impressed you've managed as well as you have. If I were you, I would have blown up half of England by now. Unless you are a monk who meditates for most of the day, your willpower alone will never be enough to tame your emotions. Think of them as a forest fire burning out of control. Using willpower is like trying to put it out with water: if you don't have enough, you'll never succeed. You can wait for it to die out on its own, but then everything will be ash."

"What can I do?"

"You can make a channel and divert it away."

With that, he stands and beckons for me to join. I follow him over to the writing desk, and he places his tumbler on it and backs away. He grabs something from his pocket and puts it gently into my palm. It's a 50p coin, except it's really thick and old looking. The date on it says 1969.

"That was one of the first ever made. I love old coins – just think how many loaves of bread that has bought over the years. Amazing what you find lying around in a hotel. Metal is a fantastic conductor of heat and electricity. But to EMTs like us, it is a very helpful conductor of emotions. I want you to take this and remember it as a gift from me. It'll make using it a bit easier."

"What does EMT mean?" I ask, annoyed that I've stopped him to ask a silly question.

"Emotionally Manifesting Target. It's an old scientific name. Emomancer sounds so much better, don't you think? Now let's start with smaller, less destructive manifestations and work our way up. I want you to pull the glass towards you. Ordinarily, I would tell you to covet it, but in your case, I want you to be disgusted by my very expensive crystal tumbler," he says with a chuckle.

I'm not really sure what to do, so I hold out my hand towards the glass.

"Both hands please, Magneto," Zachary says, demonstrating.

"Does that help?" I say, holding them both out like I am waiting for a ball – I assume . . . Leave me alone, I don't know sports.

"Not particularly. I just don't want you to drop it."

I'm focusing as hard as I can, but it just doesn't want to move. I try to be disgusted by how decadent it is, but it's still a very nice glass. Beautiful swirls cut into it and a rim so thin you'd swear it wasn't there.

The cup sparkles pink and then is thrown backwards off the table at an alarming speed. It hurtles toward the back wall but stops very suddenly. Then, it shoots back into Zachary's hand, who places it back on the table.

"Well, you did something. Not what we were after, but as first attempts go, that wasn't the worst I've seen. Try again. This time, picture something really revolting in your mind's eye. But keep your actual eyes on the glass. I know – who knew we'd be multi-tasking? The emotion needs to be genuine, but it doesn't have to come from what you are trying to affect. Otherwise, you'll never be able to pull a bacon sandwich toward you."

I raise my hands again, but they are shaking. He must see this because I feel a warm hand on my shoulder, shooting courage through me. I can do this. I think of the toilets on the beachfront: the unholy blockages that surely no human was capable of doing.

Somewhere in my sense memory, I uncork the smell long bottled away and too foul even for words.

That does the trick. My hands start glowing green. I stare at the glass, and it starts to wobble. Then the whole writing desk flies towards me and knocks me off my feet.

Zachary is over me, laughing. He lifts me back up and dusts my back down.

"Well, you achieved the assignment," he says, using his own disgust to push the desk back with a green wave of his hand. "Technically, the glass did come to you."

"Ugh, why am I so bad at this?" I grumble, wishing Zachary would turn away, so I could kick something without him seeing.

"This is attempt two of lesson one. Did you think you'd be perfect straight away?"

"Lesson one?"

"Surely you didn't think I'd teach you everything in one night? I assume you'll be in Grunsby for a while?"

"Until Wednesday at least. My friend is hellbent on taking me back home, but I sort of broke our car. We are waiting for a rental to arrive – but I haven't decided yet," I hastily add. If I stay in Grunsby, I could have a lesson with Zachary every day. Who really needs A Levels anyway?

"Okay, if you'd like, we can meet up tomorrow and Wednesday too? A three-day crash course in emomancy. Sound good?"

"Yes," I say a little too quickly.

He smiles at me then turns back to the desk. "Let's keep going with lesson one, shall we? Try again, but really focus just on the glass."

This time, I make a pen fly off the table and almost impale Zachary. The following attempt, I make papers fly out of the drawers, and we have to stop for five minutes to clear them up. I'm getting really frustrated, but Zachary is calm and patient and tells me I can do it.

After six more failed attempts, just when I am about to give up and throw the glass out the window, it flies straight into my hand like a magnet.

What did I do differently this time? I can't remember. It just sort of happened. I overlaid the image of the smelly toilets with the tumbler like before, but this time I felt the edges of the glass before I pulled it. Zachary's face bursts open, and he pulls me into an embrace. He smells great. I can feel his body pressed against mine and his curly hair on my neck. His chest rises and falls into mine, and his arms are wrapped around my waist.

Think of white. Think of nothing.

He pulls away just before I cause a fire or something. His hand glows green, and the glass levitates out of my grasp and plonks back on the table.

"Do it again," he says.

And I do.

Three more times, in fact. Each time is easier than the last, like muscle memory. I wonder if we will move on to pushing, but that might be too much for one night. Zachary can do it with such effortlessness, and I'd probably smash it into the wall again. He resets the glass one last time but holds his own hand out this time.

"Now that you have the hang of it, we can move on to the real first lesson and the reason I gave you that coin. Where is it?"

I fish it out of my trousers and hold it up to him.

"Perfection," he says, his voice low. "Now, being able to move things with our emotions is all well and good, but what do you do if you start manifesting the wrong thing? Changing what you feel is a tall order, as I'm sure you're aware. But what we *can* do is push that unwanted manifestation elsewhere. Into an emotional conductor, a siphon, so that it can be safely stored away."

With that, his hand glows green, but almost immediately, the aura disappears into his talon-shaped ring. "We may not carry ceremonial knives, but emomancers will always have some metal on them for a siphon. I want you to go again, but just when you feel you are at the apex of the emotion, that small breath just before the manifestation starts, I need you to send it all into the coin. Got that? Give it a go."

I summon the delightful image of an unflushed lavatory and focus on the glass. The trick begins to rumble deep inside me and rises to my chest. I feel that familiar tingle at the edge of my fingers. I have nanoseconds before it fully manifests. The cool metal of the coin rubs between my thumb and index finger. I squeeze it hard and focus, but it's a lot harder than Zachary made it look.

"Concentrate," he whispers. "Imagine the metal is a part of you. You are diverting the energy into it."

My hand starts to glow green. It's like when you try to stuff a sleeping bag back into its teeny tiny case. I push and push and push, but it never seems to end. I hold the coin up, and green is trickling into it, but it's nowhere near the vacuum strength of when Zachary did it. It's more like a hoover with a blocked pipe, just vaguely sucking up crumbs.

But I persevere. Eventually, all the green is gone from my hand, and the glass remains exactly where Zachary placed it.

I did it. For the first time in my life, I stopped a trick from manifesting. Yes, it took a while, but I can only get better. I don't know if I could feel any happier.

And then I feel Zachary's lips pressed against mine.

13

The situation has taken a curious turn. At 1800 hours, I received a phone call from Director Delphi back at HQ, detailing a detected surge in Emotion Manifestation Energy in the Grunsby-on-Sea area. Our satellites picked up this EME surge approximately forty minutes after Junior Agent Wren engaged a suspected EMT. I would be a fool if I didn't think the two events were related. To detect such a power surge here is disconcerting, to say the least. It suggests either a high concentration of EMTs manifesting simultaneously or one exceptionally strong EMT experiencing the utmost extremity of human emotion.

But this is not unheard of. Three years ago, five children in Brazil were detected after they caused enormous damage to the Amazon following the death of their mother, and the prototype satellite, launched in 1969, blew up in orbit when it detected the

EME coming from Woodstock. No, finding a rare and powerful EMT is unusual but not curious.

What is curious is that during the surge, Director Delphi received a phone call from Agent Samantha Fowler. The same Agent Fowler who has been MIA for almost four years. The number was withheld, but we could trace it within a five-mile radius.

The phone call came from Grunsby-on-Sea.

This cannot be a coincidence. Whatever was manifested by the rogue EMT must have affected Agent Fowler somehow. Why else would she wait four years before contacting HQ? If she is being held captive, this surge might have provided her a window of opportunity to make the call. This is all speculation, but something tells me there is more to this than meets the eye.

Below is a transcript of the recording. In total, the call lasted nine seconds.

<u>Transcript of phone call to Director</u>
<u>Delphi from</u>
<u>Agent Fowler</u>
<u>23/11/2020 1515 GMT</u>

DD_ Hello?

AF_ Del . . . phi?

DD_ Yes, this is Director Delphi. Who is this?

AF_ F . . . Fowler. I . . . warn . . . I'm . . .

```
DD_   Agent Fowler? Is that you? Where are
      you?

AF_   Lam    . . .    Pen    . . .    W-w    . . .
      Com    . . .    Ment   . . .    Ess    . . .
      Wa . . . Ni . . . Too . . . oh

DD_   What? Fowler, what's your position?
      Are you hurt?

AF_   D-Den . . . Pruh Den . . . Den
```

              - End of Transcript -

Her voice was hoarse and drowsy, so she may be drugged. DEMA
analysts have been assigned to dissect the audio for any further
clues.

In light of these developments, Director Delphi has escalated
our case to Priority Delta, and I've also been assigned to track
down Fowler and bring her into HQ. Officially speaking, Director
Delphi has instructed me to keep these as separate lines of inquiry,
but he shares my suspicions that they are linked. I have not
updated Junior Agent Wren yet: partly due to her bungling of the
current investigation and partly because I wish to establish a more
concrete connection first. In any case, she is currently on patrol,
and her phone is still broken despite its immersion in packet rice.
When she reports back, I will inform her of the EME surge.

The lateness of this entry is primarily because I have been
examining the reports Agent Fowler made before she vanished.
Fowler was assigned to surveil a minor EMT in Sheffield. She
had narrowed the target down to an office building near the city
centre and suspected a man working in an accountancy firm.

From the looks of things, it was a by-the-numbers case. She was about to begin Phase Four of the Neutralisation Protocol when the logs in her report stopped. Nothing suggests the target would be too much for her – in fact, DEMA gave the case a priority rating of Zeta, the lowest possible. There is no reason to believe that a Zeta EMT would best an agent as talented and as experienced as Agent Fowler.

There must have been a complication. Something she didn't foresee. Something that HQ missed during their investigation into her disappearance. And then there is the mystery of how she came to be in Grunsby-on-Sea.

Fowler was a great agent who shared Junior Agent Wren's *gusto* for field assignments. Before joining DEMA, she trained as an actress, so often gave her work a theatrical flair. Fowler was particularly adept at Phase Three (Infiltration), living believably as her cover identity and going the extra mile to make it watertight: working other jobs, making friends, going to social gatherings. While some thought this a waste of time, she believed it added a layer of authenticity to make Phases Four and Five easier.

She kept a personal diary as her character, utterly devoid of any mention of DEMA – I assume as part of her "method" acting. Many of these diary entries detail long, tragic backstories, contrived motivations, and overstated character quirks – I assume in case her cover story was ever in doubt or for her own self-indulgence. The psychological ramifications of this exercise in delusion aside, this does give us an insight into what Agent Fowler was up to when not scoping out her target.

The diary for her last case was impounded as evidence after her disappearance and digitised on DEMA's central server. Here are some passages I feel might be relevant to her disappearance.

The diary of "Jessie Hannover"

Extract One – 7 January 2016:

That's it. All my stuff is officially moved in! I can't believe I got such a beautiful flat for so little – yay me! I just wish Daddy was alive to see this. If only he hadn't died tragically in that kayaking accident. It was a struggle to move out of Mum's place with my other seven siblings, but now I am finally going to have my own life.

Moving boxes is the worst. At least I will have burned off all those mince pies (my favourite treat – weird, I know) from Xmas. I got soooo sweaty, and the cute guy downstairs also moving in saw me like this! So embarrassing. He helped me move most of the boxes, so I can't complain. His name is Frank, and he is a serious hotty. Tall, dark, and handsome – Mumma likey! He's new in town too and invited me out to dinner tomorrow. Eeeek!

Extract Two – 14 February 2016:

Frank got me a beautiful diamond bracelet for Valentine's! I was on my way to a new client across town when he surprised me. No idea how he knew I'd be there, but I'm not complaining – I feel like a princess. He really liked the ring I bought him too – it's the one he was looking at the other day. It may just be the shiny thing on my wrist talking, but I am seriously starting to fall for this guy. Especially now that his hair has gone all salt and pepper. He's like a young George Clooney.

We are going back to Luigi's, and I know he's got something romantic planned. Maybe he'll whisk me away to somewhere exotic for a weekend, or we'll go to the ballet. You know I almost was in the Russian Ballet, but I had a secret affair with the choreographer and was told to never return . . .

Extract Three – 12 March 2016:

Day three and still no sign of Frank. Weird that he would disappear and not tell his girlfriend. He had mentioned how his mother was sick, so he might have to return home soon, but he would have said goodbye before leaving. Right?

Have I done something wrong? We said "I love you" to each other almost a month ago. And he meant it. I meant it. Why would he suddenly be afraid of commitment now? He makes me feel wanted, and beautiful, and like . . . well, me. I forget everything else but him.

Extract Four – 13 March 2016:

Frank called last night. Panic over. He had to rush back because his mother took a turn for the worse. With everything going on, he hasn't had the brain space to call, and apparently, the signal in Grunsby is terrible. It's fine. I understand. I just wish he'd told me sooner, so I would stop panicking.

\- End of Extracts \-

From these extracts, a few deductions can be made. Fowler was in a relationship with "Frank" from "Grunsby" – which I assume is Grunsby-on-Sea and not the Isle of Grunsby in Scotland. The full extent of their relationship is unknown; however, I suspect that the feelings of "Jessie Hannover" towards this Frank began to bleed over into Fowler. Her later diary entries seem more candid and less demonstrative, reading less like she's in character.

The diary stops on 17 March, and her DEMA reports are filed until the eighteenth. She wrote the former at night and the latter every morning, indicating that Agent Fowler went missing sometime after 0900 on the eighteenth. Given her relationship with Frank and where she made the call from, we can assume she came to Grunsby-on-Sea in search of him, driving down after completing her morning report. From there, it is possible she was compromised and has remained in this town ever since.

Tomorrow, I will return to the library to check records and local newspapers from March 2016. Hopefully, that may yield some clues as to what befell Agent Fowler. If Frank is from Grunsby-on-Sea, his school records should also be available. Once I have the list of possible Franks, it will be a case of questioning them. We must find out if "Jessie" ever made it to him.

– End of Log –

14

Steven

What was that?

I . . . I just.

He.

We.

Woah.

Was that . . . ?

Did Zachary just kiss me? Did I kiss him back?

Yes, and yes.

I'm staggering down the corridor, my head floating at least nine metres above me. What does this all mean? My heart feels like it's got a vendetta against my ribs and is pounding as hard as it can to crack them. I'm at the lift again. Pressing the button and sinking against the back wall as it begins to descend.

This is mad.

He kissed me. And I wanted to kiss him back. I *did* kiss him back.

At first, I resisted – the terror from the last time I did this gripping my body. The memory of lips searing hot followed by a bang like a popping balloon. But Zachary held me tight like I was the only thing keeping him upright in a storm. And I gave into it. Yes, it might have been a bit clumsy on my part, but I just wanted every part of me and every part of him to fuse together. I wanted more of him than I could have ever got from just a kiss.

And nothing bad happened. No exploding heads. No blood. Just me and him together held in a moment.

And then it stopped.

"It's probably best we leave it there for today," he had said, boring into me with those sapphire eyes. It had taken all I had not to pounce on his face again. "Homework: fill that coin with as many emotions as you can. Anytime you feel a manifestation, put it into the coin. Here, I'll do this one for free. My fault, anyway."

I hadn't even noticed I was fizzing yellow, but he swiftly stopped it with his talon thing. A wink and one last kiss on the cheek, and then he shut the door.

And just like that, I'm standing in the lobby looking like a doped-up idiot.

What does this mean? You kiss one guy, and it's a fluke. You kiss a second (A LOT), and it's a pattern.

I don't ... I can't ... I can't even ... All these things are swimming like tangled seaweed in my head. I really shouldn't have drunk that whisky if I knew I were confronting deeply personal conundrums.

Facts. Facts will steer me through – no need to worry about labels and things if I stick to facts.

Fact: I like Zachary. He's nice and genuinely trying to help me control my powers.

Fact: I kissed Zachary.

Fact: I want to kiss Zachary again. And again. And again.

Fact: FREYA MUST NEVER KNOW, OR I WILL NEVER HEAR THE END OF IT.

As I leave the Regalia, the cold sea air wakes me up like a smack in the face. Alright, Cinderella, you've had fun at the ball, but it's now roughly midnight. If you don't return soon, you'll turn into a pumpkin. I cut up and through town this time – no need to dawdle.

At this time of night, Grunsby doesn't seem so bad. When the grubby pink buildings are bathed in the soft amber glow of a streetlamp, it almost seems quaint.

Almost.

When there are no apathetic residents to shrug and ignore your existence, the town almost feels homely.

Again, almost.

Let's be honest; this town is a steaming hot turd. How Zachary can stand to stay here out of choice is beyond me. Mind you, if I lived in an apartment that nice, I wouldn't care what the town below looked like. He must be loaded. I wonder what he does for a living. Is there a uni nearby? I probably should have asked him. Probably should have asked him hundreds of things, but I was a bit distracted. You know, with the trying to stop myself from killing people thing. And with how handsome he is. And with his tongue in my mouth. A lot of things to be distracted by. I'm seeing him the same time tomorrow, so I'll ask him then.

Oh god, will he kiss me again?

Was it just a one-time thing?

Did I do it wrong or something? I felt like I was doing it right, but it was all a sort of a blur. My body just responded in the moment, and I can't remember what it did. Argh, overthinking this for sure.

I round a corner and stop dead. Agent Pixie is standing in the middle of the road, waving what looks like a Geiger counter around. She's got her back to me, so she hasn't seen me yet. But I've got seconds before she swings that device round and spots me.

Piss biscuits!

I turn quickly and power walk back the way I came.

Super obvious, Percival, come on.

My heart is hammering again now, but for very different reasons. This time, there's nothing to help me: no Freya and no car. A blue glow begins to softly creep up my fingertips. I'm starting to sweat in my jacket. Immediately, my hand goes to my pocket, and I grip the coin so tightly I swear I'm going to crush it.

I can hear footsteps clomping behind me, getting faster. A whir of something electrical. Maybe that device is tracking my powers. An emometer? No time for wordplay – get moving!

I'm at a jog now, heading the complete wrong direction, but I can hear Agent Pixie on my heels.

"Wait!" she says in a loud whisper. "Come back!"

Yeah, like that's going to work. I'll just hand myself in to be dissected because you asked nicely.

The clip-clopping stops only to be replaced by the revving of an engine. I glance behind and see headlights flicker on. Since when do secret agents drive Mini Metros? Crap, she's gaining on me. Slowly, though. It seems like she has a problem getting out of first gear. I run as quickly as my unfit, noodle body will let me. There's a footpath between two houses just ahead. I barrel down the narrow passage, distant car noises getting closer every second.

The path takes me out to an industrial estate. Three purpose-built grey buildings are connected by a small pot-holed road and a huge car park. As if on cue, I see headlights turning into the estate ahead of me. Doesn't she ever quit?

I make a break for the unit to my left and run to the back of it. Pressing myself against the back wall, I peer around. The Pixie-mobile crawls past, and I pull my head back just in time. It keeps going, reaches the end of the road, and turns back. I hold my breath until I hear it roar away.

She's gone.

Jesus, I am unfit – Freya needs to take me running or something. I take a moment to catch my breath, and that's when I notice something. Behind this unit is a barbed wire fence with another building beyond it. An austere-looking place made of grey brick like a school or something. Unlike the units in the estate, this building is pretty messed up: smashed windows, a huge scorch mark down one of the walls, and a rusted sign hanging above the entrance that looks like it was designed in the fifties. On it is a faded logo of a helix in an eyeball, and in big letters is one word:

DEMA

15

Troy

I get woken up by the smell. It's like an explosion in an Old Spice factory. Has a murderer bathed themselves in cologne before coming to stab me? Heavy breathing too. An asthmatic murderer? I would open my eyes to check, but I'm so tired I can't. I'll just take the murder if it means I get five more minutes to sleep.

"Crap!" I hear someone whisper, accompanied by the sound of furniture being kicked. Fine, I'll peep.

I open my eyes and see a dark shape hopping around, clutching their toe.

"Steven?"

"Sorry, Troy! I was trying not to wake you up."

"It's okay. I've been up for hours," I lie between yawns as I check my watch. Why is Steven rolling in 2 a.m.? "Put the light on if you need."

"Cheers," he says, despite not having a drink in his hand.

Oh, why did I say that? The light flicks on and burns my retinas, and I feel my precious sleep sizzle away to nothing. Guess I'm awake then.

Steven strips off his clothes and starts wandering around, brushing his teeth in his underwear. I make a show of looking away – last thing I want is to freak a straight boy out by ogling him. That being said, I do sneak a peek as he heads back into the bathroom. He's slim with broad shoulders, so he's unintentionally got that Dorito thing going for him. And a cute butt.

He comes back out, wiping the toothpaste from his mouth, and our eyes meet. I throw him a smile, and he returns it – it makes my insides burn like hot tomato soup. He perches on the edge of the couch and whispers, "Are you sure you want the air mattress? I don't mind swapping if you'd be better off up here?"

"No, I'm fine here. Thanks, though," I reply. Truth is, I would much prefer it up there; the air mattress has a puncture somewhere. But at this precise moment in time, I can't really . . . you know . . . stand up. At least while Steven is sitting there in his underwear. Oh my gosh, this is so embarrassing.

"How was work?" I ask, trying to deflect as much attention away from me as I can.

He takes about four seconds to grasp what I'm saying.

"Oh, yeah! It was errr . . . It was great – good. Yeah. As good as work can be, I guess. How was your night?"

Now it's his turn to deflect. Why do I always feel like our conversations revolve around keeping things from each other? He obviously doesn't want to tell me where he really was or why he smells of aftershave, so I play dumb.

"Good too. We found a bunch of old games in the closet in the hall, so we played KerPlunk and Monopoly. It was fun."

It was not fun. Freya is so competitive that she takes all the fun out of the games, and Marcus sulked the entire night. They got into *another* argument over the free parking rules, and then Freya flipped over the board when she landed on my hotel on Mayfair. Also, there were like six sticks in the KerPlunk box, so we never managed to play a game. I also found a dartboard. But after Freya lodged the little top hat piece in the wall during her ragequit, I didn't want to give her any more projectiles.

"You played board games with Freya McCormac? Do you have a death wish or something?" he says, turning off the lights then cocooning himself in blankets on the oh-so-comfy couch. "Good night, mate."

"Good night."

*

At 6 a.m., a seagull with what sounds like a throat infection squawks loudly outside the window. It's super light already, but there's still that morning stillness, like time hasn't quite woken up yet. I'm too awake to go back to sleep, but I don't feel particularly rested. Something about Steven kept me up – I mean awake . . . not up . . . You know what, never mind.

Steven is still asleep, catching flies, unaware of the demonic bird. He's twitching like when a dog dreams. It's cute, but I'm ninety per cent sure he's having a nightmare. I'll leave him to sleep a bit longer. Guess it's time to raid the cupboards in search of coffee. In the kitchen, I find Freya in a full running outfit, stretching with her earphones in. She turns off her music and sings me a quiet but cheery, "Morning!"

"Morning," I whisper back, suddenly aware that I'm wearing nothing but my underpants and a tank top. "Did you bring your gym stuff with you?"

"Nah, I left my kit in Marcus's car last week. Pried it out of the boot to go for a run along the beachfront. Fancy coming along?" she asks without a hint of irony. Do I "fancy" running in my underwear at 6 a.m. down the beach in the middle of winter?

"I'm good. More of a go-to-the-gym-in-the-evening type guy."

"Suit yourself." She shrugs, downing the last remnants of a cup of tea on the counter.

"Hey, do you know where Steven went last night?" I ask as casually as I can. There's a flicker in her eyes – she probably sees through my ruse. I've never directly told Freya that I like Steven, but I am pretty sure she's worked it out by now. I mean, I try to be discreet, but there are only so many times you can bring a person up in conversation before people realise you might have a mild obsession with them. Very mild, of course. Like a Kraft Single level of mild.

"Errm, didn't he have work or something?" Freya says, avoiding my eye. Jeez, talk about subtle.

"No, it's just he got back late and was all out of breath and smelled of aftershave."

Freya turns away and begins retying her shoe. Even if her dad wasn't a cop, Freya would make a terrible criminal. At least it's super obvious when she is lying to you.

"Oh yeah. He was probably, errm, unloading boxes of perfume … at the docks. Yeah, that's probably it. Right, I need to run. Bye," she says, darting out of the apartment.

Like I said, subtle.

I locate the instant coffee (the worst thing about Great Britain – don't come for me) and put the electric kettle on to boil. As it gently whistles away, the sleepy form of Steven shuffles into the kitchen, still very much in his underpants.

"Morning," I say, suddenly very interested in reading the label of this coffee.

"Morning," he replies while stretching. "Sleep well? Sorry if I woke you when I came in, I just – Jesus!"

"What! What is it?"

"Oh no, it's just . . . I didn't realise your . . . nice guns."

Now he's very interested in the coffee jar. Aww, his ears have gone red. Now that I think of it, Steven hasn't seen me in anything other than button-downs.

"Thanks," I say, playing it cool. "I started bench pressing my feelings in sophomore year. Do you want a drink? Kettle's just boiled."

"Coffee if you're offering. Milk . . . and two sugars," he adds, weirdly triumphant. "Take it Freya's gone for her run?"

"Yeah. Exercising before breakfast, what a freak."

"Exercising at all, what a freak. Oh, wait. I didn't mean . . ." he stammers, thinking I'm offended.

"Oh no, I am a freak for exercising. Here you go," I say, passing out our coffees.

Oh my gosh, this is the most disgusting thing ever. I immediately spit it back into the mug.

"Yeah, should have warned you; it tastes like dirt," he says, shuddering as he drinks it.

"Well, it was *ground* yesterday!"

Steven tilts his head, confused, and says, "No, it's not ground – it's the instant stuff."

"Yeah, I know. It was just a joke. Ground like 'the ground' because you said it tastes like dirt." He nods and offers a small laugh. A pity laugh. How embarrassing. Get me out of here before I rip my face off. "Well, I think I'll have a shower now."

"No worries. Towels are in the cupboard. I'll have one after you, and by then, Freya should be back from her suicidal beach run, so I'll do breakfast. You still up for learning how to fry an egg?"

"Absolutely!"

"Great. If you're a good student, we might even get onto scrambling," he says, giving me a wink that turns my insides to goop. Pure liquified goop. That's it; I'm now a gelatinous blob of unrequited homosexual angst. Pity my existence. And pray for me.

Steven

Freya gets back from her run (the mad cow), and I try to corner her while she makes her post-workout tea (the madder cow.) Obviously, I'm keeping the whole Zachary thing to myself, at least for now. I'd hoped that sleeping on it would help me understand how I feel, but alas, I'm still a tightly smushed ball of confusion and arousal. When I see him for lesson two tonight, maybe I'll get some clarity.

So yeah, unanswerable existential questions about my sexual identity aside, I still need to chat to Freya ASAP. But as soon as I open my mouth, Marcus shuffles into the room with a grunt. He really does have the worst timing. Prick.

Actually, this is the perfect opportunity. I fish out my coin and really indulge in what a prick Marcus is. He's always getting in the way – I can't even talk to my best friend about controlling my powers for the first time because he's here. A conversational dead weight personified.

Yes! Red mist starts to coil around my hand, and the room suddenly feels colder. Step one, check! I focus everything on the coin and stuff the anger into it like an over full suitcase. It takes about three minutes until all the red vanishes, but no one cowers away from me in fear. Not a bad start – could be quicker, but it's only the third time I've tried to do it.

I'm going to practise with it all day, just as Zachary said, and I can't wait. Even Marcus's prickishness can't keep me down today. I'm finally allowed to feel. Allowed to be happy without the fear of murdering someone. I feel alive again for the first time in months.

I lend Troy a T-shirt of mine, which looks hilarious. Like he hulked out but bottled it midway through his transformation.

"Better than freezing to death, I suppose," he says, rolling up the sleeves so it looks like a vest. If I had arms like that, I'd never wear a shirt again. "Okay, breakfast 101?"

"Let's do it! I think if we wait any longer, Marcus might eat us."

We head to the kitchen, and I get the frying pan ready while Troy puts on the toast and gets the eggs.

"Uhh, are you sure they'll be okay? I thought you're meant to keep them in the fridge?" he says, rummaging through the larder.

"Do you see a refrigerator? This flat hasn't been updated since it was built. Well, apart from the washing machine. They'll be fine. Right, have you ever cooked before?"

"I've put frozen stuff like pizzas in the oven, but I've never used a stove. So please, patronise away. Wait, what's that you put in the pan?"

"Just a bit of oil. It stops the food sticking to the metal. Have you cracked an egg before?"

"Nope. Is it hard?"

"Incredibly. You need a sledgehammer and a chisel ... That's a joke," I add, seeing his face all serious. He takes things so seriously sometimes, and it's both adorable and hilarious. "Just a knife or the edge of a bowl or something. Like this."

I break an egg on the edge of the pan and slop its contents into the oil. I put three more in, accidentally breaking one of the yolks.

"Piss biscuits. Marcus can have that one," I whisper and Troy giggles. It's weird to see someone so big giggle, but also kind of endearing, like when a Great Dane is afraid of a mouse. "Salt and pepper make everything tastier. Unfortunately, we have neither. I hope you're taking notes, you have to do all this tomorrow, and I will be marking out of ten."

"Hope I don't *crack* with the pressure."

"Full of puns this morning, aren't you? These look about done, so let's flip them."

I do one and then pass the spatula over for him to do the rest. He's a bit cack-handed and breaks another yolk.

"Darn it!"

"It's okay. They're just eggs," I say, smiling as I steady his hand to flip the remaining eggs. "Don't like swearing, huh?"

"It's how I was raised. You can be just the worst, most awful human being as long as you don't curse. And always say ma'am and sir and please and thank you."

"Wow. Last Christmas, my mum told me to piss off because I gave her a pick-up-four during Uno."

"Oh my gosh! I don't think I've ever heard my mom say butt."

We lift the eggs onto the toast. Really should make bacon – Freya will riot without it.

"Bonus challenge. Bacon time!"

"See, now you're speaking my language," he says. "Even if it is the weird British kind of bacon. How do we cook it?"

"You've never cooked bacon? Isn't it like your national vegetable or something?"

"Hey! I have cooked it before. But like in the microwave."

I stop lowering the rashers into the pan and fix him with my best comedy look of disgust.

"So you won't swear, but you'll commit blasphemy." He laughs at that a lot. "This is the same deal, but you want a higher heat." I bung the bacon into the pan, and it sizzles away. God, that smell is incredible. Some fat spits out, and Troy jumps back with a yelp. "See, Troy, that's the bacon gods smiting you for your heresy."

"It can't hurt you in the microwave," he says, rubbing the red spot on his forearm. "Man, I wish I knew this stuff."

"I only know because my mum taught me. She thinks I'll starve to death at uni next year otherwise."

"I don't even think my mom knows how to turn on the stove. I lived on a diet of Twinkies and Pop-Tarts pretty much till high school."

"And yet your teeth are so white, and your muscles like that. Genetics just aren't fair."

"Clearly, didn't get the cooking gene."

"Me neither! I can cook breakfast, but I'm hardly Gordon Ramsay."

"No, you've only cussed like twice."

"Cussed," I repeat in my worst American accent.

"What's wrong with cussed?" he says, pretending to be defensive.

"Nothing. Just sometimes you sound like one of the Brady Bunch."

We laugh as I plate the bacon. He is such a dork, but he makes for good company.

We take the plates through to the living room and plonk them down on the coffee table. Marcus is watching morning television while he scrolls through Instagram absent-mindedly. Doesn't even say thank you, just sits forward and inhales the food. You're welcome. Prick.

Freya emerges from the bedroom in yet another woollen monstrosity but with her hair plaited into a bun like Princess Leia's ginger cousin.

"Oooh, what did you whip up this morning?" she sings as she immediately attacks her bacon.

"Just bacon and eggs. No caviar, I'm afraid. We've run out," I reply, tucking into my own.

"And was Percy a good teacher, young padawan?" she asks.

"Yeah, only mild amounts of cussing," Troy says, giving me a wry smile.

Once the plates are licked clean and Marcus has come up for air, Freya offers to do the washing up. I follow her to the kitchen, then fill the kettle up to the top and stick it on – yes, not the most eco-friendly thing to do, but the noise will give us some cover. That's definitely some 007 level of espionage.

Freya seems to be on my wavelength because she waits for the roar of the plastic kettle before sidling up to me and whispering, "So how'd it go?"

And I tell her everything. Well, not *everything*, obviously. I breeze over Zachary in case Freya catches on using her best-friend insight, but honestly, it's hard. Half of me wants to talk about him until I run out of breath. How his stubble was soft and framed his sculpted face perfectly. How his hands held my back like I was the most important thing in the world. How his lips felt pressed into mine.

But I don't. Instead, I finish off by telling her about Agent Pixie chasing me halfway across town. She looks . . . frightened.

"I don't like this. That's twice this woman has chased after you. Until we know for certain what she wants, it's probably best you stay in the house."

"But I have another lesson with Zachary tonight," I protest.

Freya's hands rest on her hips, and she gives me that mothering look she knows I hate.

"If she catches you, you could be carted off and vivisected in a lab! Or arrested, Steven!"

"Definitely should have led with arrested. Look, I'll be careful. I'll go down the backstreets."

"I'll come with you," she decides like it's the end of the conversation.

"No! No, you don't have to do that," I say a bit too hastily. Play it cool, Percival.

"Why not? I want to see this Zachary guy," she says a bit too coyly. Oh God, does she know? Was I accidentally livestreaming last night? Thankfully she changes the subject. "Do you reckon you can stop them from happening now?"

"I need to practise more," I say, pouring the now boiled water into my mug. "But yeah, once I've mastered it, no more unexpected tricks!"

"Show me!" she says eagerly.

I pick up an empty mug from the sink and place it on the countertop opposite. Alright, just like before. Just remember those toilets and—

The mug flies straight into my hand, green mist swirling around my fingers. Freya's eyes bulge, and she suppresses a squeal of excitement. I place the mug back but this time hold onto my coin. I feel the disgust wash over me. The mug begins to wobble. My hand glows green, but I push it into the coin. Slowly but steadily. Like walking against the tide.

The last of the green vanishes, and Freya actually does squeal this time. She throws her arms around me for a quick squeeze, then inspects the mug.

"That was fantastic, Percy! I am so proud of you."

My stomach burns and not from the eggs. I can tell my ears have gone red too. Freya is an overachiever, highest GCSEs in our year, head girl, and the life and soul of any party she walks into; she's had so much to feel proud of. Me – I do okay at school, a handful of good friends, but no obvious discernible talents. I've never had something to feel truly proud of. Until right now. I just stopped a trick and my best friend thinks it's the greatest thing in the world. And for once, so do I.

Freya recoils suddenly, her eyes wide in shock. She moves her head side to side, searching the room and whispers, "Percy!"

"Err, yeah? What is it?"

She jumps and clutches her chest.

"Bloody hell, where are you?"

"What are you talking about? I'm right here."

"Steven. I think you're invisible."

16

Excerpt from the report of
Field Director Fareborn: DEMA Case 1569GOS
Priority Delta
TUE 24/11/2020
1224 GMT

Junior Agent Wren has broken the Neutralisation Protocol *yet again*. Last night whilst doing a routine sweep of the area, Wren discovered a significant EME spike in an individual seen walking alone. However, rather than covertly watching to ascertain their destination (as Phase One dictates), Junior Agent Wren proceeded directly to Phase Five. She chased the suspected EMT, losing their trail in the eastern housing estate area (sector J). Once again, Wren has jeopardised this mission and put herself in grave danger from an EMT of unknown power level. She has been reprimanded *again* and told a further infraction will result in the immediate termination of her role in this mission and a disciplinary hearing at DEMA HQ.

I want to see her succeed. When I first started field duty, I had something to prove too. I was the first black woman to be a Field

Director, and I had the eyes of the entire department on me, or at least I felt I did. Of course, DEMA is a lot more inclusive now than in 1998, but I can still relate to Wren's need to prove herself. However, this cannot go in the face of the Neutralisation Protocol: Investigation, Identification, Infiltration, Conversation, Confrontation, Neutralisation – in that specific order, no exceptions. For now, I have Wren doing sector sweeps with EME detection drones to triangulate areas our EMT might frequent. With any luck, we can move on to Phase Three: Infiltration by the end of the week.

The EME readings Agent Wren detected from the suspect (58 kilodents) are high enough to warrant raising the classification of this case to Delta. Unfortunately, she could not identify the target due to the poor lighting, but she suspects it was either the male or female she pursued from the arcade yesterday.

As for my side investigation into the disappearance of Agent Fowler, I have just returned from the library in town with some very interesting developments.

DEMA HQ has pulled a list of forty-five Franks from school and census data. By cross-referencing these names with various records, I have whittled the Franks down to four. All were known to be residing outside of Grunsby at the time; however, since 2016, one has emigrated to America, one has died, and the trail on the last two has gone cold. It is safe to assume "Frank" was as much a cover story as "Jessie" was to Agent Fowler. But if that is the case, *who is this Frank?*

My research into the local newspapers at the time of Agent Fowler's disappearance was far more fruitful. Here are selected clippings:

LIGHTNING STRIKES GRUNSBY'S HISTORIC PIER
At 11 p.m. last night, fire crews were scrambled to put out a blaze that tore through Grunsby-on-Sea's historic Victorian pier but were too late. Ten minutes after they arrived on the scene, the grade-A listed structure collapsed into Grunsby bay. While no one was hurt, the damage to the pier and the JP Theatre has been declared irreparable. Eyewitnesses report seeing a man and woman running from the direction of the pier just moments before lightning struck the historic theatre. Curiously, the fire seemed to spread along the support struts, largely avoiding the theatre and boardwalk, which Fire Chief Boldan believes damaged its structural integrity enough to collapse.

Talk will inevitability turn to the subject of rebuilding. However, this might just be the mercy the pier needed. The JP Theatre had been suffering from declining audience numbers for years. In fact, the current production of Julius Caesar *has sold dismally, with last night's performance only having four audience members. The last time Grunsby Council commissioned a significant rebuilding of a historic site was Dysley House, a foster home for evacuated children, in 1941 following the fire that tore through the west wing. When asked, the Mayor's office stated –* cont. on page 4.

- End of Extract -

This account was published a few days after Fowler failed to report in. While not conclusive proof of EMT involvement, the fact that the fire only spread to the struts indicates that this might have been a targeted manifestation. My gut tells me that the two spotted fleeing the scene were Agent Fowler and "Frank", although as accomplices or enemies, I do not know. To speculate further, I believe "Frank" could be an EMT and targeted Agent Fowler specifically. Did he know she was DEMA? Or was that just a coincidence?

<u>Extract Two – *The Grunsby Echo* – Page 18 – 5 April 2016:</u>

LOCAL SIXTH FORMER GOES MISSING
Danni Walters was last seen in her home in Rosemount Avenue, Monday at 7.30 a.m.. Her father, Gregg Walters, woke her up just before leaving for work, but Seaview High claims she never made it in for classes.

Danni is described as being 5 foot 3 inches tall and of slender build, with tight curly ginger hair. The eighteen-year-old was last seen wearing black leggings and a navy denim jacket.
Danni is now the twenty-fifth young person to disappear in Grunsby-on-Sea since 2000, in what many have described as the "Grunsby Curse. If anyone has seen Danni, or a young woman matching the description, please get in touch with Grunsby Police Department immediately."

- End of Extract -

The timing of this disappearance is most curious: just two and a half weeks after Agent Fowler made her way to Grunsby-on-Sea, another young woman vanishes. Perhaps in isolation, they could be unrelated, but when viewed in the context of this so-called

Grunsby Curse, then the connection is almost certain. From 2000, there have now been over thirty cases of young people disappearing without a trace. It is now such a common occurrence that the newspapers hardly report them anymore (the excerpt above was relegated to page 18). Is this a case of endemic young runaways or something altogether more sinister?

When compiled, the missing people have a few things in common: all were between seventeen and twenty-five, resided in a fifteen-mile radius of Grunsby-on-Sea, vanished in plain sight, and none appear to have been taken by force. Curiously, there is no denominator underlying those taken that would indicate a type. Both young men and women alike have vanished from various ethnic, social, and racial backgrounds. Most of these cases received two to four articles in the local newspapers before being forgotten about. It strikes me as odd that the families would give up the searches for their loved ones after a few months.

I have had Danni's school records pulled by HQ. She appears to have been an average student with a reasonably stable home life and an aptitude for competitive diving. Following a hunch I had, I pulled weather records for days when Danni took part in diving competitions. Almost without fail, the days she came first were unnaturally hot and sunny, whilst the competitions she failed to place in were accompanied by rain. While not conclusive proof, it indicates that Danni could be an unregistered EMT – Epsilon grade if I had to stake a guess (due in part to the minor nature of her manifestations). It is too soon to conclude that is why she disappeared, but I have asked DEMA HQ to run background tests on the other thirty-one missing people to ascertain their EMT probability.

One final clue came not from the library but DEMA HQ. Whilst analysing school records of the area, they came across Lilian Pollecutt, daughter of the DEMA scientist Julian Pollecutt, enrolled in a local first school. In 1974, she was placed in foster care following her father's disappearance and was taken to London shortly thereafter, never returning to Grunsby-on-Sea. Why is this relevant? Because in 1989, Lilian married Thomas Fowler and had a daughter, Samantha, who would go on to become an agent with DEMA and return to her mother's hometown.

Two generations of the same family have disappeared in the same town over forty years apart. This cannot be coincidence. I will conduct further research into Julian Pollecutt, her grandfather, and request his file from DEMA HQ.

Something key is missing, but I can't quite see what yet.

– End of Log –

17

Freya

"I'm invisible?" says Percy's disembodied voice.

"Shhhh! I don't think the upstairs neighbours quite heard you," I whisper back.

Honestly, sometimes that boy has zero perception of his own volume. The last thing I need right now is for Marcus to come barrelling into the kitchen, demanding to know why he can hear but not see Steven. Maybe he'll buy that Steven can throw his voice like a ventriloquist? God, I'm bad at thinking on my feet.

But yes, Steven Percival is currently invisible. I assume. He may have gone to another dimension or something. I reach out my hand, and it hits something squishy in the air.

"Yes, that is my face, McCormac."

"Sorry! Just needed to check you hadn't gone full ghost. Can you touch me?"

Something hits my forehead and makes a hollow sound. Little prick just flicked me!

"Ow!"

"Come off it! That didn't hurt."

"Even when I can't see you, you still find a way to annoy me, Percy. So you are invisible but not intangible."

"Good to know."

"Pick something up."

"Why?"

"Just do it!"

The mug he just made fly across the room suddenly starts to levitate. Steven then accompanies this with ghostly "ooo" sounds because, apparently, he's twelve.

"Stop that! If Troy comes through, he'll think we have a poltergeist!"

"Fine. I've picked up something. What now?"

"Honestly, Percy, sometimes you really are blind to the obvious. Look down at yourself. It's not just you that is invisible; it's your clothes too."

"So?"

Time for a sigh and eye roll combo.

"So, logically, it means you can make other things invisible too. Not just yourself. Can you focus on the mug – like you did when you pulled it towards you?"

"I'll give it a go."

There are a few straining noises like he's trying to force out a fart. Then the ugly floral mug floating in the air gets fuzzy around the edges. Steven grunts from the aether, and with a surge of white sparkles, it pops out of existence.

"This is brilliant!" I say as I reach out a hand to where the mug was. I can still feel the smooth porcelain despite my eyes telling me nothing is there. Even pinching the rim, I can see my fingers squishing against a hard surface, but there doesn't seem to be anything between them. "Think of all the spying we could do. We could rob a bank, and no one would know."

"Isn't your dad a police officer?"

"I said we could, not that we should. Any ideas what caused this?"

"Not sure. I was happy I stopped the cup moving, and then it sort of happened."

Hmm, a mystery. I love a good mystery. It's mainly why I want to be a forensic scientist – that, and I think I'd look fetching in a deerstalker hat.

"So, you said your powers are the reverse of what other emotion manifestors do, right?"

"I believe the correct term is emomancer, but yes."

"Yeah, that's stupid, and I am never saying that. Anyway, you also said emotions come in pairs, opposites. So what is the opposite of being invisible?"

"Being seen?"

"Being the centre of attention – yesterday, you did one of your tricks, and I couldn't stop looking at you—"

"Must have been my dashing good looks."

"Do you mind? When Sherlock is deducing, Watson doesn't interrupt him with stupid comments."

"Why am I Watson in this scenario?"

"Because I'm the brains, and you are the bra— actually, never mind. You can be their housekeeper." I assume he's sticking his fingers up at me because that's what he would normally do. "Anyway, whatever you felt then is probably the opposite of what you feel now. It's probably something that makes you want to be seen."

"Pride? I guess I felt proud I could control it," comes a sober voice. "And yesterday it was shame."

Shame? Why would he be feeling that? I wish I could remember what we were talking about at the time. Just what is going on in Percy's head? He's hiding something, and I'm not leaving Grunsby-on-Sea until I find out what. Yeah, I am definitely Sherlock in this scenario. And most scenarios.

"Can you just do the coin thing now? I'm getting bored with having a conversation with your cabinets."

Just at that moment, I hear footsteps from the living room, heading for the kitchen.

"Abort! Abort! Stay invisible," I hiss as Troy comes in, looking like a sad middle child who had a growth spurt in his hand-me-downs.

"Hey, what's up," he says.

"HEY!" Okay, I tried to be cool and ended up super loud. He gives me a quizzical look but doesn't question it. He just heads for the sink. Exactly where Steven is. I assume.

Crap.

"What are you doing?" I blurt out.

"I was just going to make a coffee. It's gross, but my brain is demanding caffeine. Have you seen my mug? I thought I left here?"

Yes, it's currently half a metre away, being held by an invisible sixth former.

"Nope, haven't seen it. I'm going to make myself a tea. You sit back down. I'll bring it through."

"That's okay. I don't mind making it," he says. God, why does he have to be so bloody lovely all the time?

"No, go sit through! You . . . You helped make breakfast, so it's my turn."

"I only flipped a few eggs, but—"

"No! Steven told me you were a right little sous chef."

He perks up at this. Thought he might.

"Oh, did he? Where is Steven anyway? I thought he was out here with you?"

"He was, but he . . . went to buy more eggs."

"But we have a dozen right there?"

"Oh, maybe he didn't see them. I'm sure he'll be back soon."

Troy looks conflicted. Like he wants to say something but isn't sure how. Troy, I love you, but please piss off. Now really isn't the time for a heart to heart. Steven's manifestation can't last forever, and lord knows what we'll do if he suddenly reappears in the kitchen.

"So, what's Steven's deal?" he asks awkwardly.

"His deal?"

"Yeah. It's like. Okay, full honesty, we've been hitting it off, and I get a . . . vibe from him. And I can't tell if that's just how he is with everyone or if there's . . . something there."

I knew it. Sherlock McCormac solves another case. Troy is such a sweetheart but wears his heart on his sleeve. Unfortunately, Steven Percival is the most oblivious idiot and bottles everything up. Of course, he's missed the flashing neon signs Troy has been sending him. Every time Steven is in the same room, big, strong all-American Troy turns into a teenage girl drawing love hearts on her journal and giggling at his stupid jokes. The irony is they'd make a really cute couple, but Steven is so far in the closet he is organising Christmas decorations. At least, I think he is. Ugh, why can't boys be open about their feelings?

"Honestly, I don't know," I say, very conscious that Steven is in the room. "I've been wondering that myself for years. If you feel this way, you should try to talk to him."

"I know, but if he's not . . ."

"Then he'll be flattered, and you can move on. Win-win."

"Okay," he says with a determined face. What have I got Steven in for? At least he's had some warning; he can prepare a response . . . one way or the other. "Oh, there's my mug."

He's not wrong. The floral mug is sat at the edge of the counter next to the door. When did Steven put it down? The front door opens and closes, and Steven walks into the kitchen.

"Got halfway there and remembered we still had a dozen."

He winks at me as he settles against the counter, next to me. How much did he hear?

"Steven, I needed to talk to you about something," says Troy.

I didn't mean now! With me here! God, I hate being a third wheel, and I do *not* do well with cringey stuff – I always end up laughing nervously. I need to bail – now. I pick up my tea and turn to make a swift exit when Troy says, "Wait, Freya! I need you here too."

Bloody hell, why does he want a witness? I already feel the giggles tickling the edges of my lips. Where is my huge scarf when I need it?

"So, remember I said that woman was asking questions about you," he continues. Not where I thought he was going with this. "Well, she gave me her card to call in case you came back. I just picked up my jacket, and the card fell out. I don't know if you want to give her a call, but here."

He holds out a plain white business card, and I take it. There's a phone number scrawled in red pen on one side, and on the other, in holographic font, is one word: *DEMA*.

*

Steven

I snatch the card from Freya and hold it to the light, but there's nothing else on it. This is huge. But I can't say anything because

Troy is standing there giving me the most earnest smile you've ever seen.

I'll give Freya her due: she is very good at picking up on things. With just the slightest glance, she realises I need to talk to her, so she says, "Thanks, Troy. I'll give her a call in a little bit – see what's up. Now I mean it. Go sit down, and I'll bring the drinks through."

Maybe she is a bit Sherlock.

Troy nods and goes back into the lounge. Freya empties the boiled kettle and fills it to the very top again. At least I don't pay the electric bill.

"Spill," she orders as the rumble masks our voices again.

"Okay, remember I said I hid from Agent Pixie-Cut in an industrial estate? Well, there was this creepy, abandoned building there with a sign that said 'DEMA' on it."

"And you think it's the same DEMA?"

"It would be a huge coincidence if not. And they have the same helix-eye symbol. See it?"

Freya examines the card again, then stares out into the middle distance, brain whirring like she's Rain Man. Then she types furiously away on her phone, pacing up and down my tiny kitchen. I take the opportunity to add invisibility to my trick cheat sheet.

"Well, there's nothing on Google," she says, biting her lip. "Unless it's a town in Kentucky or the Danish Emergency Management Agency?"

"I think we are a little out of Denmark's jurisdiction. So do you reckon Agent Pixie is part of this DEMA too?"

"Potentially. First things first, we need to find out what this DEMA is and why they want you."

"Well, I assume nothing good considering their name sounds like a demon. Are you going to call the number?" I ask, having a google myself, but it's pointless. A super-secret agency isn't going to have a website or a Twitter account: *Trying to abduct a boy in @Grunsby_on_Sea to take to our super-secret lab for experiments #DissectionLife #SecretAgent #Blessed.*

"Of course, I'm not going to call the number, Percival! They'll track where I am calling from, then the whole town will be swarming with those agents."

"What do we do?"

"I could call Dad? See if he's heard of them."

"And what will you say when he asks questions? For all we know, DEMA are hitmen that go out and kill people like me. And you're a terrible liar, McCormac. He'll know something is up."

"Do you have any bright ideas then?"

"We could check out that building I saw last night."

"No, absolutely not! It's one thing to go to your lesson at night, but going out in broad daylight? Steven, there could be hundreds of DEMA people here undercover. You ran into that woman twice in the same day already. No, it's too risky. We'll be seen."

I open my mouth to protest when an idea pops into my head. I turn to Freya, and it looks as though she's just had the same thought. She chews it, trying to find a reason not to do it, but I can tell the detective in her is dying to see what clues are there.

"Do you think you can sustain it that long?" she asks.

"Probably," I say, not terribly convinced myself, but this might be my only shot to leave the house and get some answers.

"Could you cover me too, if needed?"

"If I'm touching you, I don't see why not."

"I feel bad leaving Troy and Marcus."

"They're big boys. They'll understand. Just tell them you lost an earring yesterday, and we are going to find it. Or better yet, I'll tell them. I'm much better at lying."

"Don't I know it," she mutters just loud enough for me to hear. I ignore it. Suddenly figuring out who I am doesn't seem as important as figuring out what DEMA is and why they keep following me.

✳

Twenty minutes later, Freya is shuffling down the housing estates like she's concealing a cantaloupe in her buttocks while I walk alongside, unseeable to anyone. Turns out Marcus needs to go to the police station anyway, so I convinced Troy to go with him. He didn't really put up much of a fight. I just asked him nicely. Weird.

"Relax," I whisper, making her jump. "You look like you have something to hide."

"I do have something to hide!" she snaps but then pretends to play with her hair as a man waiting for a bus turns to look at her. Smooth. "How much further?"

"Just a little bit."

In all honesty, I can't really remember the way, so we've been zigzagging through the streets, hoping I find the footpath. Why does every house in this town have to look the same? All terraced Victorian buildings with long alcove windows and a severe case of paint flaking.

I turn the corner first, then immediately dart back and put my hand on Freya's shoulders. She jumps again. Jesus, every time.

"What is it?" she whispers out of the corner of her mouth as she readjusts her rucksack.

"There's a woman in a suit; looks official. Might be DEMA," I reply.

With a quick glance to check no one is watching, I start to vanish Freya. I let the trick flow from my fingertips down to Freya's shoulders. It's sort of like what Zachary taught me to do with the coin, but instead of pushing it into Freya, I'm stretching my pride over her. Wow, this is a lot harder than a mug. I push harder, and her arm begins to look hazy. Then her leg and torso. I need to hurry because I'm sure the woman in the suit will be here any second now.

Focus, Percival, focus. Think of how proud Zachary will be when you tell him you did this. His smile flits across my memory, and my stomach burns. I can feel happiness germinate, but I can't let that be the focus, or Freya's hair will fall out or something. Instead, I use it. I push that happiness into the pride I'm feeling like redirecting a flowing river.

With a surge, the invisibility covers Freya completely, just as the woman in the suit rounds the corner.

She looks like the kind of person who has an aura of power around her. A black woman in her forties with very short curly hair, an immaculately tailored grey suit, and a stern face. She reminds me of a lion, powerful, poised, and deadly. Without a doubt, she must be a DEMA agent.

"Wren, we are moving to Phase Two of the Neutralisation Protocol," she says, holding a phone to her ear. "... Identification, Wren! Confrontation is Phase Five. We have been over the phases twice since we arrived! ... No, don't write them down!"

When we have safely put some distance from Agent Lioness, I release Freya, and she pops back into existence.

"Definitely DEMA," she breathes as we take a right at an intersection.

Suddenly I see it: the footpath is just a little ways further on the left. I push my pride into the coin, and to my surprise, it slips in almost instantly. I guess I didn't have much left anyway. Freya jumps as I suddenly become visible too. We follow the footpath and come out in the industrial estate. Far less creepy during the daytime, for sure.

All that is going through my head right now are the words "Neutralisation Protocol". Jesus, are these people here to kill me? Maybe Freya was right. It was a risk coming here. Tomorrow, I will stay in the house until Marcus gets his car. That is if I am going back. With all that's happened, I still haven't made up my mind. If I stay, I might get found and *neutralised* by DEMA. But if I go I might never see Zachary again.

We get to the barbed wire fence, and Freya is already running the length of it, looking for an opening. She calls me over to a bit that has come away from its post, and we pry it open.

On the other side is the building, crooked sign proudly displaying DEMA. The front door is boarded up, but most of the planks have rotted away, so we can probably squeeze through. The upper left-hand side of the grey bricked building has been damaged by a fire or an explosion. Is it even safe for us to go in? No – this is the only clue we have. We'll just be careful.

"Ready?" says Freya, giving my hand a squeeze.

"Ready."

18

Steven

We duck under the planks of wood nailed over the entrance and find ourselves in a small lobby. Ahead is a space-age style reception desk, all curves and tarnished chrome. A retro DEMA logo is somewhat visible on the wall behind, although most of the paint has flaked away. The lobby is overgrown with weeds and creeping vines. Maybe this facility was growing super plants? And Agent Pixie and Agent Lioness are just well-dressed botanists? Yeah, because the universe is that merciful.

"Creepy, huh?" I say, examining the rest of the room. There are some chairs along the wall where visitors probably would have waited and an industrial metal door on the far wall. "What do you reckon, Miss Marple? Any clues?"

"Miss Marple? Really? You saying I'm an old lady?"

"Well, if the comfortable shoes fit ..."

She sneers at me then begins to ransack the reception desk, emptying the contents of the drawers on the floor. There's nothing interesting: just piles of browning, water-damaged paper, some chewed pens, and a tear-off calendar that still says 1 May.

"Whoever these DEMA people are, they weren't stupid enough to leave anything at reception," Freya says, snapping a photo of the pile of office supplies now strewn about the lobby.

"The door's locked. Guess we'll have to head back."

Freya's face screws up like she's trying to do long division, then she darts under the desk.

"Aha! Just as I thought. Look," she says as a manicured hand emerges, clutching a set of keys. "Nailed to the underside in case the receptionist forgot them, I'd imagine."

We match the key to the lock and unlock it. It takes the two of us to push – either it's super heavy, or the hinges have rusted – but it comes open with a horrible groan. Waiting on the other side is a corridor out of the abandoned building playbook: dingy grey walls, filthy stone floors littered with broken ceiling plaster, fluorescent light fixture swaying ominously as it dangles. The only light source is from the barred windows at the far end by some stairs, dust swirling in the shafts of sunshine. Everything is quiet but not the comforting level of quiet. No, it's the sort of quiet where you second-guess every breath, every stomach rumble, every footstep like you're being watched.

"Split up and look for clues?" Freya asks unironically, oblivious to the mortal dread I'm feeling.

"Oh, silly me, I forgot to bring our talking dog!" I snap.

"Is someone scared, Percy?"

"No," I lie, "I just think we should stick together."

"Don't be such a baby; we'll cover more ground this way. This room looks like old records, so I'll scout it out. Why don't you start next door?"

"Surely, we can both look at records," I protest. There is no way I want to be left alone in this place.

"Percy, you are such a slow reader; you'll just slow everything down."

She has a point. Why did I decide to study English again?

"Fine! But you have to come straight away if I shout, okay?"

"Alright," she says, rolling her eyes as she disappears into the record room.

*

Freya

Steven is such a worrywart. What does he think he's going to find in an abandoned building? Zombies? The curse of Tutankhamun? This place has been locked tight since the fifties! The worst he might see is a mouse or a big spider. Insert eye roll here.

This place is filthy and, yeah, a little creepy. But honestly, I am loving the retro aesthetic. All the filing cabinets are those olive-green metal ones you see in movies. There's also a really cool typewriter which I might totally steal – for Instagram purposes, obviously. I'm not a complete relic.

I go to the first cabinet, labelled A, and open the top drawer.

Empty.

Okay, next one down, B.

Empty.

I pull out all twenty-five drawers with letters on them (XYZ were lumped together), but there isn't a scrap of paper in any of them. So, they obviously didn't abandon this place in a hurry. That's still useful information. And if they had a drawer for each letter of the alphabet, I assume they were storing information on people in them. But why? Staff? Patients? Targets?

The next lot are labelled by month, so probably had invoices or salary stuff in them. January is empty, but February has two folders crumpled on the bottom. I guess whoever cleared out these cabinets didn't double-check them. Their careless-ness is my clue! I grab it and shine my phone's light on its contents.

Oh, come on! What super-secret organisation writes all their notes in pencil that fades after sixty-odd years? Nothing left on most of these sheets of paper apart from the odd echo of a word – certainly nothing legible. Onto the floor it goes, and on to the next folder I go.

Pen on these ones but only at the bottom. A signature, perhaps? Signing off on invoices? I can make out "Pr ZD", "Dr DT", and "Pr JP" – nothing too helpful, but I snap a picture on my phone all the same.

I'm just about to move on to the rest of the months when I shine my light at the bottom of the February drawer, and it catches on an old photograph. It's black and white (duh) and shows the outside of the building back in the day. Standing in the foreground are two men, one blond and broad and the other with dark slicked-over curls like an Italian James Dean. Both are wearing lab coats with huge grins on their faces. On the back, in beautiful cursive writing, it says:

ZD & JP
Opening of DEMA Epigenetic Research Lab
Dysley House
21 April 1956

Bingo! So this is a laboratory, and they were studying "epigenetics". Why do I know that word? I feel like I saw it during my Biology revision. Something to do with genes, I assume, but I can't google it because my stupid phone doesn't get signal here. I take a picture of the back, just in case, then slip the photo into my rucksack.

I'm just about to start on March when I hear Steven scream.

*

Steven

I am going to kill Freya. That is if I'm not killed by whatever is here first. Hasn't she ever watched a horror movie? Rule number one of surviving a horror movie: you NEVER split up. It's a guarantee that the murderer or monster will pick you off one by one!

I take the next door on the right. The plaque outside says it's Lab Suite A, but there doesn't seem to be much of a lab left. It's a square room with chrome benches in two neat lines, sort of like if the *Bake Off* tent were designed by Dr Frankenstein. No weird machines or apparatus, though. Not even a Bunsen burner.

At the far end of the lab is a small office labelled "Professor Dent". The door is already ajar, so I gently nudge it all the way open, but there's very little to see. All the furniture has been dragged out, so it's just an empty box with peeling fleur-de-lis wallpaper. A little extravagant for a lab, maybe?

As I push the door all the way to the wall, I feel resistance – something must have been left behind it. There's a small leather satchel, like a washbag. Inside is a rusted hammer, some pliers with what looks like old, dried blood on them, and a leather strap with the imprints of many bites on it.

I throw the bag away from me. Maybe this place *was* designed by a mad scientist.

Creepy atmosphere: check.

Instruments of torture: check.

Overwhelming feeling that a lot of evil was committed here: double check.

I leave Lab Suite A as quickly as I can. Where to go next? The stairs to the first floor or down to the basement?

Rule number two for surviving a horror movie: NEVER go to the basement, especially alone. That's always where they keep the monster or the torture chamber. Guess I'll check out the room opposite: Lab Suit B and Professor Pollecutt's office, according to the rusted plaques.

I pull open the door, but what greets me isn't another lab – it's a war zone. The floor above has collapsed, and the entire room is filled with rubble. Huge chunks of brick and plaster make getting to Professor Pollecutt's office on the far side a near impossibility. I'm about to step inside when the rest of the ceiling gives way.

I scream and jump back, shutting the door and narrowly missing the debris. That was close! This place is too unstable. We need to find stuff quickly and then get out before it comes down around us.

"What happened? Are you okay?" says Freya sprinting out of the records room.

"Yeah, I'm fine. The ceiling almost fell on me," I say, my heart pounding like mad.

"I leave you alone for five minutes!" Here comes the eye roll. "Did you at least find anything?"

"Just a creepy bag of tools. You?"

"A few names and an old photograph. But I found out they were researching *epigenetics*."

"Isn't that the thing racists and Nazis believe in? Like selective breeding and the master race?"

"That's *eugenics*. Epigenetics is something different, I'm sure. I remember my biology textbook mentioning it at some point . . . What was it? Something about affecting genes, maybe? I've got no signal, so I can't look it up – what about you?"

"No bars."

"Okay, we'll check when we get home."

"Speaking of which, are we done? We need to get out of here before Freddy Krueger redecorates the floors with our organs!"

"Would you relax? Think about this logically: the door was locked before we arrived, so obviously, no one has got in. And even if someone were trapped in here with provisions, they would have died of starvation sometime around Thatcher's second term. As for the structural integrity, let's just walk carefully and avoid the left side of the building."

"But—"

"It'll be fine!"

"Okay." Literally no point arguing with her. Even if the ceiling had fallen on me, she wouldn't have changed her mind. Let's just get this over with.

"Now, where to look next?" Freya says, mainly to herself. "We can keep looking in the records room, but most of the cabinets are empty. I reckon they cleared the place of anything incriminating when they sealed this place up. So that leaves the first floor and the basement."

Don't do it.

"It's very possible they might have left something behind," she continues.

Don't do it.

"I mean, lugging equipment up all those stairs . . ."

She's going to do it, isn't she?

"Okay, let's start with the basement."

Piss biscuits.

19

Steven

Has Freya lost her mind? You don't go in the basement. Ever! Next, she'll be saying things like, "I'll be right back", "I'm going to investigate that creepy sound", and "Steven, let's open this evil book of curses". As we head down the stairs, the way forward illuminated only by the lights on our phones, I can hear myself shouting at the movie screen, "Don't go in there!" But of course, we are going to ignore every bad omen and worrying feeling and head into the goddamn basement.

Note to self: don't touch *any* magical talismans, ancient sarcophagi, or tubes of alien goo.

The staircase is narrow with concrete walls that make it feel like heading into a bunker. At the bottom is a thick metal door with one of those wheel handles like submarines or bank vaults have in movies.

"Look how cool this door is!" Freya says as she runs her hand over it. Only she could find this undeniable warning sign "cool". She tries to turn the handle, but it doesn't budge.

"Well, we tried. Let's check out the upstairs now? Or better yet, leave."

"Are you kidding? A big ominous vault door is tucked away in this super-secret research facility, and you don't want to know what's inside?"

"No, I don't."

"Seriously, Percy? You're not the least bit curious why they didn't want people to get in?"

"Maybe they didn't want something to get out!"

"You are being ridiculous! There's probably just research data. *Valuable* data that could help us figure out who these people were – are. There might even be stuff about your powers."

She has a point, although I can't shift this unease I feel. Answers would be nice. There is so much I don't understand about myself right now; even just one piece of the puzzle might help me find the rest.

"How do we open it?" I ask.

"*We* don't. *You* do. It opens inwards, so use your powers to push it open," she says like it's the most obvious thing in the world.

"I'll try," I say, unconvinced. Desire is a hard emotion to make yourself feel – it's a lot easier to summon the negative ones like sadness, anger, or disgust. I pass my phone to Freya and awkwardly hold my hands out in front of me. I really should workshop what to do with my hands when I use my powers. Spider-Man has the monopoly on the two-fingered wrist bend, and Freya would laugh at me if I put my fingers on my temples like Professor X.

Okay, admire the door. It's a nice door. A bit retro. Probably quite sturdy. Nothing yet. Okay . . . I want the door. I want it so badly.

"Nothing's happening," Freya sings.

"I know!" I sing back to her, annoyed.

I change tack. Think of something else but focus it on the door. But what do I want? I could try Zachary but that might be too close to happiness. Zachary's apartment! That place was stunning. Everything decadent but classy like it was from an old Hollywood movie. And I want everything in that room.

I get the tingling. The trick is starting to manifest. My fingers glow pink, and I can feel my power pressing against the door.

But before I know it, I am being thrown through the air and land on the hard stone steps.

"Are you alright?" asks Freya as she helps me back to my feet.

"I'm fine. Just hurt my back a bit." There's still a smidgen of pink light around my hands, so I shove it into the coin.

"What happened?"

"I don't know. I tried to push it, but it was like the door pushed me back."

"Weird. Maybe your emotion wasn't strong enough to push the door. Instead, you sort of pushed off from it. What were you thinking about?"

"Oh, just, you know, how nice the door was." Her eyes narrow, but she doesn't question it. I've already told her how gorgeous Zachary's flat was, but I'd just rather avoid the subject altogether with Detective Freya.

"Why don't you try something stronger?"

"It's a lot harder than it looks," I snap. "You try forcing yourself to feel a certain way. Trying to summon a genuine emotion on cue isn't as simple as pulling out a batarang from my utility belt."

"Is there another power that's easier to access?"

I'm about to tell her that I am not a performing monkey when I realise there is something I could try. But it would be very dangerous. And the last time I used it . . .

"Yeah, I . . . Happiness might do it," I mumble. There's a lump in my throat that I just can't shift. "Stand back, though."

My mouth is dry, but my palms are dripping. A deafening pop replays over and over in my mind. The same pop I hear every night when I'm trying to sleep. I can't do this. Not again. I can't willingly use the same power that made me a fugitive. That made me a murderer. What if Freya is next? She's looking at me like I've got another head. She just doesn't understand. One errant feeling, and I could be looking at her headless corpse.

"Sometime before the inevitable heat death of the universe, Percival."

I take a breath. Stop shaking, you stupid hands. I just need to focus very carefully and start off small – diet happiness.

Without saying anything to Freya, I focus on the slab of steel in front of me until everything else goes away – total tunnel vision. In my mind's eye, I picture Zachary. His blue eyes blink slowly at me, and his stubbled face bursts into a perfect smile.

There is a flash of yellow, then the heavy metal door shatters into millions of pieces like it was nothing more than a brittle pane of glass. Freya screams and shields her eyes, but she needn't have bothered; the shards are gone before they hit the ground. Fizzled away into the aether.

"Jesus!" Freya says, running her finger along the neat edge where the door once stood. "Come on, let's see what DEMA are hiding away in their basement."

Still a little shellshocked, I follow Freya into the foreboding dark of the basement. I will never judge the stupid decisions of a character in a horror movie ever again.

✳

Freya

Ugh, it smells awful. Like raw chicken left out in the sun for a few days. I guess sixty years of stale air will do that. Maybe some rats died too?

We scan our lights over the room. Strange apparatus and scientific equipment is strewn about the floor like a tornado hit. In the very centre, next to the signs for the loos, are long, opaque plastic curtains concealing something big and square.

I was right! Everything is still here. Giant machines line the right-hand wall, their gauges and valves silent: retro computers, a hundred times the size and a thousand times slower than the phone in my hand. I walk over to it and flip some switches, but more for the fun of doing it than anything. Even if there were power, I wouldn't be able to work this thing – everything would come out on tape. Still, it would've been cutting edge at the time, so that means DEMA had a lot of money. Government-funded?

Steven is going along the other wall, checking out the filing cabinets and throwing fearful glances at the plastic curtains from time to time. Honestly, that boy is such a wuss.

"Anything?" I shout over to him.

"No. There's just a load of ash. It looks like everything was firebombed."

He's right. Huge scorch marks decorate the cabinets. Obviously, whoever worked down here didn't want their secrets leaving the building.

I pick through the detritus, but nothing is jumping out to me as a clue – just hunks of metal, broken glass, and an old Hula Hoops packet. On the back wall is a rack with some safety goggles and dusty lab coats hung up. Inside one of the pockets, I find a key. Great clue. Love a key. But what is it for?

"Here's something!" Steven calls. "Got half a memo – slightly singed, but I can make out some of it."

"What does it say?"

"'Confirmed by intelligence at the Kremlin ... something something Soviets have ... something something ... EMT ... East Berlin.' Nah, that's about it. Rest is too burned. I'll take a picture for you."

"Kremlin? What's that?" I ask.

"It's Russia's White House. I mean, East Berlin, Soviet, Kremlin ... All very Cold War, isn't it?"

"Uhuh," I agree vaguely. I know next to nothing about history or foreign politics. "Zachary told me EMT was the proper word for emomancer. Maybe they were trying to turn people like me into weapons against the Soviets?"

"Very possibly."

"What do you reckon that is?" He points to the big plastic-wrapped elephant in the room.

"Shall we find out?"

I step over the broken equipment and grab the plastic curtain. Steven looks like he wants to say something, stop me perhaps, but all he manages is a small whimper. Honestly! He can make doors vanish, but he's afraid of what's underneath a plastic sheet? Heart of a lion as always, Percival.

Behind the curtain is a huge mesh cage. Inside is a raised chair with leather arm, leg, and neck restraints, all of which look like they have been ripped open.

"Looks like a torture chamber – or a secret sex dungeon," I say. "The scorch marks on the chair look controlled. Maybe they were electrocuting them? Jesus, just what the hell were they researching here?"

"Remember when we went to the science museum in year nine? There was that cage that blocked out electromagnetic fields?"

"Yeah! We stood in it, and they hit it with electricity, but we didn't feel anything. God, what was it called? I think it was in *Doctor Who* at some point too."

"A Faraday cage!" Steven says, suddenly remembering. "Why would they have one here? Were they doing experiments with electromagnetic stuff? Oooh! Or do you reckon it protects them from emotions as well as – OH MY GOD!"

I whip my head back around at Steven, who has his phone pointed at the bottom of the cage.

Oh my god!

There's a dead body. Like, an actual dead body. It's wearing a lab coat and lying on its back by the door to the cage. Obviously, it's been decomposing for a while because there is nothing but a blackened skeleton remaining.

This is amazing! The clue fairy came in the night and left me a big fat juicy one. Yeah, respect for the dead, blah blah blah, but to someone wanting to be a forensic pathologist, this is the motherlode.

I try the key in the lock, and the door opens. Just as I'm about to step inside, Steven hisses, "What are you doing?" in an unnaturally high voice.

"Taking a look," I reply. "What's the problem?"

"What's the prob— Freya! You are stepping into a cage with a skeleton!"

"So? It's not going to hurt me – it's dead. Zero muscle mass."

"Yeah, well . . . We don't know what the cage is for. It might be dangerous!"

"You said it yourself: it's a Faraday cage. So it's just there to protect the inside from electro-stuff."

"Or keep all the electro-stuff contained to protect the outside! For all we know, they filled the cage with electricity, and that poor sod got fried."

"Steven, it'll be fine. This building hasn't had electricity for years," I say, stepping inside the cage. "See? Nothing to worry about."

I pop a squat and inspect our skeletal friend.

"Don't touch it! It could have evidence or something," Steven says, shuffling round to the door but keeping his distance.

"Percy, you're telling the daughter of a police officer not to disturb the evidence on a dead body. I know you're scared, but it's no excuse for mansplaining. Right, let's see here. No way to tell how long ago they died without testing, but it's hardly recent. There's a badge on their lab coat . . . Why did everyone have to write in cursive in the fifties? Looks like . . . Julian . . . Pollecutt."

"I saw his office earlier before the ceiling fell!"

"He must be the JP in the photo too. One of the lead scientists. But why is he here? If one of the facility heads goes missing, people would ask questions."

"H-how do you think he died?"

"Hmm, not sure. No broken bones or obvious trauma. Weird – his lab coat is dusty, but it's still pretty white. There are no stains, no blood. Even if he starved to death, his body would've decomposed and made some sort of mark. All his bones are in the right place, so he died where he fell. It's like he was sucked dry."

"Do you reckon he was strapped into that thing?" Steven says, pointing a shaky finger to the raised chair.

"He's facing the wrong way for a start, and I can't imagine a weedy boffin breaking free from leather straps."

"Maybe someone trapped him in here and zapped him with something?" Steven offers. "Both doors were locked from the outside, so there must have been someone else here."

"Oooh, very possibly. You're saying that someone lured him into the cage then locked him away to try to kill him? Still doesn't explain how he died so clean. If there was a death ray or something, wouldn't it still be in there with him, or it'd defeat the whole point of the Faraday cage?"

Questions, questions, and not a lot of answers. I take some photos on my phone. Bit weird, but you never know when something might be important. Even something as small as the positions of his arms – one stretched across himself like he was cowering or trying to protect his body.

I walk the perimeter of the cage looking for something: drag marks in the dust, a trail of blood, a signed confession from a murderer, but there's nothing. Just one of the broken straps on the floor by the chair. Bloody hell, these are thick! No way someone could get out without tools unless they are Wonder Woman.

"Freya, I really think we should get out of here!" says Steven, shining his light on me. "This is really freaking me out and – OH MY GOD! LOOK UP!"

Jesus tits! The top of the cage has been twisted and ripped open like a feral beast has burst through it. But what can rip through steel like that? Perhaps the same thing that broke free of its leather straps.

Steven has started to hyperventilate. I know he's scared because he's chewing his nails. He pretty much chewed to the bone watched *A Nightmare on Elm Street*. Is it getting hot in here too? It's silly. Monsters don't exist, and a sixty-year-old cadaver isn't going to hurt us.

Okay, one last quick photo of Professor Pollecutt's body. This is without a doubt the most bizarre corpse I have ever seen, and – I AM GOING TO KILL STEVEN PERCIVAL IF HE KEEPS BITING HIS STUPID NAILS.

*

Steven

"WOULD YOU STOP CHEWING YOUR PISSING FINGERS!" Freya suddenly shouts, so loud that I jump.

"What?"

Is she joking? Bit of a weird time to be joking. I can't see her face; she's shining her phone at me like an interrogation. She storms out of the Faraday cage and shoves my shoulder hard.

I'm speechless. What's happening to her? Why is she so angry?

I shine my light on my hands and see blue smoke emanating from them. With everything going on, I didn't realise I've been manifesting my fear. I've been too busy freaking out about the dead body in the creepy abandoned laboratory. Now, where is my coin? I shove my hand in my pocket, but I can't find it. I just had it a second ago.

"I WARNED YOU!" Freya bellows as she throws a punch.

Jesus Christ, McCormac can do some damage. My shoulder blazes with pain as she reels back for another blow. I grab her wrists, still clutching my phone. We are at a stalemate. She can't hit me, but I can't get the coin. I can't get to anything metal to . . .

I am such an idiot – my phone!

I do just as Zachary told me: I push all my fear into the phone, but something feels weird. The coin felt like I was squashing and stuffing my emotions into it. My phone, however, is actively fighting me. Whatever I shove in, it pushes back out, like trying to keep an inflatable ball underwater. Now I'm locked in two struggles: keeping a wild Freya from ripping my face off and trying to force my fear into a vessel it clearly doesn't want to go.

Okay, time to try the old way.

I clear my mind. Breathe in. Think of white. Breathe out. Nothing but white. A void of pure nothingness. The fear ebbs, diminishing to a tiny puddle, but doesn't completely evaporate. Freya's arms slacken slightly. I push the remaining fear up my arm and into my phone. It puts up resistance, but this time it can take what I'm trying to give it – like a thimble holding a drop of water and not a torrent.

The blue wisps away to nothing.

Freya's eyes refocus on mine, and she pulls herself away.

"I . . . I'm so s—"

"Don't," I interrupt, rubbing my shoulder. "It wasn't your fault. I lost control."

"Steven, I would never—"

"Freya, I'm fine. Honestly."

She nods, but her eyes give her away. She can't look at me because now she's the one who's afraid.

Not afraid of what *I* can do, but of what I can make *her* do.

I've tried to warn her how my powers hurt people, but I don't think she really understood it till now. And she still doesn't know

159

what I'm capable of . . . what I've done. If I told her the truth, I'd probably lose her forever.

Good. At least now she'll take it seriously. She won't scoff when I warn her how dangerous I am. I fish the coin out from my jacket pocket. I must have put it there earlier. I'm not letting this out of my hand for the rest of the day.

"We should probably get out of here," Freya says shakily, rubbing her wrists which look like they've been burned. Was that me too? "Let's go investigate the upstairs."

*

Freya

Bloody hell, my wrists hurt. I guess fear also produces heat. I roll down my sleeves and try not to touch them.

"What should we do about the body?" asks Steven, looking back at the cage as we head towards the door.

"Leave it. We can report it anonymously to the police later."

Just as we near the doorway, a noise stops us both dead. A clunk like metal hitting wood that came from the toilets behind us.

"What was that?" Steven whispers. It's probably a bit late for that, Percival. I just shouted myself hoarse a minute ago.

"Pipes?" I offer, although I guarantee the water has probably been shut off. Steven doesn't look convinced by that either. The noise happens again, and the ladies' room door sways slightly.

"That didn't sound like pipes. What if . . . whatever killed that scientist is still here?"

"And how would it survive for sixty years without food, Percy?" I reply, but part of me is spooked.

"You're right. Let's leave."

We step through the doorway, and Steven is halfway up the stairs when I yell up to him, "Wait! Can you ... bring the door back?"

"You're asking me to bring the door I atomised back into existence?"

"Can you do it or not?"

"No! That's not how my powers work – I think."

I chew my lip. My rational side knows I am just being silly, and there is nothing in the ladies' loo. But the side of me who reads her horoscope every week is a little bit freaked out that the Demogorgon will jump out at me.

As I walk up the steps after Steven, I notice something is stuck to my trainers: a dirty, browned scrap of paper. I peel it off once I'm at the top and shine my light on it as Steven peers over my shoulder. In hastily scratched biro is one word:

LEECH

20

"Leech?" I read aloud. "What does that mean?"

"No idea. Code for some experiment? Name of one of the workers? Label for a jar of leeches?"

"If that was the case, it would say, 'Leeches' plural, not 'Leech' singular."

Freya considers this and starts looking over the photos on her phone as we climb the stairs to the first floor. The light coming through the long, barred windows melting away the fear still griping my insides – things always seem much less scary in the light. Really, we should be leaving, but I know Freya would never forgive me if I didn't let her explore everywhere. She's relentless. But it means we are getting closer to the truth. I can feel it.

We reach the landing and find ourselves in an equally dilapidated corridor. Freya marches over to the nearest door on the right and pushes it open. This must have been the epicentre of the fire damage we saw from the outside. The room is huge but almost entirely blackened and missing a considerable amount of floor.

"Epigenetic Activation Chamber – authorised personnel only," I read from the rusted plaque on the door. "What the hell does that mean?"

"Nothing good, I would imagine. Whatever they were doing here obviously went wrong. Did you see anything from the room below?"

"Just rubble and broken bits. It's too dangerous to go check, anyway," I add firmly before Freya asks me to somersault my way over there.

She huffs, annoyed that she's missing clues, then snaps some photos, and we close the door carefully.

"What's wrong?" I ask. Freya is chewing her lip and pulling at the skin on her neck absent-mindedly.

"Just thinking."

"I gathered. About what?"

She rolls her eyes and relents.

"The head scientist is dead, trapped in a cage in a sealed vault in the basement. And upstairs, half of the building has been blown up. So the question is: which came first? If Professor Pollecutt was murdered first, then maybe whoever locked him in came up here and sabotaged something, so everyone would abandon the building. If the fire happened first, the building was already abandoned, so no one would check the basement. But then why did the professor come back?"

"The calendar!" I suddenly remember. "From the reception desk. The receptionist wouldn't have torn off any more days after they abandoned the building. So whatever day it said—"

"—is probably the day of the fire. Let me see if I can find the ..." she says, trailing off as she furiously flicks through the photos on her phone. "Yes! Here. The first of May ... It's so small, but it looks like 19 ... 61. Great! Well done, Percy, we'll make a Watson out of you yet."

"See! When we aren't in a spooky basement, I can be quite useful."

I try a door on the left, but it's just an empty supply cupboard. Next to that are the loos, but we find nothing there besides some ivy aggressively bursting through the windows. The final two doors before the smashed window at the end of the corridor are right next to each other. One of them is another industrial-looking vault door. Freya gives it a shove, but it doesn't move.

"We might need to use your powers again on that one," she says like it's no big deal.

"Freya, I really don't think it's a good idea, especially after . . . You know."

"That was an accident. You didn't have your coin."

"Still, manifesting happiness is super dangerous. It worked once, but next time I could burn down the building. We also don't know what's behind it. There could be more dead bodies or a genetically modified super-plague."

She opens her mouth to fight back but then just says, "Okay." I know what she's doing. She's letting me think I've won, so I'll shut up, then she'll bully me into doing it later. That's what always ends up happening. "Let's try this door then," she says, gently creaking it open.

"After you."

She gives me another eye roll, flicks a stray hair behind her ear, and crosses the threshold.

*

Freya

It's very light in here, so I turn off my phone's torch. I'm running low on battery, anyway. It's a small room with a few chairs and a desk, but there's a smashed glass screen that looks into a much larger room with barred windows.

"Some sort of observation room?" I guess.

"But who were they observing?" Steven replies as he rifles through the desk.

I peer through the dirty glass at the room beyond. It's colourful, or at least it was before the paint bleached and cracked away. Now it's mainly green from the invasive creeper plants, but there is a mostly intact painting of . . .

"Pooh," I murmur.

"Trying to curb your swearing?" Steven chimes in as he scans through a folder.

"As in the 'Winnie The' variety. Look! There's a painting of him. And Tigger . . . Rabbit's on the ceiling. They look like the old illustrations, like pre-Disney . . . Oh god."

My stomach falls out of me as it dawns on me what I am looking at.

"What? What is it?"

"Children."

"What?"

"It's a nursery. They were experimenting on children, Steven."

Steven joins me at the glass. I can see an old-fashioned teddy bear with matted fur, wooden blocks, and a severely damaged edition of *Peter Pan*. Four small beds and a crib falling apart with rot are pushed up against the walls. The room carries on slightly further to the right – no doubt to the vault door. These people kept children locked behind a metal door like they were in some sort of cage . . .

"The glass! Steven, look. There's thin wire in the glass. It's another Faraday cage to stop manifestations getting out."

"Would that work?"

"Not now that it's smashed, I assume. If we're right, that means these children were like you. Or they were trying to make them like you."

"How would they do that?"

"Honestly, I dread to think."

I feel sick. Was everyone a monster back in the day? The thought of scientists using kids as emotional weapons is just revolting. But I need to know exactly what happened here.

I leave Steven to pour over the file and head next door. It's another observation room, but there's a door next to the glass that someone forgot to close. Beyond it is what looks like a ward or old-fashioned infirmary. Six stained hospital beds made of rusted iron lie empty. Full size, too big for children. So, who were they for?

I step through the open door next to the window. Under the first bed, I find a medical chart on a clipboard. Bingo! As clues go, this has to be S-rank.

Goddamnit, why do all doctors have to write in chicken scratch? There's a lot of medical stuff I don't understand: monitoring of blood levels, different cocktails of drugs prescribed – oh Jesus, they gave this person thalidomide! No name, just a number (EMC06), and try as I may, I can't find a date of birth or gender anywhere. At the bottom of the first page is something that catches my eye:

EMT Status: Negative
Genetic Marker Present: Unconfirmed, but brother has been
identified as EMT, so highly likely.

Very interesting. So DEMA thought these emotion powers were hereditary, despite this patient not being one. Like someone with black hair carrying a ginger gene.

I flip the page and am about to sit down on the bed to read when I remember the revolting stains. Standing is fine. No major clues on this page, just more drug prescriptions, but on the next, I find a very strange log:

Attempt #1

EMC06-A

F

B. 03/12/1957

Trauma: ECT administered at months 4, 6, and 9

Subject's first attempt is unsuccessful. No noticeable EME has been recorded from EMC06-A within 2 months.

EMT Status: Negative

Attempt #2

EMC06-B

M

B. 21/05/1958

Trauma: ECT administered monthly, Sleep Deprivation

Attempt 2 has also resulted in failure. Lack of sleep paired with monthly electric shock sessions has resulted in the premature termination of EMC06-B. Extreme defects also present – unknown if trauma-related.

EMT Status: Unknown

Attempt #3

EMC06-C

F

B. 21/03/1959

Trauma: Controlled Starvation, enforced use of narcotics

*After a suitable recovery from Attempt #2, patient has successfully
been brought to term. Zeta levels of EME detected in EMC06-C.
Further observation will now continue.
EMT Status: Positive – Zeta*

Jesus, what did they do to this poor person? Electric shock
therapy, starvation . . . Who knows what else they might have
done. My brain is definitely cooking something up. Pieces
of the puzzle are lining up, but I'm still missing something
important.

I take pictures of the clipboard on my dying phone, and I'm
about to bung it down on the bed when something grabs my
attention. Something shiny and metal by my feet. A tool of some
sort shaped like a duck's bill that I'm sure doctors use for looking
at your . . .

Oh, god.

Everything clicks. The medical logs, the nursery, the . . .
speculum – that's what they call it!

"PERCY!" I yell, and within seconds he has burst through the
door.

"What is it? Are you okay?"

"I'm fine. I've just figured it all out."

"What is this place, like an infirmary or something?" he asks,
joining me on the other side of the glass.

"It's a maternity ward," I say, trying to fight the revulsion
creeping up from my stomach. "I don't think they were turning
people into EMTs; they were breeding them."

Steven opens his mouth a few times but can't quite find the
words. I offer the clipboard, and he starts to scan it.

"They were ... Oh god, Steven, they were torturing them – pregnant women. I think they were trying to make their children EMTs."

"How would that make them EMTs?"

"I don't know. Maybe they need trauma to activate it or something? They talk about this woman having the gene marker because her brother was an EMT, even though she isn't one herself. Maybe it's a recessive gene like blue eyes."

Steven is quiet for a few seconds, then says, "Do you think they tortured the kids too?"

"I don't know. Nothing in here says they did." I feel a lump rising in my throat. "Let's check the nursery. There might be records about the children through there."

Steven opens the door at the end of the ward, and we step through into the children's room. There's another mesh door, like in the Faraday cage in the basement, but this one is unlocked. The window is black and mirrored from this side, so the children couldn't see the scientist observing them. Creepy.

My heart aches thinking about these poor kids in a cage. Still, there's nothing in this room to indicate they were treated as badly. Books, toys, somewhat conformable looking beds – they at least give off the semblance of care.

"What's this?" Steven calls, holding up a glass bell with a rubber ball on the end, not unlike an old-fashioned bike horn.

"I think it's a breast pump, Percival."

"A what?"

"Honestly, do they teach men nothing? A pump. For pumping out milk."

"Like a cow?"

169

For that, he gets a good five seconds of eye-rollage. Boys are idiots.

"No, like a human female. I assume they didn't want the mothers breastfeeding in case they bonded with DEMA's little science experiments."

Steven puts the breast pump down like it's an unexploded bomb and keeps searching the room. I'm in the process of looking under each of the kids' beds when there's a knock on the heavy vault door at the other end of the room.

We both freeze.

Scraping. Something is scraping down the door. Everything is silent for a moment before Steven whispers, "What was that?"

"The wind?"

"The wind can't bang on a metal door!"

"Well, maybe it's just a cat or something?"

"Cats don't have opposable—"

"Yes, I know, cats don't have opposable thumbs, Steven! Let's just go out the way we came and . . ."

I stop talking because the unmistakable sound of slow, heavy footsteps reaches my eardrums.

And it's coming from the maternity ward.

Whatever was just at the vault door has just taken the long way round and will be bursting into the nursery in less than ten seconds.

I attempt to prise open the vault door, but it won't budge. Steven tries his powers, but it's no use. He can't seem to summon the right emotion.

A long, withered hand reaches around the door, followed by its monstrous owner. Standing in the threshold is what looks like a freeze-dried corpse – a skeletal figure with gnarled, blackened skin like burned tree bark. Its face, if you can call it that, is devoid of eyes and a nose, but its mouth is a dark hole dripping with saliva. It shuffles into the room, its head moving from side to side and its long, clawed hands out in front of it like it's playing blind man's buff.

We back against the wall, hardly daring to breathe. The creature drops to all fours and crawls forward. It's suddenly getting really hot in here again, and a blue aura covers Steven's hands. He's afraid.

The creature snaps its head in our direction.

Oh crap. How does it know where we are? Echolocation? Or maybe it can sense Steven's fear. Just what is this thing?

It opens its mouth hole even wider and lets out an ungodly shriek. Its mouth lights up with grey sparks.

Oh god, I feel . . . woozy . . . and . . . numb.

21

Steven

What the actual hell is that thing? And what is Freya doing? She's fallen to her knees, swaying like she's drunk. The creature's mouth is still sparkling like it swallowed a Catherine wheel. The blue's also gone from my hands – that's weird.

This is my fault. All the warning signs were there: abandoned Cold War lab, creepy basement with skeletons and cages.

"Get up," I say, trying to pull Freya to her feet. Is the creature doing this?

I need to stop it quickly. My hand curls around the coin in my pocket, and I raise the other one at the monster. Desire ought to do it – I can blast it back and make a run for it with Freya.

Crap. This is really hard to do under pressure. I'm trying to think of Zachary's flat like before, but I just can't do it. Staring at this blackened, twisted creature, my brain just won't go anywhere else. Fight or flight is surging through my body. Desire something. Anything. But it's no use.

But I can feel something. Not in my body but outside it. I can feel a familiar desire, but like it's separate from me now. An emotion preserved in amber. The coin! It's coming from the coin in my fist. I reach down with my mind and draw it into myself.

My hands glow pink, and I send the manifestation out towards the creature, but it rolls off it. I try again, but it won't work. It's like when magnets repel if you put the same poles together.

Freya starts convulsing as sparkle-mouth tenses its muscles. It's feeding. Feeding on Freya. It's sucking her dry like . . .

Like a *Leech*.

Holy crap. This is the thing from the basement that killed that professor and tore a hole in the cage. And now it's trying to do the same to Freya!

Okay, screw powers. I grab the nearest thing and throw it. A teddy bear hits the Leech with all the force of a light cough. I try some of the books, but it ignores them and continues its feast. With one last desperate attempt, I seize the breast pump and lob it as hard as I can.

Bullseye!

It smacks the Leech in the face, and the glass horn smashes. It stumbles, screeching in outrage and clawing at the shards of glass stuck in its face hole.

Freya raises her head and lets out a breath.

"Wh-what? Steven?"

"On your feet, McCormac, NOW!" I pull her up, and she takes in the sight of the screaming Leech as we run past it. She snaps back to herself, but her eyes have lost their usual hazel colour and look grey.

We are almost at the door when the Leech does something else unexpected. It screeches again, like when a bell pepper squeaks on your teeth (but obviously, worse and more murderous). Green sparks swirl in its mouth hole and the mesh door slams shut.

Piss biscuits.

Freya tries to pull the door open, but can't. The Leech crawls towards us, then rears up like a cobra.

"STEVEN!" Freya cries out. "DO SOMETHING!"

But I can't think of anything. My powers don't seem to work on this abomination. But if I don't think of something in the next ten seconds, it will suck us dry like it did to that bloke in the basement.

It's true what they say: your life really does flash before your eyes. Well, it's more like your brain is scanning desperately for something useful to save you. My search brings back a big fat zero results. Just Freya rolling her eyes at me, Mum packing my lunchbox for school, Dad teaching me to use a pen knife, Troy's face when he flipped an egg, Zachary pushing his curls from his face . . .

My stomach burns at the thought of him. Of course, the universe gives me the happiest night of my life, then kills me the next day.

Of course.

Happiness.

I try to remember everything from last night. The smell of his perfume, woody and spicy. His hips pressed into mine as we kissed. Laughing at all my stupid jokes. It's working. Despite the monster looming over me, I can feel a nugget of happiness form within me. But it's not enough. So I imagine. I whip up a fantasy of me and him together, lying on a couch. He wraps me in his arms and kisses me on the head. Then he's in front of me, drawing me close. His shirt falls away. He draws near, lips parted and . . .

Yellow light erupts from my hands and swirls around my body. I push it all towards the door behind us, which starts to crack. I push harder, the yellow pouring from my eyes now too, but something is stopping me – like a powerful wind is blowing my trick back.

Grey sparks swirl in the Leech's mouth hole again, but this time, it's aiming it at me. All the happiness I am manifesting is being pulled towards it like an emotional black hole, gobbling everything in sight. But I'm not feeling faint like Freya. I guess my trick is protecting me for now. Once the Leech's finished feeding on it, I'm done for. Need to hold it a little longer.

"Oi, ugly!" Freya yells from somewhere out of my eye line. Something zooms past my face and straight into the Leech's mouth hole. It topples backwards and thrashes about on the floor, trying to dislodge the foreign object. Freya is by a box of breast pumps, throwing them one after another. I feel like this is some sort of cosmic feminist moment.

My powers flare again, no longer being redirected toward the Leech. I swing my hand out to the door, and it crumbles to dust. But the trick is still going. I shake my hand like I've got something stuck to it, but the yellow won't turn off. The floor starts to rumble and crack. Freya grabs my arm and pulls me through the observation room just as the maternity ward falls into the lab below, taking the Leech with it.

No time to bask in getting rid of it. The glass to the nursery shatters into a million pieces, and more of the floor disappears. Crap, turn it off, Percival. Turn it off!

"Steven, your coin!" Freya yells as we run for the stairs. I'm gripping it tight, but it's not working. Either the trick is too strong, or I'm not focusing hard enough. In fairness, it's tough to do calming breaths and visualisations when you are one broken support beam away from being crushed.

And as if things couldn't get any worse, prowling up the stairs is the Leech. It steps into the sunlight cascading through the window and recoils, arching its back and screaming like boiling water was just thrown on it.

"Other way!" I cry, turning about and running back up the stairs. "The window!"

Freya points to the small window at the end of the hall. What are we supposed to do with . . . oh, right.

I clench my fists, yellow ribbons still streaming from them, and punch a massive hole out of the far wall.

The Leech jumps to the top of the landing, avoiding the sunlight. It breaks into a run like a wolf hunting its prey.

We are nearly there – so nearly there. The ground starts falling beneath our feet. The Leech is less than a metre away. It reaches its long clawed hands to strike, but we jump. Our feet leave the floor just as it crumbles away from us.

The Leech falls.

I grab Freya's hand and clutch my coin in the other. We are a lot higher up than I thought. The pavement below looks hard. If I don't do something quickly, we are both looking at broken bones.

Then I feel it again.

The emotion trapped in the coin. The desire I tried to send at the Leech, depleted but still there. I grab it, let it flow through me, and then I throw it down to the nearing pavement. A pink aura replaces the yellow around my hand and slams into the ground below.

I shoot upwards, Freya being yanked with me. There isn't enough to keep us airborne, so we slowly descend. Our feet touch terra firma, and we collapse into a heap, out of breath and flushed with adrenaline.

Not a second later, the entire DEMA facility implodes, burying its secrets and the Leech in a cloud of dust and rubble.

"Jesus tits!" Freya swears.

Jesus tits indeed.

22

Excerpt from the report of
Field Director Fareborn: DEMA Case 1569GOS
Priority Gamma
TUE 24/11/2020
1900 GMT

I have asked for the reclassification of this mission to Gamma status. I fear there may be stronger forces at work here than first theorised. Forty-five minutes ago, I was alerted that HQ had detected a shift in the ambient Emotion Manifestation Energy levels within 20 miles of my location. However, unlike the recent surge that seemingly awoke Agent Fowler, this shift was a noticeable dip in EME – from a slightly below average 2.5KD to -200KD for approximately ten minutes. Minus kilodents indicate a substantial depletion or leeching of energy (typically from apathetic manifestations in an unregistered EMT). Such a significant dip suggests we are facing a far higher risk than previously estimated. Therefore, I once again request additional assistance from DEMA HQ. I know we are stretched thin, but I fear the situation could soon develop into a Beta or even Alpha priority level.

I have also decided to move to Phase Two of the Neutralisation Protocol: Identification. Wren's investigation of the area has led her to believe that the EMT resides in sector seven or nine. It would seem her eagerness to make up for previous mistakes has led to some exemplary surveillance.

HQ has finished analysing the other missing people and determined their EMT probabilities range from forty to eighty-nine per cent (Danni receiving a score of sixty-seven). This is exceptionally high, and I feel it is a vital clue to why these people vanished. They were very likely targeted for their powers, but by whom we do not know.

It is also imperative to note that our researchers noticed a trend emerging whilst analysing the data. All the missing people in Grunsby-on-Sea had an adopted or fostered parent. Even Agent Fowler's mother was briefly sent to an orphanage before being fostered following Julian Pollecutt's disappearance. I have asked them to trace adoption records and find commonality, whether it be a particular orphanage, region, or shared tragedy. If there is a denominator to all these disappearances, we may be able to prevent another and follow it back to find Agent Fowler.

I feel like the truth is a jigsaw puzzle. I have most of the pieces, but it's just a matter of figuring out where they go. I will brief Junior Agent Wren tonight about all of this. While she has been somewhat of a liability, her propensity to think abstractly might be just the thing needed to line the pieces up.

– End of Log –

23

<u>Freya</u>

"Are you okay?"

It's the first thing Steven has said to me in twenty minutes. I nod, unsure how articulate my feelings. In the past few hours, we've discovered a dead body, seen cages where people experimented on mothers and children, survived a building falling on us, and escaped from some freaky science experiment. Don't know if there's a particular word for how that makes someone feel – no doubt there is one in German. They love a long compound word. Probably OhmychristIexploredanabandonedlabandalmostdied.

It's late, and the winter sun has already set. We've been wandering down the housing estates, putting as much distance between us and the facility. We don't bother with invisibility: hardly any cars come down these streets, and I think using his powers so much has tired Steven out. I spot a bench on the other side of the road and pull Steven over to it. With a synchronised groan of fatigue, we sit.

"Oh god. Remember sitting?" I say, letting out a long, pleasurable moan.

"You really need to take me running sometime."

"In case you get chased by a different mutated monster?"

"I mean, I don't plan on making a habit of it."

"Just what the hell was that?"

"I don't know. I assume it was the Leech the note warned us about."

"I hadn't even thought of that!" I say, kicking myself for missing the obvious. "Maybe it was developed to be an anti-EMT weapon or something?"

Steven doesn't look convinced. I wait for him to say something, but he seems too conflicted to speak.

"What is it?" I prompt.

"I just thought ... you know what? It's probably stupid. Anyway, Sherlock, what did we learn from our jolly day out?" he asks, rubbing his eyes with the heels of his palms.

"A whole bunch. I'm still not sure what eighty per cent of it means, but I have some theories. Can I borrow your phone? Something's been bothering me."

Steven obliges, and I start searching the internet at lightning speed.

"What was it?" he asks as I return his phone.

"Epigenetics. I knew I'd heard the word before. I don't get all of it, but from what I can see, it's all about gene expression: turning genes on or off. It's like, all your cells have the same DNA, but your epigenetics turn on or off particular genes so that a skin cell functions differently from a liver cell – even though genetically speaking, they are made from the same thing. So they change the expression of the genes but not the genetic code itself. Make sense?"

"Kind of," Steven replies, but his face says otherwise.

"Think of your genes like a big switchboard. Epigenetics decide which switches are on or off, but it doesn't change what is already there. I think that's right. It's incredible that DEMA was researching this before the genome was mapped out."

"Why were they researching this?"

"My guess is it's something to do with your powers. Maybe there's a gene that needs to be activated for them to occur."

"That room that was blown up!" Steven exclaims, sitting up. "It said it was an epigenetic activation chamber! So that means they were trying to activate the gene that causes powers like mine."

"Oh my god!" I say as the penny drops. "The maternity ward . . . all those tests we saw. They weren't breeding children to get the right genes – the kids already had the EMT gene. They were torturing those pregnant women to activate it. Trauma in the womb must somehow turn on the gene in their offspring."

I can see my words hit Steven like a punch in the gut. He's probably thinking about his own mother, wondering what caused him to have his powers. He goes very quiet and fiddles with his fingernails. We've got some answers, but obviously, the questions they threw up are even worse.

My mind is still trying to understand the scene in the basement. So if the Leech was in the Faraday cage, why was Professor Pollecutt there too? Was the Leech always kept there? Did the other researchers know about it, or was it an experiment gone wrong? Did the professor die before or after the facility was abandoned? Somewhere, there is a clue I missed. Something inconsequential that would explain this bizarre scenario. Once I'm home and my phone is charged, I can review my photos.

"Troy and Marcus are probably wondering where the hell we are. Let's head back. What time is your lesson?"

"Oh crap!" he says, jumping to his feet. "It's in fifteen minutes."

"Wait, Percy!"

"What is it? I need to go."

"Just really quick then. I know it might be tempting, but don't tell Zachary anything about today, okay?"

"What? Why?"

"No, it's probably fine. But just in case, you know."

"No, I don't know. Freya, what are you saying?" he says, his temper rising. Oh dear, I seem to have struck a nerve.

"Like I said, it's probably fine. But we don't know much about him."

"He's offering to help me, Freya!"

"I know. Don't go being a moodymancer with me. All I am saying is what we saw today . . . well, it's a lot. If the wrong people find out we know something, we could be putting ourselves in danger. I'm not saying you can't trust him, but let's keep it between us for the time being."

"Surely I need to warn him DEMA are here," he protests.

"That's fine. Just don't go shouting that we found a dead body and a B-movie monster."

"Fine."

He's pissed off, but he doesn't have time to argue, thankfully. He checks his phone again, then runs faster than I've ever seen him run. Before he turns the corner, there is a small flash of white, and he vanishes instantly.

"Bye then," I call after him.

He's still being super cagey about this Zachary guy. I might have to swing by the hotel after dinner to see him for myself.

Dinner! Marcus was doing fajitas tonight – if I'm late, I will never hear the end of it. With that, I also jump to my feet and sprint off in the other direction.

∗

Marcus

"Where the hell have you been?" I ask as Freya saunters through the door.

"Nice to see you too, darling," Freya says, rolling her eyes. I hate that.

"Not answering the question. You've been gone for hours, and you turned your phone off. What am I supposed to think?"

"That I'm an independent young woman and can go wherever I want without your permission," she fires back, clearly sporting for an argument – as usual.

"That's not what I meant, and you know it. Where were you? Why didn't you answer your phone?"

"I didn't have signal, and then it died. Okay?" she says, waving a black screen in my face. She pushes past me and plugs her phone into the wall, then plonks down on the couch beside Troy.

"You've been gone hours!"

"We were trying to find my earring."

"Where's Steven?" asks Troy.

"Oh, he had to go work his final shift."

"You think I believe any of this? Something is going on here, and I want you to tell me the truth."

"We were investigating an abandoned laboratory on the other side of town but got attacked by a mutated experiment that tried to use its magical powers to kill us. Happy?"

"Ha ha, very funny. Look, if you're not going to be honest with me, then I'm not going to waste my breath talking to you."

"Fine," she says, picking up her phone.

"Fine," I say. Guess we are in for another night of not talking to each other. Why can't she ever see things from my point of view? I get that the feminist in her rages at the thought of being told by a man where she can or can't go, but that's not what I am doing. She can't keep disappearing like this without telling me. Of course, she has the right to go where she wants and the right to keep secrets, but that doesn't mean she's immune to the consequences. The annoying thing is, if this were the other way round, she would go ballistic. Not the going off on my own part – she's not a jealous girl – but keeping secrets.

"Did you find your earring?" asks Troy, clearly trying to defuse the tension.

She hesitates, and her eyes bug out. She would honestly be the world's worst poker player.

"N-No. We did find an earring, but it was the wrong one. That's why we took so long. We had to hand the other one in."

"That's weird. We didn't see you at the police station," I snipe.

"Well, we obviously were there after you were! How'd it go there anyway?"

Changing the subject, Freya? I grunt and let Troy answer – he's done enough talking for the both of us these past five hours.

"They're making Marcus pay for the streetlight to be fixed. I mean, his insurance should cover it, right? Still, there was soooooo much paperwork to sort through, and I'm pretty sure they've only just discovered the fax machine there."

"And the car?"

"Totalled. Way too costly to fix, so they are just going to give him the value of the car. It took them forever to tell us, though. We were waiting in the garage for an hour and a half."

Really? It felt like nine. I swear Troy's mouth was starting to fray at the edges by the time they got me to sign the paperwork.

"Dinner's in the kitchen," I say. "It's cold now."

Freya gives a very polite, "Thank you," but stays put. I know she's hungry, but she'd rather cut off her nose to spite her face. In twenty minutes, she'll get up stuff her face with cold fajitas, but right now, she needs to save face.

Sometimes that girl drives me up the wall.

*

She manages to hold out for thirty minutes, but then she "pops to the loo" and comes back with salsa all round her chops. She sits down on the couch next to me and mutes the TV. Troy was watching old episodes of some American comedy before he went for a stroll to the corner shop, and I had barely noticed it was on.

Freya snuggles into me like a cat pining for attention. She's full, so at least the claws have retracted. I lock my phone and put my arm around her.

"Sorry," she mumbles, putting her head on my stomach.

"It's alright. I was just worried about you."

"I know."

"I'm sorry too. I got a bit heated. I know he's your best friend, but a lot of the time, I feel like you pick Stevie over me. And that's fine. But it does get to me."

"You're right," she says. "From now on, I'm going to put you first. I promise."

I wrap her in my arms and kiss her hair. We'll see how long that lasts.

The front door opens, and Troy steps in, clutching a blue carrier bag.

"Okay, they didn't have the largest selection, no Doritos or any ice cream, but I did get smoky bacon chips and something called Hula Hoops, which looked fun."

"Chuck us a packet, would you?" I ask, and Troy throws one my way. I offer Freya a Hula Hoop when suddenly she gasps, grabs her phone, and starts frantically typing away.

"Yes!" she says victoriously before zooming out of the room to get her trainers on.

"What's going on?" I ask.

"Long story! But I've just worked something out. Something important. I'll be back soon. I just need to tell Steven something."

Wow, barely two minutes before she ran off to do something for Stevie. A new record.

24

Steven

Can't believe I'm late! Even when chased by a murderous emotion-sucking monster, I couldn't wait to see Zachary again. And now here I am, running down the seafront, five minutes late already.

As the gaudy hotel looms into view, a thought strikes me: how the hell do I play this? I want nothing more than to kiss him again, but what if he doesn't feel the same? He might pretend the kissing never happened – we'd both had a whisky, after all. Maybe I should pretend it didn't happen too. Play it cool. He's also supposed to be teaching me to use my powers. Kind of hard to do that when our tongues are having a wrestling match.

I'm just about to head into the hotel when I run into Zachary leaving.

"Running late, are we?"

"Just a bit," I pant. God, this is so unsexy.

"It's a beautiful night. I thought we might have class outside."

"Won't people see us?"

"Don't worry about that. Come, let's take a walk down the beach."

So we do. It's dark, but I can still make out his handsome face and tonight's snappy outfit. He's wearing a black fitted T-shirt under a leather jacket, tailored trousers and loafers. Why can't I ever dress as cool as that? He's walking close to me, and I am extremely aware of our hands being near each other. Just one movement, and he could grab mine, or I could grab his. But neither of us does, and I try my best not to be disappointed.

"How are you feeling after last night?" he asks.

"Err, yeah. Good. I've been practising all day, so I should be much better at it tonight."

"Practising all day, huh? With the back of your hand, or have you gone full narcissist and been kissing the mirror?"

Thank God it's dark because I can feel my ears burning red.

"Oh no! I didn't mean . . . I mean, the—"

"Relax! I know what you meant. I was just teasing you, little emomancer. Good to hear you've done your homework. Do you still have the coin?"

"Right here."

"Good, you'll need it in just a moment. But first, here is our classroom for the night."

He's led me to where the wreck of the burned pier still stands. Just a few columns of timber, really. The main part of the pier is submerged. How are we meant to practise emomancy there?

"Are you ready to see something rather splendid?" he asks, to which I nod.

He raises his hand, and purple sparks flutter out of his talon-shaped ring. Immediately, a thick fog descends over the seafront, blotting out the lights behind us from view but leaving a wide berth around us and the pier. Then, the purple vanishes, and a yellow glow envelops his hand. There is a creaking sound, and lumps of blackened wood rise up from the sea to fly back onto the pier, filling in the gaps of the walkway and the struts underneath. Zachary tenses his hand, and a huge structure, an old theatre or arcade perhaps, bursts out of the ocean, dragging seaweed and a few fish with it. It soars through the air then lightly comes to rest at the very end of the pier, still charred but like it never left. One by one, big metal letters fly into place along the top of the facade until it spells "Grunsby-on-Sea Pier".

I'm speechless. Zachary has rebuilt the ruined pier in a matter of seconds. He is, without a doubt, the most incredible man I know. There is one issue, however. We are on the beach below, and there aren't any steps to get up.

But Zachary isn't done yet. He grabs me around the waist and says, "Hold on tight," before his hand glows green, and we too soar into the air.

We are flying! Actually, flying! He brings us down on the wooden walkway and lets go of my waist.

"Shall we?" he says like he hasn't just defied gravity. I glance down at the charred and sea-warped wood now supporting the pier. Zachary notices and says, "Oh, don't worry. It's being held up with my powers. Well, actually, that little ray of happiness came from you yesterday."

Okay, ears are fully crimson now for sure. I turn my phone light on to illuminate the path ahead, and we stroll along the magically suspended pier.

"That's actually what our lesson is about today," he continues. "Extracting and using the emotions stored away in your siphon."

"I actually did that earlier." He raises his eyebrows. I'm about to tell him about using stored desire to slow my descent, but then

I would have to mention the DEMA lab and the Leech, and I promised Freya I wouldn't.

"Excellent!" he says, and I can tell he means it. The way his face lights up makes my legs feel wobbly. "You are ahead of the class. Hopefully, by the end of the lesson, you'll be able to store and access different manifestations at will."

We reach the end of the pier, and in front of us is the old Victorian building. It was obviously quite a grand thing before its extended bath in the English Channel: ornate archways and pillars, two domed turrets, and a statue of some Greek god holding a bunch of grapes. Now, the paint and finer details have corroded, and several barnacles have taken up shop on the facade. Zachary pushes open the doors with a spark of green from his hand and ushers me inside.

I was right: it was a theatre! Was being the operative word. It's not a massive lobby, just a refreshment stand, a small cubbyhole for a box office, and some stairs leading up to the balcony. A once-golden chandelier hangs from the ceiling, although the seaweed dangling from it reminds me of cobwebs in a haunted house. I might just be a bit jumpy from running around an abandoned laboratory all day, but this place gives me the creeps.

"I do love the theatre," Zachary declares. "Such a shame – this used to be Grunsby's only cultural landmark."

"What happened to it?" I ask.

"About four years ago, it was struck by lightning. The support struts broke, and the whole thing slipped into Grunsby bay. There wasn't much call to have it rebuilt. Still, I come back here from time to time," he says wistfully. "I wish you could have seen it in its heyday."

Zachary leads us through the rotting foyer and opens the door to the stalls for me. I'm just about to step through when I notice a small, rusted plaque.

Julian Pollecutt Theatre

Holy crap! That was the guy whose corpse I was staring at a few hours ago.

Zachary sees me staring and says, "He was the patron of this place. Local guy. Went missing a while back. They never did find him."

I'm not surprised.

The theatre itself is just as pickled as the lobby. The velvet-covered chairs now grey and deteriorating, and the wooden stage warped and swamped with algae. Zachary brings me on stage and proclaims, "Welcome to lesson two!" like an over-the-top Shakespearian actor.

I mime a big theatrical bow, and Zachary continues.

"Lots to get through tonight. But first, let's have a bit of light, shall we?"

White mist billows from his ring, and his whole body glows. Then he shoots it out of the top of his fingers, and a ball of light hangs above our heads.

"How'd you do that?" I ask eagerly.

"Pride – well, an alternative use for it that I discovered. So for you, it'd be guilt that manifests that. But first things first, how'd you get on with the coin?"

"Honestly, it's changed my life. I woke up today, and I wasn't afraid that I might hurt someone. I let myself feel for the first time in so long."

"That's wonderful! And what did you manage to store?"

"Well, I stopped some anger from manifesting at breakfast. I think there's some disgust there too. I did have desire, but I used it all up. Oh yeah! And I turned myself invisible with pride."

"That's a fun one. My first bout of invisibility was when I was eight, and I smashed my foster mother's antique vase. She didn't find me for six hours."

"There was something weird," I say. "I didn't have the coin to hand, and I tried to use my phone as a siphon, but it kind of fought me."

He considers this for a moment, then says, "Well, it could be the electricals in your phone interfering with the conduction, but it's more likely the sentiment of the siphon. Your phone is such a practical tool, and while yes expensive, it's ultimately disposable. It doesn't hold any sentimental value, so it's harder for you to push your emotions into it. With practice, you'll be able to use any old scrap you find, but while you're starting out, it's best to use something you have a connection with like a gift.

"Now to start off our second lesson, I want you to pull specific seats down with disgust. Let's start off easy with that one," he says, pointing to a salt-devoured seat in the front row.

I allow myself to feel revulsion at the rotten velvet, and almost immediately, every chair in the first five rows springs open like a mighty wind has blown them.

Zachary shudders and says, "Good. Let's try to focus it now."

Again and again, I try, but it's tough. Sometimes I flip down all the chairs in a line, and sometimes it's a cluster. I'm focusing hard on just one chair, but my powers spill over the side like a shotgun.

"Ugh, why can't I do this? Yesterday I managed the cup!"

"Yesterday, there was one thing, and you were much closer. Don't stress – you're improving."

He's right, of course. The overspill is getting smaller, but not as much as I want it to.

"Try this," he says, pointing his index finger and thumb at one and making it fold instantly.

"Finger guns?"

"You'll look cool. Just like Fonzie," he says, shooting me two of them. I shrug, and he shakes his head. "*Happy Days*? No? Tsk tsk, the youth of today."

I stick my tongue out playfully and then try the finger guns. To my amazement, I only unfold about three chairs.

"See? Never doubt the fifties cool-guy finger-guns," he says with a smirk.

"Does it focus my powers or something?"

"Not really, but it focuses your mind on one thing."

"Why can't there be an instruction manual for these powers?" I lament.

"It would make life a lot easier, but that's what mentors like me are for. I was taught by someone who was taught by someone else."

"How did you find your mentor?" I ask, trying again and this time narrowing it down to five.

"Same way you did."

"In the men's toilets?"

"No," he chuckles. "By happenstance. There's this theory: the *Serendipity of EMTs*. For some reason, EMTs attract one another like super magnets. There are very few of us in the world, yet fate always conspires to bring us together. From a scientific standpoint, it's probably an evolutionary defence system: it stops the gene dying out. It is also why EMTs can't use their powers on other EMTs. That, and you'd get stuck in a never-ending loop of manifesting at each other."

"I didn't know I can't use my powers on other EMTs."

"For the most part. There are two notable exceptions, but we will save them for lesson three. That's not to say you couldn't use your powers against other EMTs, but you'd just need to be creative. I couldn't push you off the stage, but I could push a chair at you to push you off. I can't make your leg fall off, but I could make the ceiling fall in on you. That sort of thing."

"Jesus, can you please stop thinking of ways to murder me," I joke.

"Trust me, I wouldn't want to hurt a single hair on your head."

Cheesy line, but it works. I'm like warm butter in his hand. I try once more, and this time, only one chair unfolds. Bullseye.

"Amazing! You are really getting the hang of this. Now, my little emomancer, I want you to do it again, but with the emotion in your siphon. Let your mind's eye travel to the coin like it does when you're storing. You should be able to feel what's stored there, like echoes of past emotions. It's hard to explain, so it's probably easier to learn through doing. Once you find what you want, let it come to you, don't grab for it."

It's definitely hard at first to get my head around. It's so easy now to reach out and grab the emotion already there. Instead, I close my eyes and let my mind wander down to the coin. There are bumps, not physically but in my head. I can feel the reserves of emotions I shoved into it, but rather than being all jumbled together, each is in a crystallised lump – separate and contained, even if they are the same emotion. I let the fossilised nugget of disgust from this morning come to me. The coin sparks green, and I point my finger gun at the seat in front of me, which unfolds then snaps back up again.

We keep going. Zachary points at different chairs all around the auditorium, and one by one, I pull the seats down. I eventually burn through that nugget of disgust, so I find another. We keep this up until all my reserves are gone. I'm short of breath, and my muscles ache, but I feel alive. Really alive.

"Fantastic!" Zachary says, brushing his curls from his face. He walks towards me, and my body tenses. Is he going to kiss me?

No, he just pats me on the back. Ooft. That'll leave a bruise on my ego. Maybe he's trying to keep it professional.

"You said you are out of desire, so we can't move onto that, and trying happiness or sadness here might be a bit too risky. It's too cold in here already to try your anger out, and this place has already burned down once, so we won't try fear."

"Wait. What?" I say, thoroughly confused. "I thought anger and fear made other people angry or fearful?"

"True, but they also give off and suck in heat, respectively. When focused on an inanimate object, you can use them to freeze or burn. But as I said, let's try not to wreck the place anymore. That means we are left with guilt and pride and the other two. Fancy turning stuff invisible?"

For the next ten minutes, I refamiliarise myself with turning invisible, using small amounts of the pride reserved in my siphon. While I experiment vanishing different body parts, Zachary pops backstage and reappears with a silver briefcase.

"Anything exciting?"

"No, I just left it behind last time I was here. Righto, let's move on to stage two!"

He then makes me turn seats invisible by touching them, which is pretty easy, considering I did it on a whole Freya earlier. The next step is much more challenging: vanishing things I'm not touching without turning invisible myself.

"You can manifest most of your powers completely separately to yourself," he explains, pointing at a seat and making it hover up into the balcony. "See? I'm using disgust to push against the ground, but it's centred on the chair. It's the same principle here. Just recall that pride and instead of directing it at the object, imagine you are the object."

He makes it look so easy.

"I can't do it," I whine, turning myself invisible and not the seat I'm pointing at for the twentieth time. "I just can't empathise with a sodding folding chair."

"Keep trying!"

Even after fifty attempts, the seat is still as visible as ever, and I have run out of stored pride.

"Let's call it a day," he says placing his hands on my shoulder. "Great work, Steven. With a little more practice, you'll be in complete control in no time."

I try my best not to look put out, but the truth is, I want to keep going. I want to get this right. Then again, if the lesson is over, he might be more inclined to kiss me.

"Any homework?"

"Keep storing emotions and try to remote manifest," he says as he leads me down from the stage and back out to the lobby. The hand not clutching that briefcase brushes the small of my back, and I have never been happier for physical contact in my life. We leave the rotting theatre and start a leisurely promenade down the pier. I'm shivering in the wintery sea air, but I don't really care. All I can think about is the three inches between my right hand and his left. Just grab it, please for the love of God.

"Have you ever heard of DEMA?" I ask. I've been trying to find a good time to ask about it, but honestly, trying to shoehorn in a malevolent organisation that tried to make emotional atomic bombs is a lot harder than you think.

"DEMA?" he repeats. "How do you know that name?" He is keeping his cool, but his eyebrows shoot up into his hairline.

"Someone from DEMA was asking about me back home. And I'm pretty sure I had a run-in with another agent here in town. I just wondered if you have heard of them before?" I really want to tell him all about the old facility and the Leech, but I don't. Freya's right, although I hate to admit it.

"Yeah, I've heard of them. They're an organisation that go around 'neutralising' EMTs. If they are in town, stay as far away from them as possible. If they find you, keep your cool and try not to manifest – they have ways of detecting your Emotion Manifestation Energy. And above all, don't trust them. They may try to trick you to take you quietly."

"It sounds like you've dealt with them before."

"You could say that," he says bitterly. Maybe they tried to "neutralise" him too. I don't push him for answers in case whatever happened was traumatic. "Just promise me you'll avoid them."

"Promise."

"Good. I don't want anything bad happening to my little emomancer."

I grin stupidly. We walk on, the gentle crashing of the waves the only sound between us. Two things are bubbling up within me: one is wonderful and unlike anything I've ever felt before. The other is a deep shame that I still haven't come clean. I need to tell him what I've done before it consumes me. We reach the end of the pier where the thick fog starts, and I turn to face him.

"Have you ever . . . hurt someone with your powers?" I ask, the words catching in my throat like a dry biscuit.

"Yes," he replies. Poker face.

"Have you ever . . . killed someone with them?"

I can't bear to look at him. Tears burn my eyes, and my shoulders are twitching.

"Hey now, hey," he says, scooping me up into an embrace. "It's okay. Steven, you are a good person. I know you'd never intentionally do something bad."

"I killed someone," I say, sobbing into his leather jacket. "I didn't mean to, but it sort of happened. I did it. He's . . . dead because of me."

"It's okay." He pulls me away and wipes my tears with his thumb.

"We were talking, and then he kissed me and then he . . ."

"It wasn't your fault, Steven." He pauses for a moment as if weighing up something. He takes a deep breath, then continues. "When I was ten, I lost both my parents. The grief I felt caused a fire that killed a lot of people. You can't blame yourself for every disaster wrought by your powers, especially before you learned to control them. These deaths will probably never leave you, but don't let them dictate your life. You are a gift, Steven."

"I am?"

"Absolutely. Never apologise for what you are or what you can do."

I don't know what to say. I've never had anyone say such nice things about me before. He wipes my tears away again and cups my cheek.

"Now, last lesson for today. Tear it down."

It takes me a moment to realise he means the pier. I look into Zachary's eyes: so blue you'd swear they were fake.

A breath in. Eyes close. His lips are on mine. Everything that I am melts in his embrace, and there is nothing else but this moment.

Then, my entire body lights up, and an atomic bomb of happiness bursts from me. I pull my lips away and throw my hand out to the pier. The wooden structure trembles then collapses all at once – the sea reclaiming its prize.

I barely have time to celebrate before Zachary pulls me in for another kiss. I try to find my coin, but his hand grabs mine, and I feel the cool metal of his ring as he siphons off the happiness I'm manifesting.

We pull apart, and my face feels like it's been ravaged by sandpaper. Guess it's going to be hard to hide the stubble rash from Freya.

"Can I get your number?" I ask. Jesus Christ, what is wrong with me?

He chuckles and replies, "Don't have one. I'm old school. Besides, you know where to find me. I'll see you tomorrow, okay?"

"Unless you want to ... err ..." I don't really know what I'm suggesting, or maybe I'm not willing to admit it. I just don't want tonight to end.

"I've got an early start tomorrow," he says, and my heart sinks. "But I should be done by noon, so come over any time after that. Are you still heading home tomorrow?"

"I guess so. To be honest, I had completely forgotten about it. Marcus said the car should be delivered by three."

Do I really only have three hours left with Zachary? I could ... stay. I've been quietly stewing on that as an option ever since last night. But it would mean dropping out of school and leaving behind my parents and Freya. But wasn't that already the plan? If Freya hadn't turned up on my doorstep, I would've stayed in Grunsby until I inevitably smiled and caused my house to fall in and crush me to death.

"We will just have to make the time count," he says, turning to go.

"Zachary, wait!"

Now, it's my turn. I grab his face and pull him into one last passionate kiss. And then he leaves. The fog has completely vanished by now, and I stand there watching him disappear into the Grand Regalia, hoping he would look back and wave. But he doesn't.

I turn around to start walking home but immediately stop. My stomach plummets down through my feet and starts boring its way to the centre of the earth.

"Good evening," says Freya, wrapped in her mountain of wool and grinning like the cat that got the bloody cream.

25

Freya

Christmas has come early.

*

Steven

Shit.

*

Freya

Steven Percival was just locking lips with Mr Tall-Dark-and-Handsome. Locking lips with another guy!

*

Steven

Shit.

∗

Freya

I knew it! I bloody knew it!

He's stood there like a lemon, unable to speak. I guess there isn't much he can say.

∗

Steven

Just what the hell do I say? I guess there isn't much I can say.

Yes, you were right all along – I think I am attracted to men, but I haven't worked out all the labels because I've only kissed two guys, and one of them exploded immediately after.

I can't even deny it. She just watched me grab Zachary's face and kiss him. There's no way around this other than running into the sea.

Actually, that's not a bad shout.

No. Drowning can't be my only option here. But what do I say? Right now, we are just staring at each other outside the hotel like a Mexican standoff. Who is going to say . . . *gay* first?

This is not how I wanted this to happen. Or is it? I guess I wouldn't be able to keep it a secret forever. And I'd like her to know, but just without me having to tell her. It's the telling that's the scary part. If people already know, they don't actively pass judgement on you then and there. But telling someone you like boys, you are asking them to re-evaluate who you are in the space of a nanosecond. The stupid thing is that I know she'll be super supportive (after she's had her fill of mocking me, of course, but I'd expect nothing less). Still, there's this part of me that doesn't want to cross the Rubicon – that wants things to stay as they are. I know nothing will change in the grand scheme of things. I'll still be me.

But the thing is, once it's said out loud, that's it. No takebacks. The moment I admit who I am, I become it, and that's an enormous step to take. My mind fills with hundreds of what-ifs: what if my parents find out? What if they don't want to speak to me again? What if people treat me differently? What if the world ends?

*

Freya

He's overthinking this, isn't he? I do the only thing I can think of doing: I walk up to him and hug him.

*

Steven

She has her arms around me, and I feel . . . safe. All the what-ifs evaporate, and I know I have my rock. My wool-clad ginger rock.

"So," she says, pulling away, "monstrously large elephant in the room aside, shall we get moving before we run into DEMA?"

I nod, and she links her arm in mine as we stroll up the beachfront.

"What are you doing here?" I ask in a hoarse voice.

"I came to walk you home. Thought it might be best, just in case that agent found you again. I also made a huge discovery. Well, not *huge* huge, but it answers some questions which I would argue is—"

"Freya. What is it?"

"Hula Hoops."

"The children's toy?"

"No, the crisps! There was a packet of them in the basement, but Hula Hoops didn't go on sale in the UK till the seventies! Over ten years *after* the facility was shut down."

"So? We can't have been the only people to explore that abandoned lab. Maybe someone else dropped it?"

"The basement door was locked shut. Whoever left the packet there must have had the keys!"

"And you reckon that was the professor?"

"Or whoever fed him to the Leech."

"I saw the professor!" I say, suddenly remembering. "Well, not him, but his name was on the old theatre at the end of the pier. He was a patron of it before he disappeared."

Freya's eyes light up, and a bulb practically appears over her head.

"So we might not know when Pollecutt died, but at least we know it happened way after the place shut down. There's so much to research! Why can't revision be this interesting? Before we head off tomorrow, I'm going to the library to see if I can pull some records and look up epigenetics. Wait, how do you know Pollecutt's name was on the theatre?"

I tell her about my lesson and how Zachary reassembled the pier, leaving out the more . . . *homosexual* aspects. She's seriously impressed that Zachary has that kind of power. I can already hear her mind spinning with hundreds of applications for it. I also tell her how I couldn't quite manage remote manifesting, but she waves away my doubts.

"Typical Percy. 'If I'm not good at something straight away, I must be terrible.' In two days, you've already learned how to stop these manifestations. Cut yourself some slack! We can practise together. I'll be your Yoda."

"You do have the ears for it," I say.

"Ha ha," she says, dripping with sarcasm. "I mean it, though. Whatever you are going through, Percy, I'll be there to support you. Literally *anything*."

A lump forms in my throat. Does that include accidental murder? One day soon, I will have to tell her, but not now. One life-changing secret at a time.

*

Freya

"Sooooo," I say, seeing as Steven has been quiet for the last three minutes. "Do you want to talk about . . . anything?"

He opens and closes his mouth like a fish struggling to breathe. *Floundering*, I think is probably the best word. Honestly, men really are terrible at talking about their feelings.

"You don't have to, of course," I continue. "But, just know I love you and support you. God, it sounds like I'm doing an intervention."

He smiles and mutters. "I really like him."

I'm not looking, so Steven's voice startles me.

"And I think he likes me too," he goes on.

"How long have you known?" I ask, keeping it vague, so he can elaborate.

"Have you seen him? I mean, I fancied him the moment we met!"

"You know what I mean, Steven."

"I don't . . . I don't really know. A while. I guess I was trying to fool myself, so I didn't have to face it. Guess that makes me a bit of a coward."

"No, these things are . . . complicated," I say, but I am totally assuming. I've always known I was straight and cis, so I've never really had to question my identity. "I don't mean to put you on the spot, but what do you reckon you are? Gay? Bi? Pan?"

"Errr, I don't know," he replies to his shoes.

"Well, do you find women attractive? That might be the best place to start."

"I guess not."

"You guess not? Jesus, I'm asking if you are sexually aroused by women, not asking if you want butter on your toast."

"It's hard to really know. Up until yesterday, I would cause natural disasters every time I even thought about sex, so I've learned to shut it down."

"Sure, but gun to your head?"

"Gun to my head, I'd say I'm . . . I'm gay."

There it is. The big G-word. It splits the night like a crack of thunder. And just like a storm, the air feels so much better afterwards. Steven looks up from the floor and breathes deeply like he's just discovered the bottom of his lungs. Part of me wants to gloat that I've been right all these years, but I'll save it for another time.

"Were you ever going to tell me?" I ask.

"Probably. But I've never really had a reason to."

"Despite the fact we share literally everything about our lives with each other?"

"You're right. I'm sorry."

"Don't say sorry. You haven't done anything wrong. I'm just surprised you didn't say anything sooner."

"To be honest, you've always made jokes – and I know you didn't mean anything by it, and it's how we are with each other – but I think they've just made me hesitant. Or at least, they made me push back the other way and pretend like I wasn't."

"So literally anything to prove me wrong?"

"Basically."

We laugh, and everything feels normal again. I mean, normal like normal for us, not that being gay isn't normal. This is a minefield.

"I was also worried that things might change," he says.

"Of course they will, you tit. But that isn't a bad thing. The sun isn't going to fall out of the sky. I mean, I already have one gay friend. What's one more?"

"Who's your other gay friend?"

"Troy."

"Troy's gay!"

"Jesus Christ, Percival! Of course, he is. You think the universe would let someone that attractive be straight?"

He considers this like I've just told him that Troy has a peg leg, and he is flicking through his memories to see if it's true.

"Never noticed," he mumbles with a shrug. Of course he hasn't. Troy could be walking around in full Village People cosplay, and Steven wouldn't notice. Men.

"So, did you know?" he asks. "About me, I mean."

"I've suspected for a while."

"Really?" he says with a note of panic.

"But don't worry! I am a very good detective. And your best friend. Combo."

"Oh, was I that obvious?"

"Princess Peach was the giveaway."

"She has the best stats!"

"Uh-huh. So what's going to happen with you and Mr Mediterranean Heartthrob?"

"He's not Mediterranean ... I don't think. I actually don't know a huge amount about him, to be honest. I guess tonight was our second date. But yeah, I don't know what's going to happen. Maybe I'll come visit him or whatever."

"You're going to take four buses to see a guy? I mean, he is drop-dead gorgeous, so fair play."

We reach the top of the stairs to the flat – not a single woman in a trouser suit in sight. Just before we head in, Steven stops and says, "You won't tell anyone, will you?"

"Of course I'm not going to tell anyone, you colossal breast! You can let people know when you are good and ready."

"Thank you," he says, visibly relaxing his shoulders.

"Anyway. If a long-distance thing doesn't work out with Mr Perfect, I know a certain American would be *very* happy."

"Huh? What do you mean? Freya?" he hisses, but it's too late. I'm already through the front door.

Like I said, men are terrible at talking about their feelings – even the ones who can use them like superpowers. Sometimes you just need to give them a nudge in the right direction.

26

Excerpt from the report of
Field Director Fareborn: DEMA Case 1569GOS
Priority Gamma
WED 25/11/2020
0900 GMT

I have barely slept. At approximately 0200 this morning, DEMA HQ fulfilled my information request regarding ex-employee Professor Julian Pollecutt. Since then, I have been combing through stacks of confidential files, the majority of which have been redacted in some way. While I am not usually a fan of speculation and guesswork, I feel if I am to uncover the truth about Agent Fowler, it is vital I uncover the truth about DEMA's history with this town. Given that Pollecutt is not around to answer questions, this is the best line of enquiry. Find below an Internal DEMA Communication (IDC).

TO: Agent Pollecutt & Agent Dent
FROM: [[REDACTED]]
SUBJECT: New Project.
Following your recent presentation, the Board of Directors has deliberated and decided to approve your proposal. You both will be joint leaders in this project and responsible for overseeing a team. We have agreed to allocate [[REDACTED]] towards the running of this, but should additional funds be required, this can be brought to the board.

We are very excited at the prospect of [[REDACTED]]. It would be a game-changer for DEMA and the United Kingdom in these uncertain times. [[REDACTED]]

On a personal note, I would like to voice my full support for this research. Should it bear fruit, this would ensure additional funding from Parliament, and our friends across the Pond would no doubt be champing at the bit to buy anything that would give them the edge. Eisenhower has already [[REDACTED]]. To that end, we will be extensively screening all potential members of your team to ensure there are no leaks. The last thing we need is a situation like the Rosenbergs happening here.

Signed [REDACTED]

- End of Extract -

The reference to the Rosenbergs is the first clue to what the project might have been. Ethel and Julius Rosenberg were executed a year prior by the United States Government for leaking the plans for the atomic bomb to the USSR. Obviously, the paranoia of espionage was felt in all sectors during the Cold War; however, the pointed reference to the Rosenbergs leads me to believe whatever Dent and Pollecutt were researching would have an application against the Soviets. As the extract below will corroborate, I think they intended to induce in-utero trauma to activate the epigenetic switch in their subjects, artificially creating EMTs for application against the USSR.

Extract Two – IDC – 12/06/1954

TO: Agent Pollecutt
FROM: Agent Dent
SUBJECT: Lab Idea
Polly, bad news – the place in Kent has been taken. They're building an airport there, apparently.

However, as always, I have a solution. What if we used my foster parents' place in Grunsby? I know it might not be ideal, but it could work. It's large enough, and we hardly use it anymore since we are always out on assignments. We could remodel the top floor, knock through some of the dormitories to give us space, and keep the others for when the sprogs get big enough. Plus, it's far enough away from the rest of the town that we won't get locals asking questions. My only other idea was the Regalia, but I don't think Uncle Monty would care for screaming infants in his lobby.

Also, I have a compiled list of suitable subjects, with EMT Prob ranges of 75%+. HQ have said we can offer [[REDACTED]] to them if they sign up, so they'll be well compensated for their sacrifice – so stop your worrying! For that amount of money, I would gladly let someone prod me with electrodes.

That reminds me – Di spoke to her contact and has sourced two midwives for us. NDAs have been signed, and they have been briefed on the nature of the experiment. Things are moving forward!

Sorry I can't be there to talk this through in person. Duty calls.

Always,

Zeddy

PS: Thank you for the Kroon – saves me going to Estonia to complete my collection.

PPS: Can you put Bryce's test samples in a random order for me this week, seeing as I'm not here? Need to keep the tradition going.

- End of Extract -

Agent Dent refers to *Dysley House*, a foster home in Grunsby-on-Sea that was left to him upon his foster parents' deaths. Reading between the redacted lines, it would seem that Dent and Pollecutt moved forward with their experiments here during the mid-fifties and early sixties. Unfortunately, no one at HQ has ever heard of such a facility, and most records have been expunged.

At approximately 0700 this morning, I drove to Dysley House and found it destroyed, although I am led to believe, only recently so. The air was thick with residual EME, and three sets of footprints could be seen in the mud nearby.

Contained in Agent Pollecutt's file were over six hundred pages of notes from the Dysley House experiments. However, very little was of use. Dotted throughout the research were names and experiment numbers which I have compiled into a list and sent to DEMA HQ for EMT probability analysis.

Upon cross-referencing these names with local county records, I discovered that every child born in the Dysley facility was put into an orphanage or foster care in 1961. Even more pertinent, a significant portion of these orphaned children have children of their own who are currently missing. This begs the question: is someone hunting down the descendants of the experiment? If so, are they one of the Dysley children or their progeny, seeking revenge for these, frankly barbaric, experiments? Or are they kidnapping potential EMTs for another reason? It wouldn't be the first case we've seen of someone disposing of other EMTs to ensure they go unchallenged. The USSR even did it on a country-wide scale under Stalin's rule. But then why keep Fowler alive for so long? It doesn't make sense.

The Dysley Experiment was shut down in 1961 after an explosion destroyed a significant portion of the house and killed the lead researcher (and wife of Julian) Diana Pollecutt (nee Thompson). It is safe to assume the children were taken into care not long after this event. From what I gathered from the files, Diana married Julian in 1959 and had a daughter the following year. However, in amongst the research were the following IDCs.

Extract Three – IDC- 30/04/1961

TO: *Professor Dent*
FROM: *Professor Pollecutt*
SUBJECT:
She knows.

- End of Extract -

<u>Extract Four – IDC – 30/04/1961</u>

TO: Professor Pollecutt
FROM: Professor Dent
SUBJECT:
Don't panic. Continue your work, and don't talk to anyone.
I'm coming to Dysley at noon to set up the [REDACTED] for
tomorrow. Meet me at our place at 1500. Everything will work
out fine, Polly. Trust in me.
   I will fix this.
   Always,
   Zeddy
          – End of Extract –

Forgive me for the somewhat baseless speculation, but I believe
Dent and Pollecutt were involved in some romantic capacity. It is
important to remember that homosexuality was illegal in the United
Kingdom at this point in history and wouldn't be decriminalised for
another six years. The nature of their potential relationship would
have been closely guarded to avoid the risk of imprisonment or
chemical castration. It might be my own investment in the mystery
of this case that is causing me to draw this conclusion, but my gut
tells me I am right. The pet names ("Zeddy" and "Polly"), the use
of "our place," and the implication in Extract Two that Julian was
already living at Dysley House before its transformation into a lab
all indicate that their relationship was more than platonic. Extract
Three conveys a considerable weight in only two words, and the
fact that Dent immediately recognised its meaning without further
clarification leads me to believe that Diana found out about their
affair. This all happened one day before the explosion that would

take her life and cause DEMA to pull the plug on the Dysley Experiment. Surely this can't be a coincidence?

Unfortunately, the trails of Pollecutt and Dent end not long after Dysley's closure. Both were dismissed from DEMA, although the precise reasons were so heavily redacted they were nineteen pages of black lines. It could be because the experiment was branded a failure, or perhaps the full extent of what they did was revealed to the higher-ups. Whatever the reason, they didn't stay together after. Dent seemingly went north, but I can't find any records of him. Pollecutt remained in Grunsby-on-Sea to raise his daughter Lilian until his disappearance in 1974.

The legacy of Dent and Pollecutt in DEMA lives on in their research. From their findings in the Dysley experiment, we now have a much greater understanding of the epigenetic switches responsible and conditions needed for EMT activation. Their methods were abhorrent, but they have laid the foundation for most of the science DEMA operates on today.

I feel conflicted. It feels like tainted science. It is not without precedent: enslaved Africans and those in Nazi concentration camps were the unwilling guinea pigs that made western medicine what it is today. How can DEMA still use "dent" as a unit of Emotion Manifestation Energy knowing what Dent did to discover it? But if we rename it, do we lose the history, and by extension, the sacrifice of those women and children? I don't have the answer, but the moment I get back to HQ from this assignment, I will be launching a cross-departmental initiative. *Everyone* at DEMA needs to know the history of Dysley House. We must reconcile and make amends for our mistakes.

No more redacting the past.

- End of Log -

27

Steven

I sleep better than I have in a month. No crippling guilt or echoes of popping heads to keep me awake.

I wake up to the smell of bacon and the sound of someone singing. I find the culprit of both counts in the kitchen. Troy is stood over the hob with a mountain of fried eggs on a plate next to him. He's wearing his vest again, so his hulk arms are on display. I really need to start exercising more – there are muscles on his back I didn't even know existed. He realises I'm standing behind him and stops abruptly.

"Sorry! Did I wake you?"

"Nah, you're good. About time I got up."

"I made breakfast," he says with a proud grin bursting onto his face.

"For the whole town?"

"Sorry, I guess I got a bit carried away. The first batch didn't come out too good, so I wanted to keep trying till I got it right," he says sheepishly.

"Don't worry about it. They had to be used up anyway. I'm sure Marcus will eat any going spare."

The smile returns to his face, and he turns back to flip the now cremated bacon. Well, at least Troy will learn the most important rule of cooking: there is nothing a tonne of ketchup can't salvage.

"Is . . . err . . . Freya around?" I ask, trying to sound casual, but inside, my stomach has twisted in knots. She said she wouldn't say anything, but part of me is still worried that she might've. It's just Troy, but what if he knows and is treating me different? What if everyone already knows? But how do I know if they know without letting it slip in the first place? It's like Schrödinger's gay cat: I won't know if the cat is gay until I open the box.

Freya is right: I need to stop worrying so much. It's exhausting.

"No, she and Marcus went to the library. Apparently, she had some research that couldn't wait, and the library is just down the road from the car rental. Is this done?" he asks, picking up a lump of bacon-shaped charcoal.

"Perfect."

He plates them up, and we sit down to eat. Troy fixes me with the puppy-dog face, all earnest brows and bright eyes, as I take the first bite.

"Mmmmm it's great," I lie, immediately coating my plate in a sea of red sauce. At least it makes Troy happy. He gleefully tucks into his creation, seemingly unaware of the eggs' burned taste and rubbery texture. It's a big step for him: his first time cooking unaided. He looks up and beams me one of his Hollywood smiles, and I feel a flutter in my gut.

Freya did say he was . . . you know. How have I never picked up on that? I mean, I've never seen him get with a girl, but then again, I've never seen him get with a boy either. Not that he couldn't – I mean, look at him! He's . . . you know. Attractive. Very, very attractive. Muscles, a face like a Greek statue, and eyes warm and kind. Like if Hercules from the Disney movie was mixed-race and terrible at cooking. For the first time, I'm looking at Troy and seeing him as a man and not just an amorphous sexless blob for fear of a hormone-induced apocalypse. I trained for years to turn off that part of my brain. But now I have my coin and . . .

I shove my hand in my pocket just in time to catch a trick bubbling up to the surface. That was a close one! A couple seconds later, I would have thrown the eggs halfway across the room. Troy is too invested in his culinary masterpiece to notice. The morning sun bursts through the window and bathes him in a golden light. Jesus, now he really does look like Hercules.

"Typical. Our last day here's when the sun comes out," he says as he puts his fork down. "Wanna go get ice cream?"

"Sure!" I say, the word coming out of my mouth before I'd even processed it. Actually, this works out perfectly. I can kill some time with Troy before my lesson at noon, and I'll be right next to the Grand Regalia! I'll have to think of a suitable excuse to lose Troy before seeing Zachary.

"Awesome!" Troy says in the most American way you can imagine. "Should I text Freya to come meet us when they're done?"

"Nah. Leave her to her research. Disturbing Freya while she's working is dangerous."

"Yeah, she threw a book at my head once."

"That sounds on-brand for Freya. Okay, give me a minute, and then I'm ready to go."

I take the plates through to the sink, quickly run some water through my hair so it doesn't lie so stupidly, and brush my teeth. Troy's covered up the guns with the long-sleeved shirt I left out for him. The sleeves start halfway up his arm. Adorable.

"Ready?" he says, throwing on his jacket.

I nod and send Freya a quick text as we leave. Well, quick by my standards.

Me: Going for a walk with Troy on the beach. Call me if you find anything.

Almost immediately, I get a response.

Freya: OH MY GIDDY AUNT FRIDAY! IT'S FINALLY HAPPENING. And on the beach, no less. It's like one of those romance novels Mum reads. Make sure you declare your love on horseback. Before you get all Percy about it, I'm kidding, of course. Love you. Have fun. Make smart choices. Found a few interesting bits but no major breakthroughs yet. Will keep you updated, Watson.

"You okay?" asks Troy. "You've gone all red."

"Yeah, fine, just a bit ... err warm," I say, stuffing my phone into my pocket as quickly as humanly possible. Where did I put that stupid coin?

Sometimes, I really could throttle Freya.

*

Freya

Oh my God, it's fun to torture Steven Percival. Right now, I bet he is turning crimson with his mouth flapping like a goldfish. Ordinarily, I would have written him a strongly worded text for interrupting me while I'm working, but I'm waiting for this ancient PC to load a PDF. I would just use my phone, but it keeps losing signal in this stupid town.

Like everything in Grunsby, the library is stuck in a hellscape of antiquity. Everything from the austere Formica tables to the cobwebbed shelves is screaming for a remodel or a mercy killing, and the flicking fluorescent lights make me feel like a prisoner of war. The librarian, a decrepit crone who looks one cough away from keeling over, appears to have zero regard for the Dewey Decimal System. Instead, she's shoved the entire contents of the library wherever she pleases. It took me twenty minutes to find nine books on human genetics, some of which were in the children's VHS section.

Weirdly, the newspaper microfilms are in impeccable chronological order and even seem to have been dusted recently. I picked a few from April 1956 and May 1961 to see if there was anything about the DEMA building being built or when it was shut down. Unfortunately, I could only find a brief note about the fire brigade being called out to Dysley House – probably DEMA hushing it up. However, it did mention that the house caught fire once before in 1941 when it was a foster home for evacuated children. Not sure if that's super relevant, but at least we know it wasn't built by DEMA.

A coffee cup appears in front of me. Marcus plonks down in a swivel chair, a scowl already across his face. He's my boyfriend, and I love him blah blah blah, but his presence is seriously detrimental to my research. He says he will just sit quietly, but we both know Marcus will interrupt me with a meme or that annoying thing he does where he takes in oxygen and breathes out carbon dioxide. Right now, he's sat there waiting for me to ask how it went with the car rental place. Like he's not saying anything, but if I don't ask in the next ten seconds, he'll start sighing emphatically.

Cue a sigh.

"How'd it go, sweetie?" I ask.

"Stupid woman was brain-dead, I swear," he hisses. "She kept saying there were no cars available, and I was like, 'I know, but we have one coming later.' But she wasn't getting it. Eventually, she got her manager and confirmed it's all okay. It'll be here around half three. I can't wait to get out of this dump. How long you going to be?"

"A little bit longer, this computer is hamster powered, by the looks of things."

He grunts in annoyance and starts swinging around on the chair. Because that's not annoying at all.

"Can't you just wait until you get back home? Or do it on your phone in the car?" he moans.

"I told you: this can't wait. If you're bored, go wait at the flat."

That keeps him quiet. Although he moans like hell when he's sat around waiting, I know he'd rather that than be left out.

Finally, the image loads. It's the oldest research paper I could find with "epigenetic" in the text.

"*The Praxis of Epigenetic Activation and Augmentation in Relation to Targeted Gene Expression – by Professor ZE Dent.*"

Sounds like a right barrel of laughs. I scroll the grotty wheel on the mouse, and the page chugs down, but black bars have censored parts of the document. That name rings a bell . . . I pull open a new tab and google him.

Realisation hits me, and I sit up, startling Marcus. I unlock my phone and swipe to the black-and-white photo I snapped

yesterday: Dysley House's opening. On the back, it said *ZD &*
JP – Pollecutt and Dent! The handsome, tanned face looking back
at me seems familiar, but where would I have seen him before?

I hear a buzzing noise and then a thump from behind me.
Marcus has fallen off his chair and is face down on the floor. I
scream – or at least I try to. But by the time I have inhaled, I feel
a wicked sting on my neck, and then everything goes black.

✱

Troy

Okay, I am trying to play this cool, but OH MY GOSH.

I am walking along the beach with Steven, and it seems to be
going really well! We made jokes the whole way down as Steven
showed me the "delights" of the town. It's a shame the weather has
turned so overcast now, but I eat my ice cream regardless. It's not
as creamy as the stuff back home, but it's still pretty great and came
with a little log of chocolate shoved into the side called a "Flake".

"I think mine's off," Steven says sniffing his ice cream as we
hop up on a concrete wall.

"Oh no, really?" I say, leaning forward to sniff it. With a
mischievous grin, Steven raises his cone, and my nose goes in
his ice cream. "You are *so* dead." I lift mine up to him and repay
the favour.

We laugh, little splodges of ice cream on both of our noses.
Surely, he *must* be flirting. Right? It's just the two of us on the
whole beach . . . if you ignore the old lady trying to get her stubborn terrier out of the sea. But she's a little way down, so like I
said, we're alone.

"Why did you call them ninety-nines?" I ask, wiping my nose clean.

"Dunno. Just what they're called."

"Do they cost 99p or something?"

"Maybe way-back-when. Like before running water when you didn't need a mortgage to buy a Freddo."

"Freddo?"

"It's like a frog-shaped chocolate bar that gets more expensive every year. It's how we measure inflation."

"With candy bars? Seems sensible."

"Do you miss America?" he asks between licks. He still has ice cream on the tip of his nose, which is just so cute.

"Some things. Mostly home comforts like Jolly Ranchers and In-N-Out burgers. Why'd you ask?"

"I just wondered. I don't think I could ever leave England. It'd feel weird not being on the same continent as my mum and dad."

"Are you close to them?"

He hesitates and says, "Yes. I guess I am. I'm an only child, so it's just us three. I used to tell my mum literally everything before I got all teenagey."

"And your dad?"

"He's a big idiot who keeps us laughing. Definitely inherited his sense of humour. I . . . I miss them a lot."

"Do they know you're here?"

He shakes his head.

"My mom doesn't know I'm here either," I say.

"In Grunsby?"

"I mean, she doesn't know I'm in England. My family is complicated."

"Oh, right. And your dad? Does he?"

223

"No, no, he's not with us anymore. He died in Afghanistan before I was born. These were his," I say, showing Steven the dog tags around my neck. "It's, like, the only thing I've got from back home."

Steven clearly doesn't know what to say to this. Jeez, one sure-fire way to kill the mood is to bring up dead family members. I finish the top of my ice cream and start on the cone. Steven notices and flinches.

"What's up?" I ask.

"Nothing, I just have this weird thing about people eating the cones."

"What are you supposed to do with it?"

"Throw it away and hope it never sees the light of day again."

"They are literally designed to be eaten."

"I know, it's just the texture and the ... Nope," he says pretending to retch.

"Does this mean I can have yours too?"

"By all means, freak," he says with a smirk that makes my stomach punch my lungs.

I fiddle with my dog tags and devour both cones as quickly as possible. Okay, Anderson, now's your chance. It's just you and him and the sea. Confession time ... Oh gosh, I can't do it.

"There. The offending articles have been destroyed. What do you wanna do now? There's an amusement arcade, or we could see if that Ferris wheel is working?"

"Both of which run the risk of tetanus," he quips. "I've still got thirty minutes before I need to be somewhere. We could just keep walking if you like?"

"Sure. Wait a sec. You've still got ice cream on your ..."

I reach forward and wipe his nose with my finger. Our eyes

lock, and the seconds stretch out into infinity. Holy crap, it's like a rom-com. His eyes so vivid and green. His lips twitch into a warm smile. Is it my imagination, or is he leaning closer? I could kiss him so easily from here. Just a quick lunge, and then I wouldn't have to worry about finding the words anymore. But if he's not interested, I become the creepy gay guy who assaulted him on the beach. He closes his eyes. Oh my gosh, he's going to do it. He's going to kiss me . . .

But he doesn't.

Thunder rips through the air, and we both jump. It must be right above us. When did it get so dark? Steven pulls back and fumbles for something in his pocket. A coin? What is he doing? Did I do something wrong?

"Steven, I have to tell you something," my mouth says. Oh gosh, I'm doing it. "I like you, and when I say that, I mean – oh my God!"

Okay, so I blasphemed, but with good reason. The old lady walking her dog just fell face-first into the sand, and her wiry-haired terrier is yapping at her unmoving form. I jump to my feet, and so does Steven.

"Troy, run!" Steven says, looking over my shoulder as I'm looking over his.

"Wait, what are you talking about – OH MY GOD!"

And this time is as justified as the last.

Crawling up the beach is a scaly, burned-looking thing with a hole where its face should be.

"I SAID RUN!" Steven yells as he steps between me and this thing.

But I can't. My legs are frozen, and everything feels heavy. I need to do something, but I can't. I feel . . . drained.

Steven throws out his arms and screws up his eyes. What is he doing? Suddenly a gale blows a chunk of sand towards the creature, but it digs in its taloned feet. Green sparks crackle in its mouth and the sand flies back the other way, knocking me off my feet.

Ugh, sand tastes gross. I clear my eyes and sit up. Steven is still standing, locked in a mental tug of war with the beast. I hear him chanting, "I am the sand. I am the sand," over and over under his breath. He raises one hand up like a conductor, and a pillar of sand shoots the monster sixty feet in the air. It somersaults, and as it comes back to earth, its mouth glows green again, which breaks its fall.

If it wasn't pissed before, it's pissed now. The creature screams like a mix between a banshee and the T-Rex from *Jurassic Park,* and it starts coming for Steven again. Suddenly, its head snaps up to the hotel like when a dog hears an intruder, and the creature changes course. It bounds up to the hotel entrance then starts scaling the windows.

"Zachary!" Steven calls out before running after it.

"Steven, wait!" I cry, but it's too late.

I get to my feet and run to the old lady. She's breathing, thank God! I roll her onto her side and start punching in 999 on my phone.

Steven has disappeared into the lobby now. My legs are moving that way too. I tell the operator to send an ambulance for the old lady and hang up. Should I have stayed with her until it arrived? Probably. But there's nothing else I can do for her right now. Steven, on the other hand, has just run into certain danger. Possibly, certain death. And for what reason, I don't know. All I know is that he will need me.

28

Steven

This might be the stupidest thing you have ever done, Steven Percival. Not only have you revealed your powers to Troy, but now you are running after a creature that tried to kill you twice. In fairness, I didn't really have a choice with either of those things: I had to save Troy from the Leech, and I have to warn Zachary that it's on the hunt for him now. Why does he have to be too cool for phones?

The lift rises at a glacial pace, so I hop from one foot to the next impatiently. I should really use this time to come up with a game plan, but I have nothing. The Leech is too powerful and immune to my emomancy. I guess my best bet would be to throw something else at it like I did with the sand, but I don't know if I could do that again. It was like I had a surge of power from somewhere that made everything easier to do. But it didn't come from my coin. Now I just feel . . . normal (relatively speaking). I twiddle the coin between my fingers and take stock of what is stored in it. Nothing useful annoyingly – I used up all the desire pushing the sand at the Leech. There's a lot of joy from earlier, but I don't trust myself to use it without burning the hotel to the ground.

No time to start stuffing it with anything: I'm at the eleventh floor.

The doors ping open. The hallway in front of me is silent and dark – the power must have tripped. I'm pretty sure the Leech is blind, so I turn on my phone's torch and scan ahead with it. Nothing that I can see.

I venture a step.

Then another.

I can hear a whistling, but I don't think it's the Leech. It sounds like the wind.

Before I know it, I'm at the end of the corridor, where it bends into the circular column with the curved windows. Well, where the windows once were. Obviously, the Leech decided to make its own way in because there's a gaping hole there now.

Broken glass crunches beneath my feet, and I freeze. It can't see, but it definitely can hear. I lift my foot, but that just makes more noise.

I wait, holding my breath.

No Leech appears to tear out my throat, so that's a good sign. But then again, I still don't know where it's hiding, which makes it all the more dangerous.

I sidle round the edge to the other corridor. Nothing here either, but something in the air feels thick, and I feel a pressure over my chest. It must be close.

I creep past Zachary's door to the end of the corridor and scan the staircase. Empty.

Okay, I'm safe for now. My shoulders lower themselves from my ears as I knock quietly on room 113.

Suddenly, I'm knocked to the ground. The Leech is on top of me, pinning my arms with its claws. It screeches in my face, showering me with goop. Its black maw looms over me as sparks start to swirl inside it, lighting up the room.

* * *

Troy

Come on, Freya! Answer your darn phone! I try for a fourth time, but it goes straight to voicemail again. Either she has Do Not Disturb on, or she's ignoring me. Or she's been eaten by whatever the heck that *Creature from the Black Lagoon* wannabe was. Okay, no time to text her, so I'll have to leave a voicemail and pray she's the type of young person who actually checks it.

"Freya! Call me back as soon as you can, okay? Steven is in danger. There was this . . . thing. Like a monster or something, and it was attacking us, but now it's gone into the hotel on the seafront, and Steven has gone after it. I'm heading for the hotel now to get him out, so just stay somewhere safe. This isn't a joke. Just do it. And call me back."

By now, I'm in the lobby. I expected to see Steven locked in battle with the creature, but it's eerily empty. I walk up the threadbare red carpet and peer over the reception desk. There's a young guy crumpled on the floor, just like the old lady on the beach. His chest rises and falls softly, so he's not dead.

I push the button for the elevator and get in. But which floor to try? Where are you, Steven? Okay, let's do this systematically. I push the number one, and it creaks into life. I only hope that I'm not too late.

* * *

Steven

"HELP!" I scream. "ZACHARY! HELP!"

I can hear a door flying open, footsteps rushing down the corridor, then something strikes the Leech in the head and lands on the floor with a metallic ring. A coin?

"DEE! GET OFF HIM!" roars Zachary.

Another coin pings off the Leech's thick skin, and the beast howls in pain. The speed Zachary pushes them with his emomancy must make them like bullets. The Leech releases me and charges at Zachary like a demented rhino. Zachary pushes down with a fizz of green and shoots up to the ceiling, causing the Leech to miss and crash straight into the wall.

"Come on!" Zachary taunts as he lands and starts running for the circular room. The Leech recovers and scrabbles after him round the corner.

There is a scream of pain, and I jump to my feet. Oh God, what is it doing to him?

What greets me round the corner is not what I am expecting. Zachary has his hand outstretched but not towards the Leech – towards the sky, where a shaft of brilliant sunshine is bursting through the dark clouds and hitting the top of the hotel. The Leech, caught in the light, is screaming in agony, its skin sizzling like the Wicked Witch of the West after a shower. It falls to the floor, writhing in pain. I almost feel sorry for it.

Almost.

With a spark of green, Zachary throws a tarnished coin at the creature's neck at lethal speed. It severs what I assume is its jugular, and the Leech goes still in a pool of blood.

"Are you okay?" Zachary says, pulling me in for a bear hug.

"Y-yeah, I'm fine," I say, a little shellshocked. He . . . killed it.

"What on earth happened?"

"It . . . just appeared on the beach. I fought it off, but then it started coming this way, and I thought it was coming after you, so I came to warn you, and—"

"Shhhh. You're safe now."

"Y-yeah," I stammer.

He releases me from the hug and surveys my face like I'm a child who just saw the bogie man.

"I think a sugary tea is in order," he says, and honestly, it sounds like heaven right now.

"But what about . . . that?"

"You're right," he says. "Can't leave it here. Burial at sea?"

With that, his hand glows green, and the Leech's carcass flies out of the broken window and plops into the ocean.

"Right, tea, then we'll get started on lesson three. What do you say?" he says like he hasn't just executed a demon and flung its body out the window like a dead spider.

29

Excerpt from the report of
Field Director Fareborn: DEMA Case 1569GOS
Priority Alpha
WED 25/11/2020
1245 GMT

Since my last report, I have made an enormous discovery.
Upon returning to the B&B Junior Agent Wren and I have
been staying in, I ran into the owner and was asked to sign
the guest book. As I flipped through the pages, I saw an entry
from "Jessie Hannover," the cover name used by Fowler during
the assignment in which she disappeared. The entry was as
follows:

Extract One – Azalea House Guest Book – 17/03/2016

*Didn't Expect Much At the start, but had a lovely time in
room 6.*

*very comfy, especially for journal writing, although a few
squeaky floorboards kept me awake.*

i enjoyed Seeing Everything this Nice town had to offer,
especially Dinner, but now i Have to go Elsewhere.
Liked breakfast too. Pancakes were great.
– Jessie Hannover

- End of Extract -

Although this might look innocuous to some, the cypher Agent
Fowler has used is clear (if not rather rudimentary). The capi-
talisation of certain letters spells out "DEMA SEND HELP,"
and the references to journal writing and squeaky floorboards
gave me a hunch. We have hired out the entire bed and breakfast
for security purposes, so gaining access to room six was simple.
Inside, I found four handwritten field report entries from Agent
Fowler stored in a plastic tub under the floorboards.

<u>Extract Two – Report of Agent Fowler – 18/03/2016</u>

*I've gone off-grid. DEMA has been compromised, or at least
their servers have.*

*Last night, I attempted to contact my assigned EMT as per
Phase Four of the Neutralisation Protocol. The plan was to go
to the bar I knew he would be at and strike up a conversation
organically. However, as I waited for the EMT to arrive, I
was assaulted in the toilets by an invisible assailant. I was
able to fend them off (thanks to the self-defence stuff Agent
Morgan taught us) and managed to disarm them of the syringe
they were trying to inject me with. However, they escaped out
of the bathroom window before I could see my attacker turn
visible.*

I do not believe I was attacked by the EMT that I was observing, as he is only a Zeta and does not have consistent control of his powers. But then, who was he? I am assuming male, but it could have been a woman. I told no one I was going there, but I did put it in my DEMA report from the night before. I refuse to believe this was the work of a DEMA operative, especially as we need sign-off from the higher-ups to read each other's reports if not in the same operation. So that leads me to one conclusion: someone else accessed our system. Someone compromised security, read my reports, and waited for me in that bathroom. I dusted the syringe for fingerprints, but they were wearing gloves, of course. Without access to DEMA HQ, I have no idea what is inside, but my guess is a sedative.

For this reason, I am writing these reports by hand, away from DEMA's servers, until I am sure the breach has been found. I have also left my mission zone and come to Grunsby-on-Sea. It's the only place I could think to go. Thankfully, I hadn't mentioned Frank in any of my DEMA reports, so whoever breached our server won't be able to track me here. I'll try to find Frank tomorrow and tell him the truth – well, a version of the truth. Obviously, I won't mention DEMA or who I really am, but I think it'll be safe to tell him I was attacked and that I need to stay here for a while. I hate all the lies, but one day I'll get clearance, and we can be together properly.

– End of Extract –

This breach of DEMA's servers was never reported, nor has anything similar since. If it were true, someone could be moving through our servers, reading classified information with impunity, and using it to take out agents without leaving a trail.

<u>Extract Three – Report of Agent Fowler – 19/03/2016</u>

Now that I have spent a whole day in Grunsby-on-Sea, I see that something is most definitely up with the town. Not only does it seem to be stuck twenty years in the past, but the people suffer from chronic apathy. At first, I thought it might just be a cultural thing, having spent months up north in Sheffield where saying hello to strangers isn't considered a crime. However, some of the residents I have encountered show signs of EME leeching: greyed eyes, lethargy, indifference, and abnormally low EME readings using the dentometer. What is causing this widespread leeching, I do not know. There is no precedent for this. Usually, leeching is isolated to the immediate circle of friends, family, and coworkers of the EMT. To do it at this scale would require an absurdly powerful manifestor or a coordinated effort by several. I will investigate the situation and inform DEMA when I can secure a safe connection.

I also saw Frank earlier.

With another woman.

Yes, I know I should be keeping this report professional (and I can already hear Director Delphi telling me off), but something is amiss here. The woman he was with was considerably younger – perhaps college-age – and the strangest thing was . . . so was he. His salt and pepper hair was black and curly, the small wrinkles around his eyes now smooth and youthful. I feel like I'm losing my sanity here. At first, I thought it might be his younger brother or cousin, but he told me he was an only child, so that can't be it. Something is not right here at all.

- End of Extract -

Extract Four- Report of Agent Fowler – 20/03/2016

I made contact with Frank. I used the phone in the B&B I'm staying in to tell him I was in town – I didn't bring my mobile with me in case it was traced. At first, he was confused about why I was here in Grunbsy, so I told him I had been attacked and wanted to lie low for a bit. We arranged to meet up at a café by the sea at noon.

When we met, I confronted him about the young ginger, but he says she is his stepsister, Danni, from his mum's new marriage, and they have been looking after her together. I wish I could believe him, but I don't. No one puts their arm around their sister like that, step or otherwise. But I played along to not to arouse his suspicion. He invited me to the theatre on the pier tonight – he knows I can't say no to Shakespeare, even if it is a terrible regional production of Julius Caesar.

He seems so different. Full of life in a way I've never seen before. If I hadn't watched him drink tea, I would have sworn he'd had twenty espressos.

- End of Extract -

Extract Five – Report of Agent Fowler – 21/03/2016

Frank is a lie.
An artifice.

How could I have been so stupid? In fairness, he kept the facade up for so long that there were very few warning signs.

Until last night when he slipped up.

The show was, to be expected, terrible. Let's say Caesar wasn't the only thing murdered. But I haven't seen any theatre in half a year, so it was nice to go anyway. "Frank" seemed a lot calmer than he did earlier in the day and was a perfect gentleman. He bought me ice cream at the interval and gave me his jacket when I was cold walking down the pier after. And then, just before he kissed me goodnight, he called me Samantha.

My real name.

In that moment, I knew he was the one that read my reports. He was the one who attacked me in the toilets.

He is an EMT.

For months, he'd infiltrated my operation without me being aware. That's when it hit me: he had followed the DEMA Neutralisation Protocol to the letter. He had observed me, inserted an artifice into my surroundings, and knew exactly what to say and do to woo me. That's how he knew where I was and what I wanted: he must have read my reports on the server and my character's diary that I kept in the flat – no doubt when I was out at work. Whoever Frank is, he has been using DEMA's own techniques against us. I don't know if he's ex-DEMA or just learned from his time rummaging through our servers, but either way, this ends here and now.

I let him kiss me. I pretended nothing was wrong. I knew if I attempted something there and then, he might overpower me, and I'd never get a chance to alert DEMA to him. I still can't risk contacting HQ in case Frank intercepts it and flees. I'll leave these notes somewhere safe and leave a trail for DEMA to find. I've left messages all over town pointing to this room — I just hope DEMA think to look for me in Grunsby. The best I could do in such a hurry before I left was write it in lemon juice on the back of my Character Diary.

The last thing to mention is something somewhat personal (well, more so than a pretend boyfriend who's been trying to kill me). I saw my grandfather's name in the theatre: Julian Pollecutt. I never met him: he disappeared when my mum was small, but his legacy has always been important to me. After all, he is why I joined DEMA in the first place, but I never knew he was a theatre lover. Guess that's where I get it from. I think Frank knows this connection and wanted to see if it would rattle me. This town and Grandad are linked somehow, and now, so am I. Once I've dealt with Frank, my next order of business will be to figure all this out.

- End of Extract -

This last entry was written just a few hours before lightning struck the pier and sank the theatre. It is plain to see that this resulted from an EME battle between "Frank" and Agent Fowler — one she did not walk away from.

In her penultimate log, Agent Fowler notes the name of the girl "Frank" is with as "Danni" — a match for the sixth former who went missing in town fifteen days after the pier caught fire (as detailed in my previous log). It is my firm belief that "Frank" has been using classified information from DEMA's severs to kidnap DEMA agents and suspected EMTs — most of whom are the children or grandchildren of the Dysley House experiments orphaned after the facility shut down.

It is my estimation that he is linked to the Dysley House experiments (perhaps a descendant of one of the orphans?), and Agent Fowler was specifically targeted due to her being the granddaughter of one of the architects. As for the reason why, I currently do not know, but it is clear that "Frank" is a dangerous EMT. As such, I have escalated this case to ALPHA level.

Junior Agent Wren and I will regroup immediately and await further DEMA assistance.

- End of Log -

*

1250 GMT

Upon calling Junior Agent Wren, she has informed me that she has two suspected EMTs in custody in our field site B (a disused plumber's shop on the high street). The suspects have been placed in Faraday cages and should regain consciousness and motor skills in approximately ten minutes.

Disregarding the fact she has once again skipped crucial stages of the Neutralisation Protocol without the confirmation of her superior, I will head there immediately to oversee. Who knows? She may have captured this Alpha-level EMT all by herself.

- End of Log -

30

Troy

Well, as they say, ninth floor's the charm. Right? The power's out here too, but that must have been that freaky monster thing's doing.

I step out the elevator and swing my phone's flashlight around. Nope, no signs of horrifying creatures or the dead body of a cute British boy.

I move down the corridor quickly and turn the corner. Nothing here either, just the same view out over the ruined pier as the floors below. Grey sea and dark, stormy skies – the kind that always followed me growing up. Suddenly, a burst of sunshine pierces through and strikes the window. But like, only the window – everywhere else is still covered in thick cloud.

No time to dwell on it. I've got to find Steven!

*

Freya

Jesus Christ, I feel like I've slammed nine Jägerbombs then gone to bed without water. My mouth is dry, my head is pounding, and I may have slightly wet myself. I try to move, but I can't seem to find my arms or legs. I know they are there, but whatever signal my brain sends to them is being ignored like obstinate toddlers. I think I'm sitting on a chair. My bum's gone to sleep, so it's hard to tell without looking.

I crack open my eyes, really working hard to get them to focus. Metal bars – a cage? Someone's next to me on a wooden chair: black skin, short locs sticking up – Marcus! His arms and legs are tied up. Mine are too. The feeling is starting to come back in them, so I try to wriggle free but fail miserably. Outside our cage, I can see bare concrete walls, a table with paperwork and equipment on it, and a single door. Just where the hell are we? And how did we end up here? Last thing I remember, we were in the library.

"Marcus," I hiss. "Marcus, are you okay?"

"Huh?" he moans softly, clearly still delirious. "Where ... what?"

"I don't know. I just woke up."

"Crap!" he says with sudden lucidity. "CRAP!"

"Shhh, just calm down."

"Calm down? We've been kidnapped!"

"I know, and alerting our kidnappers that we are awake is probably not a good idea!"

He considers this for a moment, chest heaving, then nods.

"Have you got your phone?" he asks quietly.

"No. You?"

"No, they must have taken it off me."

"Wait! I think I see them on the table. Okay, that's a good sign. Mine is still sharing its location with Steven. When he realises we're gone, he'll check that and come and get us."

"What is Stevie going to do? Quip them to death? Read a book? At least Troy's got muscle, even if he is soft as—"

"Steven's full of surprises. He'll get us out, I'm sure."

Marcus grunts, clearly not convinced. But this doesn't really seem like the time to tell him about Steven's powers. He wouldn't believe me on a good day, let alone when we are strapped to chairs in a weird cage.

The door flies open, and in strolls the woman in the ill-fitting trouser suit with the short brown hair we saw at the arcade.

"Oh, good! They're awake," she says in a thick Geordie accent. "Just through here, Director Fareborn."

The stern-looking black woman we passed on the street yesterday enters the room and recoils at the sight of us.

"Jesus, Wren. You tied them to chairs?" Her voice is smooth yet powerful and a little bit London.

"Yeah, the handbook said we were supposed to restrain them."

This woman, Director Fareborn or whatever the other one called her, strokes her closed eyes with her thumb and forefinger and screws up her face.

"The cage is the restraint," she says like a lioness growling a warning. If the other one had a tail, it would be between her legs right now. She smiles sheepishly before collecting a clipboard from the table and giving it to her boss. Fareborn plonks her big bag on the table then starts scouring the first page of the clipboard.

"Excuse me. What the hell is going on?" Marcus says oh so eloquently.

"Quiet," says Fareborn without looking up. Damn, this woman has some big balls. She is my new hero, kidnapper or not. "Wren, you've barely filled out any of this?"

"Yes, sorry. I'd only just got them into the car when you called, so I didn't have time."

Fareborn mutters something under her breath before composing herself and turning her attention to us.

"Right. This is not how I wanted this operation to play out, but here we are. I am Field Director Fareborn with the Department of Epigenetic Manifestation Analysis or DEMA. Apologies for the binding of your appendages – it would appear my colleague was *overzealous* in her precautions. You are here because of what you can do. What you are. DEMA is a highly sophisticated agency that works both domestically and internationally, with assistance from our sister departments, to find people like you and ensure they don't cause harm to the greater population."

My stomach flares with anger. I know exactly what they do – I've seen it with my own eyes at Dysley House. But I bite my tongue. Better for Steven's sake if I feign ignorance. As soon as they realise Marcus and I are powerless, they will let us go ... I hope. No doubt have to zap us with those things from *Men in Black* to wipe our memories, but it's probably best if Marcus forgets this.

"What the hell are you talking about?" says Marcus, thrashing against his restraints.

"Calm yourself," orders Fareborn. "It's pointless to try to manifest: the cage will conduct anything thrown at it."

Marcus ignores this, either because he doesn't understand or is too stubborn to stop, and instead strains until he crashes to the floor, legs still tied to the chair.

"You okay, pet?" Wren says, skirting around the cage like we're tigers that could stick their claws between the bars. Marcus moans in response and stops his thrashing.

"As I was saying, DEMA exists to protect the world from the misuse of emotional manifestations," Fareborn continues.

"Without our intervention, countries go to war, civilisations fall, people die. So it's our job to find potential threats and neutralise them before these things happen."

"But ... What ... You have the wrong people. We're not ..." babbles Marcus.

"We know what you can do. Junior Agent Wren was assaulted by your powers two days ago."

"I'm telling you. You have the wrong people. I don't understand anything you're saying. Please just let us go."

A hesitation in Fareborn. She turns to me. Suddenly, I feel like a mouse caught in a lion's paw.

"You're being awfully quiet."

"He's right. We don't have any powers," I reply, trying desperately not to give anything away. Curse these dinner-plate eyes.

Fareborn flips through the papers on the clipboard, giving me suspicious side-eye every now and again. An eyebrow flicks up, and the muscle in her jaw tightens. Oh God, she's going to snap my neck, and I'm sort of okay with it. After all, being murdered by a badass feminist icon is on my bucket list.

"Wren, do you see an obvious problem here?" she says calmly.

"Errr no, what?"

"'Description: young female, Caucasian, red hair. Large, grey jumper and scarf. Young male, *Caucasian*, brown hair, dark coat.'" Fareborn looks up from the clipboard and fixes Wren with an unimpressed stare. "Do you see two people before you that match those descriptions?"

"Well, one of them does."

"And the other one clearly does not! What were you thinking?"

"I'm sorry! It's just they were there together. It was just easier to take them both."

"Nice to know you are equal opportunity kidnappers," I quip but am promptly ignored by the women in power suits.

"You captured a bystander with no indication of their EMT probability nor any proof of manifestation in their immediate area?"

"Err, yes?"

"Did you take their EME readings before you stunned them?"

"Yes, both were pretty low."

"But you acted anyway?"

"Is that bad?"

"YES!" she roars.

"I was just trying to help. I saw her ginger hair in the library, and I know I've been messing up lately, so I thought I'd try to make it up to you."

"I'm sorry, but this is one mistake too far. As soon as we are done here, I will be requesting HQ to remove you from the case," Fareborn says coldly, though her eyes are burning hot.

"But I—"

"We have a potential Alpha EMT abducting members of the public and DEMA agents, and you are behaving this irresponsibly. Even if these two were EMTs, *you* are not and would be vulnerable to their manifestations!"

"But the handbook says non-EMT agents can do the confrontation stage."

"Only if the EMT is graded at below a Delta, which this case has not been since Monday. You should have contacted an EMT agent and had them assist in the capture, not just—"

"Wait, you have EMTs working for you?" I blurt out. Fareborn stops scolding Wren, and they both look at me.

Tits. Guess the cat's out of the bag.

"About sixty per cent of our staff are EMTs," Fareborn replies slowly as she eyes me up.

"So you don't . . . kill them. Dissect them in labs?"

"No, pet! We're a research agency, not the KGB," says Wren.

"Then why are we in a cage?" says Marcus from the floor.

"For our safety," says Fareborn. "We've learned over the years it's always best to contain EMTs' powers with a Faraday cage before we approach them. There's only so many times we can cover up accidents as nuclear meltdowns or forest fires."

"But you . . . you said the 'Neutralisation Protocol'. Neutralising threats . . . that's what they say in movies when they're talking about killing people."

"Neutralising as in the scientific term for restoring balance and order, like adding an acid to a base. We don't kill EMTs. We help them control their powers with siphons and keep a database of them in case of emergencies," explains Fareborn.

"No, I've seen what DEMA does – torturing pregnant women in this very town to make child-bombs against the Russians!"

God, I'm angry. How dare they lie to me. Trying to pretend they are some sort of international humanitarian company.

But Fareborn frowns at me, concerned.

"How do you know about that?"

"About Dysley House? Because I went there. I saw where they did it, and I read the reports. After you and your crony started following me and my friend, we researched everything we could about you."

"Freya?" Marcus says quietly. This is going to take so much explaining to him.

"I'm . . . sorry," Fareborn says, the fire gone from her eyes. "I've only just learned about it myself. I can assure you that nothing of that sort still happens. The poor women and children – I can only imagine what they went through."

"You didn't know?" I ask, now more disgusted that DEMA kept this quiet.

"No. I came across it while looking into the disappearance of one of our agents in Grunsby-on-Sea. When I return to HQ, I will be raising hell about it being swept under the rug for so long. Now, you mentioned a friend – I assume that's the male EMT that pushed Junior Agent Wren out to sea?"

I say nothing, but I'm ninety per cent sure my forehead muscles have contorted into the word yes.

"You have my word. We won't harm him. We only want to assist him in controlling his powers and ensure he is logged on our system."

Still, I stay silent.

"Look, it's either you or him. If it's him, we can let you out of the cage, pet," says Wren.

"Fine," I relent. "Yes, he's the EMT. But he's not going around kidnapping agents or whatever you said."

Crap, I just outed Steven. That's at least fifty bad friend points. But what else was I supposed to do?

"Can someone please tell me what's going on?" Marcus pleads from the floor.

*

Troy

Okay. Last floor. Steven has to be here, right? Man, I'm out of breath from running up and down hallways. The elevator doors open, and the lights are back on. No sign of Steven or the monster here either, or anyone else for that matter. It's weird, Freya said this place was fully booked, but I haven't seen or heard anyone else.

Wait! The rug in the middle of the carpet has been kicked up like someone ran on it, and the door to room 112 is ajar. Something's wedged between it and the door frame. It looks like one of those little bottles that doctors stick needles into when you get your shots. I carefully put my foot in the door to keep it open and pick it up. "Sodium thiopental"... No idea what that is, but it's full.

I push open the door slowly. The drapes are pulled, but a small amber light illuminates from within – maybe a bedside lamp? I step in. Oh gosh, what am I doing? I can't just go into someone's room? But I'm still doing it. Something is drawing me in. The walls are plastered with peeling floral wallpaper and dark wood panelling. An old CRT TV with a wire antenna poking out sits on a dusty desk. I can see the bathroom is that awful avocado colour people had everywhere in like the fifties or something. Why would anyone stay in this gross place is beyond me.

I turn the corner and see a figure on the small twin bed.

"Oh gosh! I am so sorry! I didn't mean to ..." But I trail off when I get a better look.

There's a girl, maybe late twenties, strapped to the bed like an incarcerated wolf-man. She's hooked up to a bunch of machines and tubes and doesn't seem entirely conscious. Her skin is pale and so dry it's cracked all over, and her hair is a matted mess. On the nightstand is a silver briefcase with little bottles, like the one I'm still holding, all lined up. There are also some needles and other medical equipment I don't know the names for. Next to the case is a larger bottle of clear liquid with a pipette attached to the lid. Its label says, "Methylenedioxymethamphetamine."

Molly.

I know because I've seen it every time I checked Mom in at rehab, in every pamphlet to throw away, on every form to fill out. By the time I was nine, I could spell almost every drug's long name . . .

What in the Sam Hill is going on here?

"Ma'am? Are you okay?" I whisper, but there's no response. I reach out my hand and touch her craggy arm. It's cold.

Suddenly her eyes fly open. The whites are yellow and cloudy. Her mouth cracks, and a dry screech emanates from it. I jump back as she thrashes at her restraints like she's possessed. One arm breaks free from the leather strap and swings wildly at me as though trying to claw my face off. She manages to grab the briefcase and send the contents flying at me. I duck, and the bottles smash against the wall. Then she holds her arm out still, and a grey aura glows from her fingertips. She opens her mouth wide, and sparks start to swirl at the back of her throat.

Everything . . .

Gets . . .

Weak . . .

I can't . . . stay up . . .

Try . . . to . . . break . . . fall . . . curtain comes . . . loose . . . sun . . . shining.

Then I'm released. The girl screams and thrashes as the light hits her face like someone threw acid on it. It's awful. She's clawing at her face and drawing blood. I want to run, but I can't just leave someone in that much pain. I shakily get to my feet and chuck the curtain over her. The screaming stops, now replaced with a whimpering like a kicked dog.

I collapse to the floor again. I'm breathing so heavily, and my mind feels sluggish. Like I've been drained. Like all my energy has been leeched . . .

31

"Here, tea makes everything better," says Zachary as he plonks down a bone china cup. He's not wrong there. I'm still shaken, but I'm not sure if it's from the Leech's attack or Zachary's execution. I sip the warm, sugary liquid and feel my heart start to settle back into its normal rhythm. Zachary's flat is just as decadent as the last time I saw it – perhaps even more so now that the sun is shining on it.

"Thanks," I say with a weak smile. Ugh, let's change the subject. "So, what's on the syllabus for our last lesson, Professor X?"

"Something extra special. But first, have you managed to practise remotely manifesting since last night?" he asks, sipping his tea in his armchair like a villain in a Bond movie. He looks different today, more vibrant. He also hasn't stopped jiggling his leg since he sat down. Maybe just put one too many sugars in his tea.

"Errr, not really," I admit. "I got a bit sidetracked with the goddamned monster attacking me. Although, I did manage to remotely push the sand underneath it. Weirdly, I had this surge of power inside me when I did it."

"Excellent! That's more than you could do yesterday. You'll be a first-class emomancer in no time! I think you're ready for the big stuff. Today, we will talk about the two most powerful emotions to manifest and the special way they work. These are the only two that I'm aware of that can work on other EMTs. Can you guess what they might be?"

I mean, there's one obvious answer, but I feel a little embarrassed to talk about it.

"Love and hate?"

"Almost," he says. "Love for certain, but the opposite of love isn't hate, despite what people might think. Love goes beyond happiness, affection, admiration and is almost ineffable – lord knows every poet in history has tried. On the other hand, hatred is nothing more than a mixture of disgust and anger. No, the opposite of love is an absence of it: apathy. Not caring about someone's existence or feelings. Humans can often cope with being hated, but indifference cuts us to the quick."

I'd never thought of it that way before, but it made sense. When Freya and I hated each other in Year Seven, of course, it upset me, but it would have been so much worse if she just stopped caring altogether.

"So, how do they manifest?" I ask.

"To answer that, we first have to understand EME or Emotion Manifestation Energy, the power behind your powers. It's a special energy that surrounds humans when we feel things.

"Love – active love – is like a turbo boost that increases the EME of the people around you. It makes our manifestations stronger and heightens the emotions of non-EMTs. On the other hand, apathy drains the EME of people around you. It makes you stronger but sucks the emotions from everyone else. Think of it like love is an exothermic reaction, giving off energy – utterly selfless. And apathy is endothermic, absorbing it – the ultimate act of selfishness. Obviously, this is all reversed for your powers.

"When I say love, I mean the active feeling: that rush of love you feel when someone kisses you – I guess the semantic difference between loving someone and being *in* love with someone.

"Apathy, however, is a rather different beast. You must shut down all other feelings and reach a state of total indifference: not caring about anything or anyone."

"And with me, it'll be reversed?" I ask, wishing I'd brought a pen to write this all down on my cheat sheet.

"For certain. You've already manifested apathy, whether you realised it or not. Your coping strategy of shutting down your emotions – 'thinking of white' – will have overridden your manifestations with a very mild apathy, too small to really register. On the day we met, you must have tapped into a stronger version, triggering an enormous EME surge in the area."

"That's why everyone went bonkers!"

Well, that's one mystery solved. But what are we supposed to do now? Am I going to sit here and try to fall in love with Zachary? Am I in love with him? I don't think I even know what it really means. Even if I was, I'm going back home in three hours – what the hell do I do then? And what about Troy? We were having such a great time at the beach, and for a moment, I thought we might . . .

I gasp, and Zachary's head tilts to one side in surprise.

"The Leech! That thing we just . . . It was manifesting apathy, wasn't it? It was sucking all the EME from Troy and that old lady. And I couldn't hit it with my powers. Is that thing . . . *was* that thing human?"

"Ah," says Zachary, placing his tea down on the coffee table and striding over to the fan-shaped window. "That being started life as an EMT like you or me. But here, you see the dangerous power of apathy. If an EMT is subjected to a large amount of negative EME, over time a second epigenetic switch activates. Eventually they mutate into a Leech."

"So we just killed a person?" My voice is small. If I've been responsible for another death, I'll never forgive myself, no matter how many times I hear the words "self-defence".

"That wretched thing was too far gone to save, Steven. If I hadn't ended it there, it would have got out and wreaked havoc on the town, killing indiscriminately. They are born from a starvation of EME, which creates an insatiable hunger: a bottomless void inside them. Why do you think it was kept in a basement behind thick metal doors? Before we start, would you like another tea?"

"Yes, please," I answer distractedly as he disappears into the kitchen. Something isn't right here. He knows way too much about the Leech, and I never told him about the basement.

*

Freya

As Wren steps into the cage to untie us, I tell Marcus (and the DEMA agents by proxy) everything I can: Steven's powers, how we found Dysley House, and our encounter with the Leech. Marcus and Wren look equally shocked by the time I'm done, and Fareborn has a grave face on.

"So this 'Leech' – there was nothing in the reports you found about it?" asks Fareborn.

"No, nothing. I don't think it was part of their experiment, maybe just a side effect or mistake or something."

"And the basement it was in was sealed?"

"Yeah, but someone visited it years after the facility shut down. There was ... a body in the Faraday cage where the Leech was kept. All sucked dry like a raisin. We believe it was one of the head researchers there: Pollecutt."

Fareborn gasps, but Wren and Marcus are still none the wiser.

"Professor Julian Pollecutt went missing in 1974. His grand-daughter is a DEMA agent currently MIA, who I suspect was abducted in Grunsby four years ago. We actually received a phone call from her two days ago from somewhere in this town, but she wasn't lucid enough to tell us where."

"The plot thickens!" I say, rubbing my hands together. I know this is *very* serious, but unravelling this mystery is the most fun I've had in a while. "So, someone bumped off Pollecutt by feeding him to the Leech, then his granddaughter goes missing in the same town forty-two years later. Do you think they are related?"

"Almost certainly. All those abducted in the past few years were suspected EMTs directly related to the Dysley House orphans. In Agent Fowler's case, both of her grandparents worked there."

"Oooh, so you suspect someone is taking revenge?" Yes! I love a good mystery to get my teeth into.

"Or thinning out potential competition."

"But wait, if your agent is still alive, then it stands to reason the rest are. And if that's the case, why aren't they straight-up murdering them? Why abduct a bunch of people with powers?"

"Make an army or something?" Wren suggests, but both Fareborn and I shake our heads.

"You don't drug soldiers," says Fareborn. I was thinking exactly the same. Maybe we should solve crime together, *McCormac and Fareborn Investigations Inc.*

"Someone clearly wants a large amount of EMTs. I take it they are pretty rare?" I ask.

"Ten per cent of the population has the gene, but less than 0.1% has it activated," explains Fareborn.

"So they obviously used the list of children from Dysley House to track down known EMTs. But how did they get their hands on that?"

"There was a breach in DEMA's server. Maybe still is. The abductor could have got the information from there?"

"But you said you have a database of all EMTs. Why only go after the Dysley descendants if there are still thousands of others in the UK, all neatly catalogued?"

This stumps Fareborn, but I can tell she's excited. She loves this just as much as I do.

"You're right. There must be a vested interest in the relations of those orphans. Something personal," she says as she perches on the end of the table in thought.

"I'm sorry, but just what the actual hell?" Marcus says, clearly having a brain meltdown. "Everything you are saying, it's just ... It's impossible, isn't it? This isn't a Marvel movie. People can't just do things with their minds or feelings or whatever."

"I assure you they can," says Fareborn as she raises her hand, and our phones fly to her from the table in a sparkle of pink.

Marcus's eyes pop out almost as much as mine do. His mouth tries to form words, but no sound comes out, so Fareborn continues.

"EMTs or Emotional Manifesting Targets have been documented throughout history, but their powers have been hushed up by DEMA or our predecessors. Many world leaders like Napoleon, Hitler, and Stalin rose to power by manifesting emotions to affect the masses. Fear and anger are powerful things when fostered correctly. But when misused, it can backfire, much like it did for Julius Caesar. Even nowadays, politicians employ EMTs to sit at their rallies and manipulate crowds."

"You mean other people know about ... this stuff?" asks Marcus.

"Strictly on a need-to-know basis. Much of DEMA HQ's time is spent expunging traces of EMT activities from the news or the internet. Given that these powers can only be induced by in utero trauma, you can see why we wouldn't want the rest of the world finding out," explains Fareborn as she hands back our phones.

"Then why are you telling us about them?" Marcus says with a face that looks like it's stuck on an error 404 brain not found page.

"Because you are in close proximity to an active EMT and should be prepared. Besides, even if you did try to leak something to the press, we would have it redacted within minutes, and you would get a knock at your door within an hour."

That shuts him up for now. I squeeze his hand gently, and I feel him do the same back. He's handling this remarkably well, considering he just saw a woman defy the laws of physics a moment ago.

"So, aside from politicians, are there any other EMTs we'd know?" I ask.

"Oh God, yeah!" says Wren. "Most boybands have at least one to drive the teenagers wild – Ringo, Robbie, JT, pretty much the whole of One Direction. Agent Styles even assists on missions when he has a free moment. Errm, who else? Steve Jobs, Joan of Arc, both of the Obamas are Epsilons, pretty sure Henry the Eighth."

"And all of them had trauma in the womb?" I ask Fareborn.

"Not all have been confirmed. We've learned recently it doesn't have to be a lot. Even just stress can activate the epigenetic switch. The level of trauma is unrelated to the power of the child. They just have to have one parent who is a carrier of the gene to start."

"Steven's powers are the wrong way round. He makes bad things happen when he is happy. Is that normal?" I say, hoping Percy won't mind that I'm asking on his behalf.

"No, that's the first time I've ever heard of that. Perhaps it's a further mutation of the ZDNT1 gene or a different combination of epigenetic switches. Even after years of research, we still don't know everything; there could be other powers locked away in the human genome that we haven't yet discovered the switches for. Ideally, we'd take Steven in for analysis – no vivisections, you have my word," she adds hastily. "Just a few tests and DNA samples. Is he managing these reversed powers?"

"Errm ... He wasn't, that's why he came here, but now he's doing better."

"Wait, *that's* why Stevie came here?" says Marcus. "I thought he couldn't hack his A Levels?"

"No. He said he didn't want to hurt anyone. He didn't have any control over his powers, but then he met this guy in town who's been showing him how to stop them or at least store them away."

Fareborn and Wren suddenly get very serious, which is weird because they didn't react as much to Steven's powers being reversed.

"Another EMT," says Fareborn to Wren.

"The Alpha?" she replies.

"Possibly. What do you know about this man? Is he a resident here or just passing through?" Fareborn asks me, and it suddenly feels like a police interview again.

"I think he lives here from what Steven said. His name is Zachary, he's early twenties, dark curly hair, tanned like he's Italian something, good looking, lives in a hotel suite – look, Steven has barely told me anything."

"Which hotel?"

"The one on the seafront, near the sunken pier."

I can see the gears whirring around in Fareborn's head. She grabs a small laptop from her bag and starts hammering the keyboard with lightning speed.

"Wren. The transcript of Agent Fowler's phone call. Read what she says out loud."

"Yes! Err one moment, ma'am," says Wren, eager to be useful. She pulls out her phone, and suddenly the room smells of Mexican food. "Here we go, she said, 'Del ... phi? F ... Fowler. I ... warn ... I'm ... Lam ... Pen ... W-w ... Com ... Ment ... Ess ... Wa ... Ni ... Too ... Oh. D-Den ... Pruh Den ... Den.' Why'd you ask?"

"Because I know where she is. Here," she exclaims, turning the screen around to a poorly rendered hotel booking page. At the top, it says, "The Grand Regalia, established 1920 by local entrepreneur Montgomery Dysley."

"I don't get it," says Wren.

"Director Delphi asked her where she was. She obviously didn't know because she was still drugged, so she described her immediate surroundings: Lamp, pen, with compliments, one, nine, two, oh – 1920. She's in the hotel! Where is Steven now?"

"He went out with our other friend for ice cream, then he was going for his last lesson with Zachary."

"Where?"

"The hotel," I answer, feeling what little colour I have drain from my face.

"Wren, pack your things. We need to go there now."

"But the protocol—"

"Screw the protocol. This entire case has been out of protocol. We message HQ on the way, but if we don't act now, it's not just Fowler we could lose."

"What's happening?" says Marcus, still utterly confused.

"Your friend is in extreme danger. We are going to rescue him. Wait here for us to return."

"Like hell we are!" I say. "If Steven is in trouble, I'm coming too. Marcus?"

"Babe, maybe we should leave this to the professionals?"

I give him my best I-will-put-your-balls-in-a-vice glare.

"Fine!" he relents. "Once again, I'll drop everything to help Stevie."

"Marcus, I—"

"We don't have time for this. If you two are coming, you do exactly what I tell you. Got it?" says Fareborn, and we nod. "Good. We are dealing with a potential Alpha. Let's just hope your friend holds out until we get there."

*

Steven

"I'll just leave it to brew for a minute," says Zachary as he sits down on the couch next to me. His arm goes around my shoulders, and I can smell his intoxicating scent. Dear God, he's attractive. But his stubble is a little shorter today and slightly patchier than usual. A few minutes ago, I would be putty in his hand, but now I'm on edge. How does he know about the basement the Leech was trapped in? I may be a loved-up, newly semi-out homosexual, but I'm not an idiot. Best to pretend I didn't notice.

"I've been thinking," Zachary continues. "I'd like you to stay."

Ambiguous, to say the least.

"Stay," I repeat.

"With me. Here. I know we only just met a few days ago, but I have a really good feeling about this. And I'd like to properly train you to use your powers. Three days just isn't enough."

"What about school?"

"Don't worry about that. You won't need A Levels if you're here with me."

"And my friends?"

"Well, you can go up and visit them, or they can come here. But you really should be with one of your own. We are so special. You are so special."

He strokes my face with his soft hand, and it's taking all I can to remain solid. A part of me wants to give in. Wants to live in this Art Deco palace and drink fine whisky and be with this gorgeous specimen of a man forever. But the Freya in my mind is folding her arms, rolling her eyes, and tutting at me. She's calling me an idiot and telling me something isn't quite what it seems.

"I'm not special."

"Oh, but you are, Steven. I've never met anyone who can do what you can. You fascinate me endlessly. What do you say?"

"That sounds so lovely, but ... I can't. I need to go back. I've been running away from my life for too long. These last few days with you have been amazing, and I really *really* like you, but I think this is for the best. I'm sorry."

Was that okay? I've never had to break up with someone before. Jesus Christ, why am I breaking up with sexy Prince Caspian? I must be mad. Or seeing sense for the first time.

He's quiet for a moment then a smile creeps over his face.

"No, no, it's fine! Just a thought I had. Of course, you'd want to go back home with your friends."

"I can come visit from time to time?" I suggest, but I'm not entirely sure I would right now.

"Of course! Anytime. And you can call the reception and get hold of me if you need to talk powers or boys. Right, I think that tea has steeped long enough, do excuse me," he says as he disappears to the kitchen again.

Quick phone check. Jesus! The fight with the Leech must have smashed my phone. I can barely see anything – it's like a Jackson Pollock painting. One little square is still working in the middle. Bloody hell – nineteen missed calls from Freya. What the hell is happening? Problem with the car? Or major discovery in her investigations? Maybe Troy told her what happened, and she's checking in – oh crap, Troy saw me using my powers. Guess that'll be a fun car conversation. I assume Freya's texted too, but that's not displaying in the destroyed portion of my phone. Okay, I'll finish up here and call her back (if the actual phone part of my phone still works).

"This is a new tea from China. Let me know what you think," says Zachary as he makes his way back over.

Not wanting to be rude, I take a big gulp of it. Oh God, it tastes disgusting. I want to spit it back out, but I don't want to be rude. Colour is funny too.

"It's a little bitter," I say.

"Oh, that's a shame. Maybe could do with another sugar. Back in a mo."

I set the cup down, and my eyes come to rest on a small scrap of paper stuck under one of the table legs. It looks like a slip from reception.

Floor 7 is now cleared of guests as per your request, Mr Dent.

My stomach drops.

Dent.

As in the scientist whose name was all over the DEMA lab. The one who tortured pregnant women. What does this mean? Is Zachary related to that monster? His grandson? I stuff the paper hastily into my jeans as he comes back over with a sugar bowl.

"Here, try now," he says.

He's put two extra lumps in, but it still tastes like diesel. I drink down another big gulp to make my cup emptier. Much more socially acceptable. With any luck, it will be cold by the time we finish the lesson, and I can leave it.

"It's a shame. I really thought I could help train you," Zachary says as he fiddles with my hair, gently pulling the curls. If Freya ever did that, I would break her fingers, but I'm not stopping him. Why aren't I stopping him?

"I've never met one like you before," he continues. "If I were to guess, I would say you had either a mutation of ZDNT1 or another gene is activated, interfering with ZDNT1's expression. Can't be ZDNT2 or you'd be putting thoughts in my head. I think a full genome analysis should be the first port of call. As I said, Steven, I'm utterly fascinated by you."

What is he talking about? And what can't I move my arms?

Why can't I move anything?

32

Steven

I'm in trouble, aren't I? No matter how hard I try, the messages in my brain aren't reaching my muscles. I'm slumped on the couch like a sack of potatoes while Zachary caresses my face. No, not caresses ... assesses. Like I'm a specimen to be examined. He lifts my arm up, and it thuds back down with no resistance.

"Perfect," he says, pushing his hair out of his gorgeous but treacherous face. I want to punch him so badly right now. Curse these limp limbs! "Total loss of motor function. It won't be long now before you slip into unconsciousness. I am sorry, Steven. I really didn't want it to come to this, but it was the only way."

"Wwhhyyyy?" I manage to say, but I'm slurring like I've downed a bottle of gin.

"Oh, Steven, I had such high hopes for you. I really did think you'd agree to stay. Most of them jump at the chance. But I can't let a gift like yours walk out before I've had a chance to analyse it, test its limits, understand what caused it. You will be my greatest discovery. If I can chart out the exact genetic and epigenetic conditions that gave you your powers, I can replicate it with a whole new generation. Combine it with others and see what new powers are locked away in the human genome. Steven, I told you that you are a gift. A gift to humanity. The next stage in our evolution."

I want to scream a gigantic SCREW YOU, but my mouth won't work now either. I manage a grunt, but ... Oh dear, now, I'm drooling like a bloodhound and can't wipe it away.

"Now, now. Just try to relax."

Maybe I can't touch him, but I can still use my powers. I let anger flare inside me. How did he even manage to ... the tea! Betrayed by a cuppa. Somehow that makes this worse. No, that's good. I turn that feeling of violation and indulge in the rage. Maybe encase Zachary in ice till the tea wears off. It's working – I feel it bubbling up inside me.

"You can try manifesting all you like, but it won't do you any good. The cocktail of drugs you just ingested dampens your abilities. Can't have any little accidents before I get you secured. Don't fret, Steven. I'm not going to harm you."

Are you bollocks. You're going to tie me down to a bench and experiment on me, just like the other Dent used to do to those pregnant women. And there's nothing I can do. I can't even cry right now because my face can't move. I'm totally at his mercy. Of course, the first guy I ever liked turned out to be a goddamned supervillain. Why does the universe hate me?

"Hmm. Still a bit too active. Let's see to that."

Zachary is standing over me, hand raised. An ugly sneer flicks across his face, and a grey mist cloaks his hand. It's like everything is sucked out of me at once: my thoughts, my breath, what little energy is left. I feel empty and numb. Cold.

Then it stops, and a wide smile cracks across his face. His eyes are bulging and obsessive. How did I ever find him attractive?

"Very conclusive," he says. "I can get a lot from you with just apathy alone. But it's nothing compared to what you'll give me as a battery. Where's my – ah, yes, I left it in Samantha's room. No matter, I should have what I need here."

He disappears out to the kitchen, but I'm facing the wrong way, so I can't see him. There's the sound of glass chinking and things being moved around. My vision's beginning to blur. I don't know how much longer I can keep awake ...

"Won't need any ecstasy with you. Tricking the brain into apathy is easier, thankfully. And just a little something to reactivate your powers. I never thought I'd make you a battery so soon, but I couldn't just let you go, Steven. Don't worry, you'll have a few months before the Leechification process starts."

He's over me. There's a jab in my arm. Things feel ... different. My powers are awake now, and my head feels weird. Before, I was tired and numb, but I kept it together with willpower. Now I feel ... nothing.

"Think about me, Steven. Only of me."

Zachary? Think about him? He ...

He isn't ...

anything.

I don't really ...

care.

I ...

don't ...

feel ...

anything.

Grey starts to trickle from my fingers. He looms over me once again and conjures his grey. This time he's not pulling my energy out of me ... I'm pushing it to him. Giving him everything I have. It only lasts a second, but I give him far more than the first time. My head is swimming. I feel . . . so woozy.

His face slides into focus for the briefest moment. His beard has entirely vanished. Clean-shaven. Not a wrinkle on his face either. How does he look so young? What did he do? But his eyes are so blue right now – they look like they would glow in the dark. As mine close, I see them burned into my retina like orbs of blue fire.

There's a knock at the door.

Then another.

A bang.

Someone shouts my name.

Then

everything

goes

black.

*

Freya

Jesus tits! As if Fareborn can't get any cooler. With one flick of her hand, she has busted down the door. And oh my god, Steven was right about this place. It's like someone threw a Gatsby party but didn't make it tacky. Evil emotion supervillains have good taste.

Said kidnapping freak is currently straddling an immobile Steven on the elegant clamshell sofa. I call out, "Steven!" but he doesn't stir. Unconscious or dead? Please, don't let us be too late.

"Step away from the boy," Fareborn orders, but Zachary doesn't move.

He seems confused more than anything, as if we've turned up too early for a party. He looks odd. Younger. Familiar. In fact, he looks just like the black and white photo saved on my phone taken in 1956. I'm talking IDENTICAL. But that's impossible.

"You! You're Professor Dent?"

The moment the words leave my lips, his face contorts into one of fear. Fareborn looks at me and then to Zachary.

"Zeddy," she murmurs like the penny's dropped. Her resolve slips ever so slightly.

And that's all he needs.

Zachary swooshes his hands like a conductor, and the busted door flies into the air and hurtles towards us. I duck to the side, but Fareborn stays where she is, and with a fizz of purple, the door breaks into hundreds of shards. Her other hand glows green, and a hail of broken wood pelts Zachary, who leaps over an armchair to shield himself. Bloody hell, she's got some skills!

Furniture and ornaments start zooming across the room, smashing against walls and exploding in mid-air. I take cover behind a dark green chaise longue, only for it to be lifted into the air a moment later. Guess I need to keep moving. Luckily, Zachary is far more interested in Fareborn than me.

I get down on the floor and start army-crawling over to Steven. A chandelier shatters above me, I curl up in a ball, but the razor-sharp glass stops just above my head. The pieces then reform into a spear and fly towards Zachary. He dodges out of the way, the spear smashing the window behind him.

I reach Steven. His chest is moving – okay, he's alive! But his face is gaunt, and ... is that a silver streak in his hair? A syringe lies on the coffee table in front of him. Just what has this freak injected him with? No time to worry about that now. I try to pick him up, but he's completely rag-dolling, and I'm not strong enough. Marcus is still trying to find this missing agent with Wren on the lower floors. All I can do till he arrives is keep Steven safe. I squeeze his hand.

"It's all going to be alright. I'm here, Percy. I'm here," I whisper as I rub his forehead. He's cold. Like hypothermic cold. Don't you dare go dying on me, Steven Percival, or I swear to God I'll kill you.

I dare to peer over the sofa. Fareborn's immaculate blazer is now torn and bloody, but she's not bothered in the slightest. She flexes her finger, and pink mist billows out of a large silver ring on her finger. She ducks out the way of a flying vase and throws her hand out. There is a loud groaning sound, then wires burst out of every wall and coil around Zachary like boa constrictors. He thrashes about and tries to free himself, but Fareborn is winding the cables tighter, binding his hands to his sides and wrapping around his neck until Zachary looks like a fly caught in a spider's web.

"Now, Zachary, Frank, Dent – whatever your name is – you are in DEMA custody. You are going to tell me where Agent Samantha Fowler is being held."

She flicks two fingers, and the wires slacken around his throat. He gasps for air, but a twisted smile grows on his face with every breath. I swear, for a moment, I see colours flickering in his eyes.

"A fellow Alpha. Been a while since I've met one," he croaks. "I see they finally made you a field director, Fareborn. You know, for such a ferocious fighter, your reports were so dull to read."

"Ms McCormac, how is he?" Fareborn shouts over to me, not taking her eyes off Zachary.

"He's unconscious, probably drugged," I shout, trying to stop my voice wavering.

"What have you done to him?" Fareborn demands, tightening the cables around Zachary.

"Just a mild sedative and something to get him manifesting apathy, so I could drain more of his EME. He'll be fine in a few hours. I'm not going to harm such an important specimen." He's talking so calmly now. Like he's not mummified in cable and at Fareborn's mercy. Like he's still in total control.

"And Agent Fowler?"

"Safe," he replies simply.

"Where is she?"

"Just down the corridor. But I wouldn't worry about that."

"Why not?"

He doesn't answer. Just smiles pleasantly, content to hang.

"Are you really him?" I ask. "Professor Dent."

His mood darkens immediately. "Yes."

"But he must have been born in the thirties! You don't look—"

"A day over twenty? Why thank you."

"H-how?" I ask.

"Because, unlike DEMA, I dared to explore the unknown. To push the limits of what we are capable of."

"By torturing pregnant women and kidnapping people," I spit.

"All necessary sacrifices for progress."

"And killing Pollecutt – was that a sacrifice?"

He didn't expect that. His eyes narrow like they are scanning me, but I stand defiant.

"Julian was ... unfortunate. I thought he'd be excited to continue the research, to see the strides I had made without him. But he wasn't. In fact, he was horrified that I had kept it going. After the ... *accident* with Diana, he never trusted me again. I tried to tell him that it wasn't her anymore, but he always was sentimental. He threatened to tell DEMA – probably hoped it would get him back in their good books. Still, I think there's something quite poetic about locking a man in a cage with his ex-wife."

Suddenly, Wren bursts through the open doorway, short brown hair ruffled like she's gone through a hedge backwards, closely followed by Marcus, his shirt nearly ripped all the way off.

"DIRECTOR FAREBORN! We need to go. They're everywhere!"

"I'm a little busy right now, Wren," Fareborn growls, her hold on Zachary never wavering.

Marcus sprints over to me and grabs my arms.

"We have to go."

"Babe?"

"There's . . . like zombies all down there. They were all strapped to the beds, but then they woke up at the same time. T-t-they did stuff. Telekinesis like some Jedi force—"

"Babe, slow down. What are you talking about?"

"Like you said at that creepy lab. All scaly. A bunch of them like Leeches sucking everything from you. We managed to lock the door to the stairs, so they're stuck down there for now, but they're strong – like *really* strong. I don't know how long that will keep them. Jesus, what happened to Stevie?"

"Long story. Basically, this guy drugged him and wants to experiment on him. Pick him up. I'll run on ahead and call the lift."

"I'm afraid I can't let you leave," says Zachary as I wend my way through the wrecked flat.

"As if you're in any position to negotiate, Dent," Fareborn says, but just as I reach the empty doorframe, a mottled, scabby foot appears, glass crunching under it. A dishevelled woman with hair in desperate need of a brush and skin paler than mine lumbers toward me, her eyes foggy and yellowed.

"See, Director Fareborn? I told you Fowler was safe," Zachary says with a smug, self-satisfied chuckle. God, I hate this prick.

We barely have a moment to react to this bombshell when another half-dead woman appears behind her with a zombie man in tow. Fowler opens her blackened mouth and screeches like a Pterodactyl. Sparks starts swirling inside her maw, and a grey mist envelops her long yellow fingernails.

Marcus was right. These people are like the Leech! Well, not entirely. They still have their eyes and their skin hasn't scaled over into the thick bark yet. Proto-Leeches then?

I feel very heavy, just like in the nursery. So very tired. My fear, anger, and sadness are ripped from me, leaving a hollowness. I can't keep my eyes open much longer.

The two other Proto-Leeches drop to all fours and crawl over to Fareborn. The cables holding Zachary begin to peel off one by one. Wren and Marcus are powerless to stop them.

I hear Fareborn hit the floor a second before I do.

*

Marcus

"FREYA!"

What has that thing done to her? Is she going to turn into one of those freaks too? I run towards her, but the zombie girl holds out her hand. It sparkles green, and I fly backwards, smacking my head on the broken plaster wall.

My eyes are spinning in my head like a *Tom and Jerry* cartoon, but I have to get up. I need to get to Freya.

Crap! Fareborn is down too. Took two of those things to get her, so she's probably a powerful wizard or whatever they are.

"My my, you are resilient," says the tanned guy with the curls, shaking off the last of the cables wrapped around him. Then that slimy prick starts laughing. Laughing at me. He's just knocked my girlfriend unconscious and drugged her best friend, and now he's laughing at me.

I run at him, which he obviously isn't expecting, and punch the smarmy twat right in the face. There's a definite crunch, and his nose starts bleeding. He staggers back, clutching his face and his hands glow red.

I WANT TO PUNCH HIM AGAIN. I WANT TO MAKE HIM BLEED. I LAUNCH MYSELF AT HIM AND THROW MY FIST OUT. THE RED DISAPPEARS FROM HIS STUPID HAND INTO HIS UGLY TACKY RING, and suddenly the anger leaves me too.

He shoots a pulse of green light out of his fingertips, and I'm knocked to the floor again like when that freaky zombie girl did it. I try to get back on my feet, but it's like there's a force field keeping me down.

Suddenly, there is a crackle of electricity, and Wren jumps at him, connecting her stun gun to his back for a brief second. He yells in pain, and his muscles spasm, but she obviously only grazed him. Not enough to knock him down or render him unconscious.

He deals a swift backhand to Wren, who falls to the ground clutching her cheek. He then points a hand at both of us, and I feel the forcefield again on my chest.

"How dare you lay your hands on me!" he roars, blood now pouring down his mouth and in his teeth. "I am an Alpha! YOU ARE NOTHING! Take the other two away. I need to find out what else they know. I'll deal with these two myself."

And to my horror, these zombies listen to him. They sling Freya and Fareborn over their shoulders and scuttle over to the gaping hole where a window used to be. I want to scream. I want to rugby tackle that freak to the ground and save Freya. But I can't. I can't do anything. I can only watch as it crawls over the edge with her.

Suddenly, a table – like a whole damn table – flies through the air and slams into the curly-haired prick.

"Get away from my friends, asshole!" orders Troy, standing in the doorway, arm bleeding, shirt ripped, and hand glowing green.

33

Troy

I have no idea what is happening or who that bleeding guy was. Steven is passed out on the sofa, Marcus and some young woman with short hair are on the ground, and Freya is nowhere to be seen. The room is a total mess, broken furniture and glass, half the plaster ripped out of the walls, and a huge hole that looks out to sea where windows must have been.

I rush over and help Marcus and this stranger to their feet.

"Where's Freya?" I ask.

"Y-y-you're one of them too?" he stammers.

"Marcus, where is Freya?"

"This thing carried her away."

"Go after her. I'll get Steven."

He nods and races out of the room.

"I'll come too, pet!" says the woman with the unusual accent. Sounds like the people in that reality show Freya made me watch once. *Geordie*, I think. Anyway, she follows on after Marcus, leaving me alone with Steven and the other E-Man, who is currently staggering to his feet. Fury burning in his bruised face like an angry beet. The floor around him is catching fire; he must be manifesting a lot of anger.

I rush down to Steven's side and try shaking him. He's ice cold and there's a streak of grey hair on the top of his head.

"Steven? Steven, wake up!"

But it's no use, and now Mr Bloody Face is standing tall. His nose is swollen, probably broken, and he's covered in red stripes like he's been bound.

"CAN PEOPLE STOP THROWING MY EXPENSIVE FURNITURE AROUND!" he bellows, his bloody spittle flying everywhere. He summons sadness from his ring, probably his siphon, and throws a wave of purple at the ceiling above me. It cracks and starts to cave in. If I don't act fast, the whole thing will come down and bury us alive!

I reach into my dog tags, find the joy I put there earlier on the beach, and throw it up. Our two manifestations collide and reach loggerheads, neither one winning over the other. The chunks of plaster and brick stay suspended in the air above our heads. I need more. I relive everything in my mind: the beach, the ice cream, but it doesn't work. We are still locked in a stalemate. Then I think of that moment just before that creature appeared. How we leaned in subconsciously. How green his eyes looked. How he took a breath before he was about to kiss me. A surge of yellow pulses through my body, and the ceiling pushes back up, mending itself like nothing was ever broken.

The E-Man staggers back, confused and angry he's been momentarily overpowered. I've never met such a strong one before, and I still feel drained from that thing in the room. Time to get Steven out of here before he does anything else. But what to do about this E-Man? He's right by the open hole in the wall; maybe I can use that? But I can't push him with disgust, and most of the furniture is broken.

He charges at me, but I give into the fear creeping up my neck and send a sheet of ice across the floor. He loses his footing and slips. Now's my chance.

I grab my dog tags and find the one emotion stored away I have in abundance. My hands glow purple as sadness radiates from my body. The sky outside turns black like the day itself has been swallowed up. Lightning flashes right outside, and thunder cracks immediately after. I summon the biggest wind I can; it blasts down the corridor, through the open doorway, and slams into the curly-headed E-Man. He slides along the ice like a curling stone and tumbles out of the broken window.

Before he can use disgust to push his way back up, I scoop up Steven and make for the corridor.

Darn it! There are more of those freaky things. No way past them to get to the elevator, and I can't use my powers on them, so they must be E-Mans too. Guess I'm taking the stairs. Eleven flights are not what I'd call a clean getaway, but it's the only option save for jumping out a window – and I'm not sure I have enough left in me to break our fall.

Stairs it is then.

*

Steven

I'm bouncing.

Lights dance over my eyelids.

I open.

Concrete zigzags above me.

Warm breath on my face.

Smells like cherries.

I'm floating.

No.

There's a face.

Warm. Kind. Stern.

Troy.

There's light above it.

Is he an angel?

But we are going down, not up.

Strong arms wrapped, lifting me. Under my legs. On my back.

Safe.

*

Troy

Steven stirs as I descend the last of the stairs. He's muttering about angels or something. Okay, that's a good sign – not the angels part but the talking. What did that guy do to him? He definitely didn't give him molly like the girl I found. Maybe something else? Roofies? Ket? He has to be alright. He just has to be! I've finally met someone like me, and I'm not going to let him die in my arms.

I kick open the door to the lobby and am greeted by four more of those things, but these ones look scalier, less human. One of which is hunched over the receptionist, bathed in a grey aura. Crap. One of them was hard enough to deal with, and that was without an unconscious boy in my arms.

One of them, a man in his late thirties, swings his head over to me. His eyes are shut, scaled over like a blind dragon, and his fingers are sharp and almost claw-like. He's like the middle stage between the one on the beach and the others. His mouth opens wider than it naturally should, and an awful screech emanates from it. The others snap their attention to me too. They launch at me on all fours like weird, scabby cheetahs. Wow, they're quick. In an instant, they have me surrounded like the velociraptors in *Jurassic Park* – one perched on the reception desk in front, two skulking at my sides, and one blocking the stairs behind. They screech at me again, and sparks start swirling in their mouths. I've got maybe three seconds before they start sucking the life from me. I find that reserve of sadness and push out as much as I can, praying for a miracle.

Lightning flashes and strikes the ground outside. The monsters howl and recoil like they've been hit with a cattle prod. It's so bright that I see spots, but I sprint past them into the torrential rain pounding the sidewalk. The creatures have recovered and are clambering after me. I know famously it doesn't, but I really need lightning to strike twice.

Headlights burst out of the stormy darkness, and a car honks its horn. Possibly the smallest, most British car I can think of, a gosh-darned Mini, pulls up next to me.

"GET IN!" shouts Marcus from the passenger seat. The storm is right overhead now, and I can barely open the car door as the wind keeps buffeting it closed again. But I pry it open, lay Steven down, then dive in next to him.

Not a moment too soon! One of the creatures pounces and lands on the roof, denting it. Another is right behind it and does the same, but the short-haired woman in the front seat slams her foot on the accelerator, and we speed off just in time. The second creature splats on the tarmac, but the first holds on.

The Geordie woman swerves and almost crashes into some beach huts, but the thing isn't letting go.

"HOLD ON!" she yells as she slams on the brakes as hard as she can.

My organs collide with my ribcage, and I swear I'm going to be sick, but it does the job. The creature is wrenched off the car and rolls along the beachfront. Wait, should we even be driving here? This isn't a road? How are we going to get back up to the town?

The Geordie drives off again, giving the recovering creature a wide berth, and we're heading for a ramp up to the road. A ramp made for pedestrians. A ramp with a metal post in the middle to stop cars from coming down. She's not slowing down. OH MY GOD, WE ARE GOING TO CRASH.

I close my eyes, but there's no scraping of metal. The Mini is just small enough to squeeze through the gap, and somehow, she managed to do it without slowing. Either she's a really good driver or a terrible one with amazing luck. She floors it down the small seaside road, weaving through traffic like cops on a high-speed pursuit. She pulls up in a parking lot behind the main street and turns off the lights. Then we wait.

Nothing.

"We've lost them," says the Geordie, then her entire demeanour changes like we weren't just murdered a bunch of times. "Alreet, pet? I'm Junior Agent Wren."

"Err, Troy. Nice to meet you. So what do we do now?"

"We need to find out where those things took Freya," says Marcus.

"And Director Fareborn!" says Wren. "I can track her mobile's last position if we get back to our base."

"And where is that?" I ask.

"A B&B around the corner. Five-minute walk from here. How's he doing?" she asks, nodding toward Steven's slumped body.

"Best to get him lying down, see if he can sleep off whatever he gave him."

Steven is cuddled into my chest, so I'm not complaining. I try to break the cloud cover with some leftover joy, but it's too strong – I suspect our curly-headed friend might be responsible.

We make a break for it. Steven shifts about as I carry him. He raises his arm and drapes it around my neck. I kiss the top of his hair, and he manages to mumble something very faintly.

"Troy . . ."

34

Steven

I'm alive.

That's a good start!

I wake from what must have been the deepest nap I've ever had but almost immediately fall back to sleep. It's just so much easier to close my eyes and drift off again. It's warm, comfy, and safe.

I don't know where I am, nor do I care. I'm too tired to care. I doze between sleep and awake for a while, content to think of nothing at all and let my whole body lie limp.

Then an ache starts to grow. Small at first, just behind my shoulder blades, but then it spreads down my back and arms. Then, I'm pulled firmly to consciousness by pain surging through my entire nervous system. I shift and roll over, but the pain doesn't stop, and with it comes thought – comes memories. I remember being unable to move, the prick of a needle in my arm. The taste of bitter tea scarred on my tongue. I remember everything.

I panic.

What if I'm still there? What if he did things to me while I was unconscious? How would I even know if I was missing a kidney?

I sit up suddenly, breathing heavily and thrashing against the mountain of blankets piled on top of me. My head is sodden with sweat. Heart is about to burst out of my ribcage like that scene in *Alien*. The room is dark. Or am I blind? Oh God, I'm going to die.

"Hey, hey, shhhhh," says a familiar voice, and a cold hand is pressed on my forehead. Another touches my back and eases me to the headboard. "It's okay. You're safe, Steven."

American.

"Troy?"

"I'm here."

"Where are you? I can't see. My eyes aren't working. I-I can't . . ."

Troy's hand disappears from my head, and suddenly the world bursts into light. I can see again!

"Hey, sleepy-butt. Just an eye mask to help you sleep," he chuckles. "You haven't gone blind."

"Where am I?" I ask. It's a tiny room stuffed with knickknacks and ornaments. Porcelain cherubs stare down at me from the shelf above the door, and a dusty grandfather clock sits still in the corner. Jesus, it's two in the morning! There's a small suitcase on the floor and a pair of pyjamas folded in an immaculate pile on the bedside table. Troy sits on a wooden chair next to the bed, a dusty romance book folded in his lap. Has he been next to me the whole time? He looks like he's been in the wars: his shirt is in tatters, and there's dried blood stuck in his hair. He's still smiling, though.

"Somewhere safe for now. A B&B near the high street. How do you feel?"

"Like I've been hit by a steamroller."

"Yeah, I imagine the hangover from whatever he gave you must be rough. Judging by how quick you woke up, it was probably a sedative like ketamine that leaves your body quicker than others. Just be thankful it wasn't anything stronger."

"How'd you know so much about ket? Bit of a wild child, are you?" I say, trying hard to be funny through the waves of grogginess and nausea.

"Something like that."

I catch his eye: brown but vivid like a burst of caramel. His smile is just so infectious.

"You look banged up too. Are you okay?" I ask.

"Nothing I can't handle. Got jumped by one of those creepy Leech-things."

My stomach falls out of my arse.

"Leech?" I ask nonchalantly.

"Well, that's what Wren calls them. I think she got it from Freya."

"Wait, who's Wren?"

"The girl from DEMA with the short hair you pushed into the ocean."

Okay, what?

A. How does Troy know about DEMA?

B. How does he know I did that?

C. OH CRAP, I USED MY POWERS IN FRONT OF HIM AND HAVEN'T SPOKEN TO HIM SINCE.

"Relax," he says, seeing my obvious discomfort. "She's totally cool with it. Says she shouldn't have cornered you – it was against 'The Protocol' or something. She left with Marcus not long after we got here ... So, do you want to address the elephant in the room, or shall I?"

Pretty sure there are a few elephants. I smile non-committally, so he can elaborate.

"You're . . . you know, like me."

Again not really narrowing it down. He rolls his eyes – Freya must be rubbing off on him – and fishes the dog tags out from around his neck. He takes a breath then a yellow aura surrounds his hands, and the tears in his shirt stitch up like nothing was ever torn.

"Holy shit-balls!"

Troy is an EMT. He has been this whole time. I didn't even know that elephant was in the room!

"Always with the cussing," he says with a laugh.

"I . . . had no idea. You hide it so well."

"Years of practice. I mean, so do you. I had no idea until you used your powers against the Leech."

"Days of practice," I reply. "I'm surprised you didn't know sooner. The whole reason I'm in this miserable town was to stop myself from blowing up half of Dorset."

"Was he helping you control it?" he asks, his gaze slipping down to the duvet.

"Err . . . yeah, something like that." Why did I say that? I'm so embarrassing. "Who taught you?"

"Oh, I got picked up by BSA after I burned down my stepdad's apartment. Bureau of Superhuman Affairs. They're sort of like the US Government's version of DEMA. Got taken to a training centre and assigned a mentor who was the worst, most racist old white dude you've ever met. But like the kinda guy who would swear he wasn't because he knows a black guy. Anyway, he jokingly called me a 'half-breed' one time, and I just had it. I got on a plane and came to live with my aunt here."

"What a dick."

"I know, right? I'd like to say people like him are rare, but . . ."

"So, wait, sorry. Still struggling to understand what is happening. Why is Marcus out with a DEMA agent? I thought they were no good."

"They are a lot better these days. Mainly just help people like us with our powers."

Huh. And here I thought Agent Pixie was going to dissect me. In my defence, DEMA do a poor job of not looking like a nefarious secret agency. They really need to work on their brand image. "So, where are they now?"

"They got a location from Fareborn's phone – that's Wren's boss. She was also taken. They're hoping Freya is with her."

"Freya's missing? What?" I say, sitting bolt upright.

"Oh boy. There is a lot to catch you up on."

And so, Troy tells me everything they know. When he's finished, I let the silence fall between us as a wave of guilt hits me.

"Are you okay?" he asks, rubbing my arm.

"This is all my fault. I . . . I let myself get carried away, and I didn't see the warning signs. Now Freya's been abducted, you and Marcus were almost torn apart by Leeches, and Zachary's escaped. All because of me."

"No. Because of Zachary. You had no idea he was a kidnapping, date-raping sociopath."

"I guess," I say, but I'm not convinced. "He called me a gift. No one's ever told me that before. I dropped my guard, let him charm me, and now Freya is paying the price."

Troy doesn't really know what to say to that. He shifts uncomfortably in his chair and passes me a glass of water.

"Thanks," I say.

"Was he going to turn you into one of those Leeches too?"

"I don't think so – well, that wasn't his plan originally. He told me the Leeches were made when people like us are subjected to extreme amounts of apathy."

"So, what did he want?"

"My powers are the opposite of normal EMTs, so I destroy when I'm happy," I say, reaching in my pocket to show him my cheat sheet and realising it's not there. Must've lost it in all the commotion. "He wanted to find out why. Run tests on me."

"EMTs? Is that what you call them over here?"

"I literally have no idea. I learned the word three days ago."

"We call them E-Mans. Like Emotion-Manifestors. Your way sounds less patriarchal, though."

"Is it a law in America that you have to rename things just to confuse the British?"

"Basically."

As we laugh together, a thought hits me. Suddenly, the pieces of the puzzle line up.

"What is it?" asks Troy.

"He drained me with his apathy, and I felt tired and numb. Then he said he could 'make a battery' out of me. He injected me with something that made *me* manifest apathy too. When he drained me again, it was like I was giving him everything. Like I was giving him my life. Afterwards, he looked . . . younger. Like years younger. When I met him on Monday, he looked early twenties . . ."

". . . and when I fought him, I thought he was sixteen. I mean, he had a bloody nose, but—"

"Why'd he have a bloody nose?"

"Marcus punched him in the face and broke it."

"Brilliant." Maybe he's not such a ginormous prick after all.

"But yeah, I was surprised someone so powerful was so young. You don't think . . ."

"That Zachary's some sort of emotional vampire leeching people's energy to stay young. Yes, Troy. That's exactly what I think. He must need normal EMTs to manifest love and at the same time hits them with apathy to drain their life and make them all Leechy. God, the whole time, he was that creepy DEMA scientist who experimented on pregnant women in the fifties. And now he has Freya. He can't turn her into a Leech or make her a battery because she's not an EMT, but . . . oh God what if he experiments on her? We need to save her!"

"Easy, easy now. You're not going anywhere just yet."

"But Freya—"

"—will be in more trouble if we rush in without a plan. We don't even know where she was taken yet, and you're still weak from the drugs. The best thing you can do for her is rest up until Marcus and Wren get back."

He makes a lot of sense, annoyingly. Right now, I don't think I have the strength to stand, let alone go toe to toe with Zachary. A shudder runs down my back. This whole time, I was snogging a man older than my grandparents – not that he looked it, but it's still weird. I was completely under his spell, and I didn't even know it. If it weren't for Troy and everyone else coming to my rescue, I could be strapped to a slab being pumped full of who-knows-what while Doctor Dracula sucked the life from me. And now he has Freya . . .

Another wave of guilt washes over me. Black smoke curls around my knuckles, and my whole body glows. At least Troy isn't staring at me like everyone else would – it's handy we don't affect each other like that. I rummage in my pocket for my coin, and revulsion grips my insides. Zachary's coin. An old coin that's still younger than he is. I try to push my guilt into it, but I can't. It's fighting me too hard, for some reason.

"What's wrong?" Troy asks. "Siphon not working?"

I shake my head and throw the coin at the wall. Stupid thing.

"Must be broken," I grunt, still glowing like a beacon. God, this is so embarrassing.

"Try something else," Troy suggests. "Something personal."

But what? I don't have a family heirloom like his dog tags. I don't think I have any metal on me other than . . .

I glance down at the cheap mood ring Freya won from the arcade. Just a small band of silver with an iridescent centre. It's currently yellow, but I don't have the bit of paper so have no idea what emotion that's supposed to be. Cheap piece of crap. But then again, it is metal, and I wouldn't have to worry about losing or spending it.

I close my eyes and think of Freya rolling her eyes at me like she always does, like when she gave the ring to me. A smile creeps across my face. I feel the guilt still sitting in my chest, but the manifestation begins to move, withdraw. It slides along my body and tips into the mood ring, like silk running over me. There's no forcing it. No feeling of squashing anything down. It slithers away with hardly any resistance. I guess Zachary was right: sentiment is important in your siphon.

"Wow! That's excellent control!" says Troy, picking up my hand and examining the ring. "And you only started doing this Monday?"

"Yeah, but it's never been that easy before."

"And that was black ... so guilt for you, right? But you manifested pride instead. Have your powers always been like that?"

"Yeah."

"I wonder what caused them to be like that?"

"Well, DEMA seems to think our powers come from trauma in the womb, but I have no idea. Mum never told me she had any problems."

"Yeah, BSA back home say the same."

"Do you know what caused yours?"

"Ah yeah ... My mom got super sad after my dad died and started drinking and taking stuff ... Got hooked while she was pregnant."

Oh crap, I've really put my foot it in. He's embarrassed, and I feel like a twat for asking him such a personal question.

"I, erm ..."

"It's super common. A lot of E-Mans are from families with addictions. It's actually the reason I want to become a counsellor."

"That's great. Not the addiction part – I meant the counselling part – not that I think that's—"

"Steven, relax. I know what you meant. Well, whatever the reason your powers are reversed, it's pretty cool they work like that."

"Not really 'cool' if you cause an earthquake every time you feel happy."

"No, but then imagine the opposite. Trying desperately to stay happy when you're so unbearably miserable in case you cause a tornado."

His shining smile is still glinting at me, but his eyes are pained. His hand is just a few centimetres from mine. I could grab it so easily, but somehow, that would take even more energy than standing up.

"Were there many tornados?"

"Mom stopped buying lawn furniture pretty quickly."

"I'm sorry," I say, mainly because I don't know what to say, and I'm British. It's what we do.

"No, don't be. That was all a long time ago. I mean, it's still there, you know. All the hurt and sadness, but for the most part, I'm the happiest I've ever been in my life."

"Even in this shithole town?"

"Especially in this . . . town."

I laugh at his stupid face. One day I'll get him to swear, and it'll be hilarious yet weird, like a dog riding a skateboard.

"In fact," He takes a deep breath and starts fiddling with the duvet cover. "Earlier on the beach, before we got attacked, I mean . . . that was the happiest I think I've ever been."

"Yeah?"

He rattles his dog tags and says, "Pretty much filled them."

I don't know what to say, but I can feel my ears burning. I must look like such a melon. My hand reaches out and squeezes his. They're rough and a little clammy, but I don't mind.

He looks into my eyes, and suddenly the world falls away. I hold his face and guide it towards me. His lips are soft and smooth, but they sink into mine so deeply and passionately that I forget everything else. I feel every part of my body screaming to be with him. And we keep going, barely coming up for breath. Troy's holding me so tightly, like I might evaporate if he lets go. Like this won't be real the moment we stop. But we do.

We separate, and I can't stop grinning. Neither can he. Yellow swirls into the pendant around his neck. I look down and do the same into the mood-ring, which is now deep purple. I don't know what else to say, so we laugh like a pair of idiots.

He takes a breath and is about to say something when we hear the latch go.

"Troy?" comes Marcus's voice quietly from the other room.

"We're in here. He's awake," Troy answers, squeezing my hand. He goes to get up, but his eyes grow wide with embarrassment, and he promptly sits back down and crosses his legs.

I laugh once more at this big doofus and cross my legs under the covers too.

35

Troy

The door flies open, and Marcus storms into the tiny bedroom, a deep scowl stuck on his face. I take my hand from Steven's and scratch a pretend itch on my face – I mean, I'm not embarrassed, but he might be. Like we haven't even talked about what that kiss means. Does it mean anything? If only Marcus had just been a minute later, I could've asked. I glance over at Steven, but his attention is on Marcus, who plonks down at the end of the bed.

"Alright, Stevie?"

"Yeah, alright," Steven replies like he hasn't just been drugged and almost experimented on by a creepy youth-sucking scientist. Why do Brits never answer how they actually are?

"No luck?" I ask.

He holds up a burner phone and throws it onto the bed in response. It's cracked, but it still looks functional.

"Fareborn's. Found it on the pavement behind the hotel. Reckon it must've fallen out of her pocket as they carried her."

"So, no leads on where they took them?"

"Nope. They could be anywhere. We were going to look around the area, but those Leeches are now all over town.

Reckon they're trying to find us. Wren detected a few closing in on us with her emotions-detector-thing, so we came back here to regroup."

"And what's Wren doing?" I ask.

"She's next door trying to send another message to HQ, but their systems are still down. Probably a cyber-attack from that guy—"

"Zachar ... Dent. His name is Dent," says Steven, his face hardened.

"Well, whoever that prick is, Fareborn reckons he had full access to DEMA's servers."

"He used to work for them in the fifties," says Steven.

"What?"

"Long story. So what is the plan then?"

"There is no plan, Stevie. We don't know where Freya is, we don't know where Dent went, and emotion-eating zombies are now prowling the streets. Both of you have magic powers but never told me. Apparently, there's a secret agency built around people with those powers, but we can't call for backup. And the one person strong enough to save the day was also kidnapped. We are totally screwed."

A silence falls, and I feel guilt growing in the pit of my stomach. Our friend is missing, and we are hiding from an Alpha level E-Man and his army of Leeches, yet here I am, locking lips with Steven like nothing else matters. I send it to my dog tags – last thing Marcus needs is for me to turn invisible.

"Marcus ... I'm so sorry I dragged Freya into all of this."

He stares at Steven for a moment, and I'm not sure which way he's going to go. I don't even think he does.

"No, you didn't. Freya made her own decisions, and hell if anyone can stop her."

Well, that's not what Steven or I expected.

"But if I hadn't come here, then—"

"Then what? You might've blown up half of Dorset? I'm not playing this game, Stevie. Freya told me about your powers – about how you came here to protect everyone. And yeah, you were a right drama queen about it, but you did what you thought was right. Freya did what she thought was right by coming here. Me and Troy did what we thought was right by following her. Now stop playing this blame game because it doesn't help our situation. It doesn't help get Freya back."

The door swings open again, and Wren bounds into the room carrying a cup of tea. I can tell from her face she hasn't been successful, yet her eternal optimism still shines through. But her eyes are different – duller than they were before. Now that I think of it, Marcus's eyes are desaturated too. Almost grey. As if being outside for an hour has drained them. Must be all the Leeches around town.

"Alreet, pet? Oh, thank goodness you're awake. I was sure he'd given you something proper strong like – thought you'd be out for hours! I made you a cuppa – thought it might help you feel better. I'll pop it down here."

She puts the tea down on the nightstand and sits next to Marcus at the foot of the bed.

"Well, isn't this cosy?" she says. "Sorry, we haven't properly been introduced, have we? I'm Junior Agent Wren."

"Steven. Nice to meet you," he says, shaking her hand awkwardly. "Errr sorry about the whole pushing you into the sea thing."

294

"Don't worry about it, pet. Totally my fault. I must've given you a proper fright, chasing you and that."

"Did you manage to get through to HQ?" asks Marcus.

"No, and I tried everything: phone, email, even a message on Director Delphi's Twitter. Everything is down. I suspect that bloke is giving them the run around to keep them busy while he tries to find us."

"It's just me he wants," says Steven as he sits up in bed. "If it means Freya and Fareborn go free, I'll do what he wants."

"Absolutely not!" I say.

"Not happening," says Wren.

"Don't be a prick, Stevie," Marcus says.

"But . . . it's the only way—"

"No, it's not!" I say, grabbing his hand with both of mine. I don't care what the others think. "It's not even one of the options. We are not trading hostages. And we are not going to let Dent experiment on you. I swear."

"Besides, do you really think he's just going to let the five of us go once he has you? No! We all know way too much about him and his sick little operation here," says Marcus.

"So what do we do?" says Steven.

"Well, the DEMA handbook says that if a case goes off-protocol, you should call for backup. If you cannit do that, you should list all the things keeping you from your current objective and deal with each one individually. So, we need to find Freya and Field Director Fareborn, that's one. Find a way to get past the Leeches – two. And three, we need to find and neutralise this Dent bloke."

Marcus gets to his feet and starts pacing.

"Okay, one – finding them. So, Fareborn's phone was a dud – what about Freya's?" I ask.

"Already tried. Her phone disappeared entirely. Either it fell out and was destroyed, or she's somewhere a signal cannot reach," says Wren, biting her nails.

"Our phones are still sharing locations with each other! I might not be able to see where she currently is, but it can tell me her last position – oh, I forgot," says Steven, pulling his phone from his pocket under the covers and seeing the screen smashed to bits.

"If you can unlock it, I could try accessing it on my computer?" suggests Wren. "Might take a little time because it has to make a virtual copy of your phone."

"How long?" asks Marcus.

"About 45 minutes? Pass it here, and I'll get it started now."

With that, she takes the shattered phone and disappears back out the door. Marcus keeps pacing but closes his eyes like he's deep in thought.

"So number two – how do we get past those Leeches? Can you two use your powers on them?"

"No," answers Steven, "they used to be EMTs like us, so we can't affect each other. Well, they *can* drain us of our energy."

"Perfect. So these zombies have no weaknesses."

"Wait!" I say, suddenly remembering my encounter in the hotel room. "They don't like sunlight. I pulled off the drapes, and one of them freaked out."

"So we just wait till morning?"

"I don't think that's going to work, Marcus," says Steven. "One of the Leeches attacked us yesterday during the day. The sun was obscured by all the storm clouds. If I know Za— Dent, then he will keep the cloud cover with his powers. Plus we can't just let them roam about town draining everybody."

"So it's obviously something to do with ultraviolet light if they were fine under clouds and lightbulbs. If we can get a hold of some UV bulbs, I might be able to make something to keep them at bay."

"But where are we supposed to get UV bulbs from? It's not like this place is full of tanning salons," I say. "And people haven't had blacklights in their homes since 1979."

"The arcade! There's a blacklight above the werewolf shooting game at the back, and I bet you they keep spares in the office," says Steven, a smile bursting across his face.

I look from him to Marcus and back again, waiting for someone to find a hole in this plan. But we don't. Instead, we call Wren back through and draw up a plan to get the bulbs. I agree to go with them this time, partly to protect them, partly because my powers should help us get into the locked arcade easier. Marcus goes and waits in the car while I hang back for a second to talk to Steven.

"Are you sure you won't need me? I can—"

"You need to rest. We'll be back in 30 minutes tops, okay?"

"Okay."

We look at each other, and I'm not sure what to do. Does he feel the same way, or was before just a side effect of all the drugs? I pat his arm and turn to leave as it seems like the least committal thing to do.

"Hey, Troy."

"Yeah?"

"Be careful. Alright?"

"Of course."

"And about earlier, I—"

"It's okay. You don't need to explain or anything."

"No, it's just, I like you . . . and stuff."

"I like you and stuff too," I say, a grin spreading across my face as Steven's ears turn crimson. Before I say anything to wreck the moment, I lean over and kiss him.

*

Steven

God, that boy can kiss. It's just as well he did because I was about to say more stupid things. *I like you and stuff* – why am I such an idiot?

He pulls away, flashes me a classic Hollywood smile, then leaves the room without another word. And I'm left alone.

I wish we'd had more time to talk. I know we have more pressing priorities – Freya, Fareborn, the fate of the world blah blah blah – but still, some clarity would be nice. I mean, I know he's not my boyfriend or anything after two kisses, so what are we? Where do we go from here?

And yeah, elephant in the room (another one), yesterday I was snogging someone else, but he turned out to be a geriatric vampire who drugged me and kidnapped my best friend, so I'm not best pleased with him. A shiver runs down my back at the very thought of kissing Zachary now. Even if he wasn't a gross freak with no concept of bodily autonomy, he really doesn't look as good without the beard.

I'm annoyed that I let myself get so carried away, but then I guess I'm not the first to be charmed by him. If all those Leeches were EMTs he seduced and used as "batteries", then he must have been doing this for years. Draining the town so people look the other way and keeping himself young by sucking the life out of other EMTs. Bombarding them with apathy while they unknowingly manifested love, until a second epigenetic switch activated and slowly turned them into . . .

No. Never again. No one else is going to be harmed by this monster. I'm going to make sure.

I know I should try to sleep, but I'm too pumped up. I get to my feet and wait for the wobbles to subside before exploring the rest of the B&B. Next door is a small living room where Wren's laptop is sat on the coffee table with my phone attached, progress bar creeping ever so slowly onwards. Near the door are a sink and a kettle with a tiny bit of counter space where an old rotary phone is sat. I catch sight of myself in a small mirror on the far wall and jump. I look terrible (but that was to be expected considering I was drugged and had the life sucked out me). What surprises me most is the line of grey running down the top of my head. Can't tell if I look like Rogue or a badger. How am I going to explain this to my parents?

I sit on the sofa, out of breath already. Jeez. Maybe I can't do this after all. Suddenly dread takes root in the pit of my stomach. If this goes wrong and I'm captured, that would be it. I'd live the rest of my life as a lab rat being experimented on until I inevitably turn into a Leech. And no one will come for me this time. My life will be over. Mum and Dad will realise that I'm not at school sooner or later, but they won't be able to find me. I'll be just another statistic. Another missing person with no trail.

Before I realise what I'm doing, I'm already at the rotary phone. I put the enormous plastic receiver to my ear, and it starts to ring. A sleepy voice answers on the other end.

"Mmmmlo?"

"Mum?" I say, my hands starting to shake.

"Hmm?"

"It's Steven."

"Steven? Steven! Steven, wha— it's three in the morning, darling," she says. I can hear Dad groaning in the background, the sound of sheets moving, then a squeak as she gets up. I feel guilty waking her up, but this might be my only chance to speak to her . . . ever. Besides, I know she worries about me – even if it means she's tired later, she would rather answer her phone at silly o'clock in the morning to know I'm safe.

"Sorry. I forgot."

"Is everything okay?" she says, sounding more awake now, but her voice is still croaky.

"Erm . . . kind of."

"We haven't heard from you in a while. I was beginning to worry."

A click. She's put the kettle on for a cuppa. Classic Mum.

"Yeah, things have been a bit manic here. I've erm . . . I've actually been struggling a lot. With a bunch of things."

"Oh, no. Well, has Freya been there to help?"

"Yeah."

"Oh, good. Couldn't ask for a better friend. She's a good egg, that girl."

Classic Mum #2 wishing Freya was her daughter.

"How're mocks going?" she asks.

"Fine," I lie. I've missed half of them. Maybe they'll let me do them another time or something? Here I am, worrying about exams when I might be dead or strapped to a slab ready for dissection by this time tomorrow. Priorities, Percival. "How's Spain?"

"It's been lovely and sunny. Uncle Pete sends his best."

"Tell him I said hi."

"Where are you? I don't recognise this number?"

"Oh, just . . . staying over at a friend's house. Look, Mum, I wanted to ask you something a bit weird."

"Okay?"

"When you were pregnant with me, did you have any problems or anything?"

There's a pause before she says, "How do you mean?"

"Like, did anything happen or were you sick or something?"

"Why do you ask?"

"Just curious is all."

"Well, I had a cyst growing at the same time as you. They thought another egg was released at the same time, but it got stuck and grew around my ovary. At one point, they thought they'd have to cut it out, which would have meant no you. In the end, we chanced it and waited till you were born. Then twenty minutes later, I was under the knife to have it cut out."

"Was it hard for you?"

"Of course. Nine months of morning sickness was bad enough, but also carrying around something that was trying to kill my baby and me was awful. Bloody hurt too. Still, it was all worth it in the end."

Goddamn you, Mum. A few months ago, I would have rolled my eyes at that, but now I'm trying not to cry.

"Was it really?"

"Well, when you finally slept at age four, it was."

Fair enough. I've always been a terrible sleeper.

"Are you sure everything is okay?" she asks before sipping her tea.

I want to say no. I want to tell her I'm tired and scared and about to attempt to rescue Freya from a man who makes Sauron look like a reasonable chap. But I can't do it. I can't worry her.

All I say is, "Everything's fine."

"Oh, good. You know how I worry about you. I'd call every day, but your father says I need to let you have your space to revise."

"You can call me whenever you like for a chat."

"And so can you. Even at three in the morning. You know that."

I swallow. My heart is beating fast, and my breath is caught at the top of my chest. I have to tell her. If this is the last time we'll speak, she has a right to know who her son is. What if she doesn't support me? Says I'm wrong or just in a phase? Disowns me? Well, I guess it won't matter if Zachary – I mean, Dent – gets his hands on me.

"Mum ... one last thing, then you can go back to bed, I promise."

"Okay."

"I ... I'm gay."

"Oh."

"Yeah."

A pause.

"... How long have you known?"

"I guess I've always known, but I haven't been honest with myself for a long time. Is err ... is that okay?"

"Of course, darling. I only want you to be happy."

"And you aren't going to disown me?"

"You're gay. You haven't murdered anyone."

Well, not intentionally.

"And what if I have?"

"Then I'll get my shovel and help you dig." We both laugh at that. "Have you got a . . . boyfriend?"

"Errrm not yet. Still working on it." Suddenly, I feel very embarrassed. My ears are burning against the receiver.

"Do you want me to tell Dad?" she asks.

"No, I'll do it. Not now, obviously. I'll call him tomorrow." If I'm not dead. "I have to go now, Mum. Thanks for . . . well, just everything. I love you."

"Love you too."

I put the phone down before she can say anything else. I should have told her about my powers, but one coming out is enough for any phone call. If I survive, I'll tell her in person – somehow, I don't think she'd believe me over the phone. I'm shaking like a dog taking a dump, and I can't stop crying. I can't quite believe I actually told her. But I have. Mum knows I'm gay.

There's nothing quite like the fear of death to drag you kicking and screaming from the closet.

36

Steven

The others burst through the front door about half an hour after I spoke to Mum, just at the point I was starting to worry about them. Marcus and Wren carry two black bin liners while Troy brings up the rear, a cut on his forehead bleeding.

"Oh my god, are you okay?" I say, springing to my feet.

"He's fine. Just hit his head on the car," says Marcus, rolling his eyes just like his girlfriend would. He and Wren set the bags on the little sofa and start pulling out a strange selection of crappy toys and electronics.

"Still not used to them being so small here," says Troy sheepishly. I grab his hand and take him to the sink.

"Everything go okay? Any Leeches?" I ask as I wet some kitchen roll and start dabbing his cut. Pretty sure he could do this by himself, but there's something intimate about doing it for him. Like I can be close to him without having to explain to any onlookers because, honestly, I don't have the energy for a second coming out today.

"Yeah, a bunch. It's like *Night of the Living Dead* out there. They are just wandering the streets. I hate to think what will happen once people start getting up and going to work. It'll be carnage."

"We'll stop them before then, don't worry," I say, not really believing what I'm saying. "Did they give you any trouble?"

"One was hanging around on the seafront, but we slipped in around the back without it noticing."

"And what's with all the toys? Did you rob a Christmas grotto or something?"

"Marcus realised we would need something to strap the bulbs to, and everything was just lying there, so we kinda helped ourselves. I made sure we were invisible first, of course, but I feel bad."

"You are too nice a person, you know that?" I tease. Had we been alone, I probably would have kissed him.

Marcus is soldering on the couch, and Wren is rifling through a toolbox on the floor next to us. She stands up, holding a spanner, screwdriver, and pair of pliers with polka-dot rubber handles.

"Knew I'd need my tools. Fareborn said I shouldn't have brought them – glad I didn't listen to her. How you feeling, pet? You look a bit brighter."

"Yeah, I'm a lot better now. Thanks."

"Oh, that's champion. I've just checked your phone, and it'll be another five minutes. I'll pop the kettle on while we wait."

By the time we have tea in hand and have sat down on the floor around the coffee table, Marcus has just finished the first of his UV weapons. It's seriously impressive. He's taken a bright pink plastic AK47, hollowed it out and jury-rigged it to shoot a beam of ultraviolet light.

"It's the best I could do with what I've got," he says, pulling the trigger and demonstrating the purple glow on the wall.

"Marcus, that's fantastic!" says Troy as he has a go. "Can you make three more?"

"Give me twenty minutes," he says, pulling another toy gun out, this one shaped like a 1920s Tommy gun, and breaking off the end with some scissors.

"While he's doing that, let's try this. Pop your passcode in, pet, and we'll see if we can find Freya's phone."

Wren passes the laptop over, and on the screen is a virtual copy of my phone. I enter my pin and navigate to the Find My Friends app. A map of Grunsby opens, and a little icon of me pops up near the high street. We wait a moment while it loads, then a picture of Freya's face appears on the map. It's on the seafront, but the other way, past the Grand Regalia.

"*Grunsby Fun Zone*. That's an oxymoron," I say, reading the label above her head.

"Why would they take them there?" asks Wren.

"Don't know. No one ever goes there, not even the tourists."

"Oh yeah, behind the hotel, there's a Ferris wheel. I'd hardly call that fun – the compartments look like animal cages," says Troy.

"That's it!" I say so suddenly Troy jumps and almost knocks my tea off the table. "They *are* cages! Faraday cages. They protect you from our powers from the outside, but they also keep our powers contained on the inside. Dent sent them there so they wouldn't be able to bust out with Fareborn's powers when she woke up. Probably took Freya because he wasn't sure if she was an EMT too."

"So he keeps them there for safekeeping?" asks Wren.

"At least until he can drug them. But he's had all this time – why hasn't he done it and moved them?"

"The Leech I found in the bed smashed a briefcase full of drugs. Maybe he used what he had left on you?" offers Troy.

"So he's fresh out. But he's a scientist, and he's been doing this for years. He must have a stash somewhere," I say, wracking my brains to remember if he mentioned anywhere. Then I remember a silver briefcase during one of our lessons. "The pier! That's where his lab must be."

"The one that's halfway in the ocean?" says Troy.

"Yeah, but he can pull it up. He took me there for a lesson."

"Fareborn mentioned in her reports that Agent Fowler fought with him on the pier the night it was destroyed," says Wren.

Suddenly her laptop makes an alarm sound, and she loads up a programme that looks like a heat map over Grunsby.

"What is it?" I ask.

"Major EME surge detected! I put these dentometers around town back when we were trying to track you down. The town's level is usually quite low, so most readings are skewed. But this is huge! And it's centred . . . right here. Where the pier used to be."

*

Marcus

We park up on the road above the seafront for the third time tonight and take the zigzag path down. A Leech tried to run after the car as we drove down the high street, but a quick blast of light from the UV guns I made, and it scarpered pretty quick. I can see a couple more down the seafront now and a few buzzing around the arcade – guess they can sense Troy used his powers there earlier. Thankfully, we aren't heading that way.

Four days ago, I wasn't involved in any of this crap. No zombies trying to drain my energy, no one with emotion powers chucking furniture around like a hurricane, no evil scientists kidnapping my girlfriend. I probably should blame Stevie for all this, but I don't. Poor guy's suffered enough, by the sounds of it. I would also blame Freya, but she's not around and would kill me if I did. So I guess the blame is on me for not walking away when I had the chance. I could've saved a lot of hassle, and my car would still be in one piece. Now that I think of it, I wonder if Stevie had anything to do with that. I was so sure I put the handbrake up.

Not the time to bring it up anyway. Everyone is so serious right now, toy guns slung over our backs, ready to fire. As we stride down the beach, no one says anything until we reach the edge of the pier. Just as Stevie thought, Dent has pulled it back out of the ocean, but only the very end where a building is perched. This is where we agreed to split up. Troy and Steven will go after Dent because they are immune to most of his powers, while Wren and I head to the Ferris wheel. She might be way too enthusiastic, but Wren's actually been really useful. She knew exactly what to take from the arcade and even helped me make the last two guns. Gripping her gun with a scowl on her face, she just looks wrong – like a Pomeranian with a semi-automatic.

"Guess you'll be swimming," I say, glancing out at the end of the pier. "Try not to get the guns wet, or they'll short out."

"Oh, don't worry, I've got a plan," says Troy, glancing at Stevie. They smile at each other. Weird. Am I missing something?

"Whatever. The batteries are crap and will drain pretty quickly, so try to use them sparingly. Short flashes."

"Good luck," says Wren, pulling them in for a hug.

"Err, you too," Stevie replies.

We leave them to it and pick up the pace as we skirt round the Grand Regalia hotel. I can't see any Leeches in the lobby – Dent probably cleared them out to find us. Let's just hope there aren't many standing guard.

On the other side is the saddest amusement area you have ever seen: a carousel with rusted horses missing most of their heads; a tiny dodgem area with crudely drawn Disney characters painted on; a ghost train that was obviously a repainted *Thomas the Tank Engine* ride; and a Ferris wheel looming over everything with its hanging cages. I can just about make out something lying down in the topmost compartment.

And that's when the Leeches attack.

*

Troy

After Marcus and Wren leave, we take a moment to stare out at the half-pier: the seaweed-covered theatre tantalisingly close. It has a soft yellow glow to it – obviously Dent's powers are keeping it from crashing into the sea. Steven swings his pink plastic UV gun down like he's doing a budget Rambo cosplay. His face is set with determination.

"We don't have to do this, you know," I say. "We could catch up to Marcus and help rescue Freya."

I know this must be hard for him. He's never told me, but I suspect something was going on with him and Zachary before all the drugging and kidnapping.

"No," he says. "We stop him here and now. We can't let him do this to anyone else ever again."

He takes my hand in his and squeezes.

I let it go.

Joy bursts out from my body in a wave of yellow, and I focus on the still sunken half of the pier. Wood and metal rise up from the seafloor and knit together as they once had until the path before us is complete.

Then there's an ungodly screech from behind us. Obviously, my manifestation has attracted the attention of a Leech ... or five. Steven glances back, then grips my hand even tighter.

"RUN!" he yells.

37

Marcus

There are six of them: four women and two men. All in various states of Leechification – in fact, one looks hardly scabby: a young girl whose face is on all the posters around town. On the other hand, one of the men has scales shutting his eyes, and the sides of his mouth have split like someone's given him a Chelsea grin. They are closing in on us like a pack of wolves. My hands tighten on the plastic Tommy gun in my hand. Need to wait till they are closer. At the far end is the Ferris wheel, its control panel sitting at the top of a ramp.

"Fowler. Can you hear me, pet? I'm Junior Agent Wren with DEMA. Director Delphi sent us," Wren pleads to the Leech that carried away Freya. The Leech cocks her head. For a moment, it looks like she understands. But then she opens her mouth and lets out a swirl of sparks. Whatever Dent has done to these people can't be undone with talking. The Leech pounces at Wren, but I yank her back and hit the monster with a blast of UV light.

"Fowler" clutches her face and falls to the ground in a heap, but two more have already clambered over the dodgems to take her place. I feel Wren's back against mine as the other three flank us from the merry-go-round. She fires her gun, and they recoil in pain at the flash of purply light, but it doesn't halt them for long. I do the same with the three on my side, stopping one of them who was trying to use his powers.

Feels just like *Call of Duty* but with plastic guns. I blast them with UV again, but the Leeches recover and keep coming. We need to keep moving.

Wren's thinking the same thing. She glances back at me and says, "Split up?"

"Let's do it," I reply. "Hit them with a long flash in three ... two ... one."

We pull the triggers at the same time, and the Leeches stagger. I take the opportunity and run, not through them, but round to the other side of the bumper cars' track. No sounds of Leeches following me yet. Almost there. Just a little farther.

Then it feels like something has caught me round the scruff of my neck, and I fly backwards, slamming my back on the wall of a small ticket hut. A Leech somersaults over my head and lands in front, its black mouth open and a pink mist dripping from its hands. The creature screams, and a green glow replaces the pink around its blackened fingernails. The little hut is hurled away behind me, and I'm pinned to the ground by an invisible force. My hands are so close to the trigger. If I can just reach it ...

There's a flash of violet, and the Leech claws at its face. It sinks down and curls up in the foetal position as the light stays on it, crying out like a wounded animal. Wren leaps over where the hut was a moment ago, her gun trained on the writhing figure. Her light flickers. The batteries are almost out. She lets go of the trigger and makes a beeline for the haunted train ride.

The moment she is clear, I get to my feet and pelt towards the Ferris wheel, not daring to look if the Leech is on its feet yet. But nothing stops me – no force throwing me around like a rag doll or sucking my energy. I dart up the metal ramp to the control panel.

There are way too many buttons. And all the labels have been eroded off. There's a big green one? That looks promising. Green for go, right? I press it, but nothing happens. Okay, let's push another. Nothing. I smack every damn button on that panel, but nothing happens. No power. Hopefully, just a breaker's been flipped, but if it's been disconnected, I'm screwed. Okay, where are the fuses? I open the doors under the panel – nope, just a ton of wires. I hop over the railings and check the back of the Ferris wheel's supports, but there's nothing here either.

Then I see a thick black cable cover, snaking its way from the wheel to the back of the toilet building. From the looks of it, each ride has a similar thing.

That must be it.

No Leeches that I can see. Guess they are too distracted chasing Wren around the ghost train, but where has the one by the ticket hut gone?

No time to worry about it now.

I follow the cable cover around the toilet block. The building has a gap of about a metre between it and the high wall that cuts the beach off from the street level. I flash my gun down the alleyway, but there's nothing down it except a metal box stuck to the side of the building. There's a big padlock on it, but it's so rusted that a quick kick and it snaps off. Thank God, no one in this town gives a toss about security.

Inside, there is a series of breakers and a switch set to off. I take a breath, then flick it on.

Immediately, every light and sound possible goes off as the amusement park bursts into life. If that doesn't attract the Leeches, it will *definitely* attract the police.

Okay. Get to the Ferris wheel. Turn it till it gets to Freya's cage. Get them out. Find Wren. Escape.

Easy.

Then, over the mind-numbingly repetitive carousel music, I hear a screech from the other end of the alley.

*

Steven

These things are relentless. I'm running as fast as my never-exercised-a-day-in-my-life body can down the rotted pier, but the Leeches are still gaining on us. Troy's being polite and hanging back, but now really isn't the time for chivalry.

"Go on ahead, and get the door open!" I yell in between gulps of air. I can't believe Freya chooses to do this for fun. The running part – not being chased down a pier by emotion-sucking zombies.

Troy nods, then sprints ahead like it's nothing. Okay, if I'm not dead or imprisoned by sunrise, I will start exercising immediately.

I throw a glance behind me. Three Leeches crawling after me on all fours and two running. Sparks are flying from their mouths, and a bunch of auras are swirling around them – green, pink, violet. But nothing seems to be happening. I guess they haven't figured out my immunity to most of their powers. Then again, I'm not immune to them ripping my face off with their bare hands.

They are less than three metres away. I sling my toy gun over my shoulder and hit them with ultraviolet light. Okay, that bought me a couple more seconds. Where is trigger-happy, sharp-shooter Freya McCormac when you need her?

A stitch stabs my side, but I keep going. Almost at those sea-warped doors that Troy is attempting to pry open. Use your powers, you tit! I would shout to him, but I definitely don't have the breath right now. He'll figure it out by the time I get there.

Suddenly, the ground beneath my foot vanishes. I fall to the decking, leg dangling over the sea. What the hell? Did I just miss a massive hole in the planks? I try to pull myself back up to standing, but my hand slips through too, and chunks of wood splash into the ocean. Patches of wood all around me are breaking and falling through. Then I hear a crack, and a gap opens up at the end of the pier just before the theatre. Of course – the Leeches are undoing Troy's manifestation! If I don't move soon, the whole walkway will collapse and take me with it.

Four of the Leeches are stood still, purple smoke manifesting from their scaly hands and sparks swirling out of their mouths. I guess it's nice they've learned the power of friendship and are working together to try to drown me. One, however, has broken free of the pack and is scampering straight for me like a reptilian jaguar. I try to pull myself free, but I don't have the upper body strength to do it one-handed, nor can I reach my light gun. So I guess my options are watery grave or ripped open like a packet of crisps.

Or there's the third option where the American guy I fancy pulls me up with one arm while he shoots the Leech with the other. That works too. Damn he's hot.

No time to thank him. The pier is groaning like Freya being forced to eat vegetables. We dart across the crumbling planks and jump the ever-widening gap to the theatre's threshold, just as a massive section of it falls into the sea.

We're safe. For now.

The Leeches stranded on the other side look furious. I mean, they always look furious, but even more so. One of them glows green and attempts to repel his way over to us, but he blasts a hole beneath his feet and splashes into the sea. Guess the ground isn't sturdy enough to push off from.

"Why isn't this bit crumbling?" asks Troy as he catches his breath.

"They're probably not strong enough to undo Zachary's manifestation," I guess. I still don't understand how all this works, but that sounds right. "Do you reckon there are more inside?"

"Could be. Best be on the ready," he says, holding up his pink, plastic Tommy gun like he's the badass in an action movie. Or at least a cheesy B-movie.

Gripping my own gun a little tighter, I think about a really juicy steak and the door flies open with a gust of pink. We step into the dark, sea-rotted lobby, long-since-suffocated fish strewn about the floor like discarded playbills. I pull the trigger of my gun, and a soft violet glow gives us a bit more light but not enough to see properly. Troy turns on his phone torch and sweeps it over the room, but there's nothing but dead fish and the refreshment stand.

I beckon Troy to come as I push open the double doors to the theatre as quietly as I can. No Leeches in there either. I flash my gun just in case, but everything remains silent. However, the UV light does catch on something on the floor in the aisle: a green splatter on the waterlogged carpet.

"Shine your light down here," I whisper to Troy, who obliges. Under the normal light, the splatter turns a dark crimson.

"Blood," says Troy.

"Let's hope it's Dent's."

I flash my gun again, but a little longer this time. A trail of green goes all the way to the stage left wing. We follow it as quietly as we can, but the floorboards are creaky and warped from their four years underwater. Nothing jumps out at us, though. No Leeches or bisexual-vampiric-psychopathic exes. Just a diminishing trail of blood that leads to a door with a green handprint smeared over it.

We creak it open and step through to a small grey corridor. Male and female dressing rooms flank us on either side, but the little green trail goes straight on towards a vault door like the one in the basement of Dysley House. On the wall next to it is a rusted plaque that says "Pollecutt Lounge", but somehow I know there isn't going to be a room with sofas and cocktails behind it. Whoever was here before us left the door ever so slightly ajar.

✱

Marcus

The Leech lunges at me before I've even raised my gun, its mouth wide and spitting sparks. Nothing else for it. I punch it as hard as I can in the face, and he staggers back.

Jesus, that hurt!

It was like punching a bag of rocks. These things really need some coconut oil. Eyes watering, I stick my bruised hand under my armpit and zap the Leech with UV. It screeches and scuttles back around the alleyway, giving me a chance to run the other way.

Everything is lit up like a Christmas market, and the carousel is playing an off-key version of "Oh, I do like to be beside the seaside".

"MARCUS!" roars a Geordie voice.

Wren almost runs straight into me. Her head is bleeding, and her sleeve is ripped, but she's still got that chirpy grin on.

"Alright?" I say. "Where are the other Leeches?"

"Ghost train! I had a feeling there'd be a few black lights inside, so I lured them in and trapped them! As soon as the power came on, they freaked out and just curled up. I've locked them in for now, but I don't know how long it'll hold them. Gun's out of battery too."

"Ferris wheel should have power. Let's go!" I say, and we set off at a sprint.

As I run past the merry-go-round, a figure leaps out behind a horse missing several legs and half its nose. I raise my gun at the Leech, but it holds out a green-glowing hand, and a sudden force rips it away from me.

I can hear Wren shouting my name, but I just yell, "GET TO THE WHEEL!" The Leech throws another wave of green my way, but I dive to the side, and the overstuffed bin next to me goes flying instead.

I scrabble up to the carousel and duck behind a carriage, just in time for a horse to explode in a purple fizz. Another catches fire, and a third disintegrates entirely. Next in the firing line is where I am. I drop down and army-crawl away just as the carriage melts into a puddle of noxious plastics. The Leech screams, and I can feel it jump onto the platform with me. A wave of purple streaks over my head, and suddenly, my cover has gone: the Leech has destroyed every horse and carriage on the ride. I flip over onto my back as it looms over me, a grey aura now swirling around its hands.

Then I feel weak.

Everything is pulled from me.

The panic.

The adrenaline.

The burning need to save Freya.

It all goes away, and a hollowness creeps over me. An icy hand reaches inside my brain and tears all the thoughts and emotions out. My breathing slows. My muscles relax. As I stare into the black abyss of this guy's mouth, my vision starts to fade at the edges. Like someone is burning the corners of a photograph. Until only a tiny sliver of light in the very centre remains. And once that's gone . . . I'll sleep.

Something whistles through the air. There's an almighty thud, and the Leech is thrown off me. I blink as my vision returns to me. On the floor, pinned underneath a dodgem car, is the Leech. And on the other side of the amusement park, still with one foot in the cage, is Fareborn, her arm stretched out and glowing green. She turns to Wren, and her stern face cracks into a smile as she pulls her in for a hug.

But there's no one else in the cage with her.

So, where's Freya?

38

<u>Troy</u>

Through the vault door, there's light, so I put my phone away. We creak it open and step through into what looks like a high school science lab with benches of equipment and locked cupboards everywhere. Huge jars of pills and vials of liquid are strapped to one of the walls, and below are three silver suitcases and a gap for a fourth. A gas-powered generator hums on the floor, its cables disappearing into another room. That must be where Dent is.

"The walls are Perspex," Steven whispers in my ear.

"What?"

"It's like an aquarium tank."

Guess that explains why everything is so dry and undamaged. If it were made of metal, it'd run the risk of being a Faraday cage. Good to know our powers will still work on the walls if we need to make a quick exit. We stand next to the doorway and share a look. Steven counts down on his fingers. Three . . . two . . . one. We push open the door.

"Good evening, gentlemen. Or should I say good morning?"

Hunched over a machine with his back to us is Dent wearing an immaculate lab coat. The room is slightly bigger than the first but has been partitioned off with a sheet of plexiglass. On the other side, strapped to a dentist's chair, is a red-headed girl, several wires attached to her body.

"FREYA!" Steven roars. "LET HER GO, DENT!"

"Dent? Come on now, Steven. I thought we were on a first-name basis?" says Dent, turning around. Jeez, he looks rough. The dried blood on his nose and shirt make him look like a feral teenager. His dark, demented eyes land on me, and he pulls an ugly smile. "But then again, I'm not acquainted with your little American friend. And you are?"

"None of your damn business," I say, clutching this gun even though it will do precisely nothing to him.

"Charming. In any case, welcome to my little lab. Well, not really mine, but I don't think Julian's around to use it anymore."

"Not after you killed him," Steven spat.

"Technically, Diana killed him. I just shut the door. I thought he'd be so happy that I was continuing the work, but all he cared about was his little sprog. It was a shame. He was . . . a brilliant mind. Still, no use dwelling on the past, is there? Not when the future is calling!

"You know, I really should have given you more credit. I thought my Leeches would have kept you busier. Honestly, I expected you around six or seven in the morning. I've barely had time to get this ready for you."

"What are you talking about?"

"Your little friend, Steven. Freya's agreed to be my guinea pig, and I wanted you to bear witness."

"What are you going to do to her, you sick, twisted freak?"

"Now, now. No need for name-calling, is there? Freya will be my first attempt at evolution. She's a carrier of ZDNT1, as

I suspected – gingers often have it. But like so many, it isn't activated. Until now, that is. I've been working on a theory of adult epigenetic activation for some years. I started my research in the Dysley children and continued it with their descendants. And now I've been given the perfect test subject. She will be the first person to become an EMT as an adult."

Steven's body is burning crimson, and ice covers the walls, dropping the lab's temperature considerably. He throws out his hand, and an icicle forms in the air before flying at Dent.

But the Alpha E-Man simply swats it away with a fizz of green, and it smashes on the wall.

"Steven, I thought you'd be pleased. Your friend will evolve. She'll be just like you."

"I wouldn't wish this on anyone, let alone my best friend, you twat!" Steven replies, punctuating his sentence by launching more chunks of ice.

This time Dent catches them in mid-air, and they float suspended between us.

"Fine. If you are determined to keep her in the mud of the evolutionary also-rans, then come claim her!"

With that, the disgust twined about his fingers flares a more vibrant green, and the ice flies back at us. I let my anger flare, sending out a ribbon of fire that turns the ice to steam. Steven dives behind one of the benches, and I do the same on the opposite side. If we can divide his attention, we might win this.

Steven's ring fizzes pink – opposite, so he's trying to push something. A centrifuge rips itself away from the wall and hurtles towards Dent, but he catches this too. Why is Steven trying this again? Then he glances at me.

Distraction.

I reach into my siphon and tap the reserve of desire I felt that night I saw Steven in his underpants – thank goodness I had my dog tags on, or they might've ripped clean off. I anchor it to the sheet of plexiglass behind Dent and pull as hard as I can. It doesn't shatter like I thought it would, but it does break free from the wall and knock Dent over. His concentration broken, the centrifuge also smacks him on the head, leaving a gash just below his hairline.

He's pissed.

Like seriously pissed.

The sheet of plastic explodes off his back, and he shakily gets to his feet. Purple escapes from his talon-shaped ring, and his hands glow. He throws one arm towards Steven, and the floor beneath him melts. Steven sinks down to his knees as vinyl engulfs him. I run towards him to pull him free, but Dent directs his other hand at me, his manifestation briefly turning crimson as he closes his fist.

My shirt bursts into flame, so I immediately stop, drop, and roll.

*

Steven

Well, this isn't going to plan. I'm stuck in a floor of melted plastic, and Troy is on fire. He's rolling around, but it's not working. I need to help him.

There's a sink on the other side. I focus on the tap and summon some disgust. It's not hard – just the thought of ever kissing Dent again does the trick. The valve wiggles. I pull it again, and it starts to turn. I keep going till the tap is fully open and water is gushing down the plughole.

I suddenly slip down to my armpits. Dent is really enjoying this. No time to focus on him. Troy needs me. I refocus my disgust on the water ... I have absolutely no idea if this will work, but it's the only thing I can think of. The stream wavers; I need to focus on it as a whole. I sink again, and now I'm just a head and two arms poking out of the floor. Focus, Percival.

It works! The water redirects its flow out of the sink and over Troy. I'm a goddamn waterbender! The fire goes out with a hiss, and Troy sits up, panting and spluttering. Without missing a beat, his hands glow green, and the water redirects again in mid-air, hitting Dent in the face.

I stop sinking – Dent's concentration is broken! Troy is over me the next moment, his strong arms pulling me up and out of the floor.

*

Troy

Steven is free, my arms smell of burned hair, and Dent is being pursued around his lab by a floating snake of water. Time to press the advantage.

I let go of the disgust I'm manifesting, and a nugget of fear rises to the top of my siphon. It's from a few hours ago when I held a fading Steven in my arms. I was terrified he might die, but now this fear is a weapon. I send it along the ribbon of water, freezing it instantly as it travels up to Dent's bloody face. Steven joins in, his hands throbbing with a red aura while mine pulse blue until ice completely encases Dent like those frozen Vikings that got stuck in glaciers.

"Will that hold him?" I ask as we stand over the young (well, young-looking) man trapped in a block of ice.

Why did I ask that? Tempting fate. The ice melts away, and a fiery flash knocks us off our feet. By the time we recover, there is nothing more than a few chunks of ice and a large puddle on the floor. Dent is gone.

"Where'd he go?"

"Don't know," I reply. "Cover me while I get Freya."

I hop over the partition where the pane of plexiglass was and rush to Freya. She's alive but drowsy. I rip the strap from her mouth.

"Freya. Can you hear me? It's Troy?"

"T-Troy?" she answers as if still in a dream.

Guess I'll have to carry her then. I've got one arm free, and I'm almost there on the second when I hear a noise behind me.

"TROY, WATCH OUT!" yells Steven.

But it's too late. A bloody hand materialises out of nowhere and closes over my face. I try to scream and throw him off, but a grey smoke obscures my vision, and suddenly I'm very ... tired. Like all my energy's been ...

*

Steven

Troy hits the ground like a sack of spuds. I forget my powers and run at Dent, ready to punch that smug twat in the face, but he pulls the pane of plexiglass off the floor and pushes it toward me. The force knocks me all the way back to the other side of the room. I shove it off me and scramble behind a bench just in time for a monitor and several medical machines to crash into where I just was.

"Just you and me again, Steven. Your handsome little American friend put up a good fight, probably a Beta, if I were to guess. He'll make a fine specimen to examine, but not as fine as you. You are an Alpha, like me. Well, with your powers being reversed, perhaps we should call you an Omega. I'll give you one last chance: come with me, and together we will uncover the mysteries locked within the human genome. We can figure out why you are the way you are."

"I don't care! All you want to do is make others like me."

"But Steven, if I can understand what caused your powers, then I can stop the gene from expressing. By isolating the epigenetic switch that reverses your powers, I can undo it – take them away. Give you a normal life."

I don't know what to say. I stare at the mood ring round my finger – cheap and cracked and forever a failsafe I'll have to live with. If he can take this away, then I'll never have to worry about it ever again. Never have to catch a smile before I wreak devastation or avoid getting angry like I'm Bruce bloody Banner.

I could kiss someone I care about and not worry about their head exploding. I imagine Troy's smiling face popping out of existence just like Harry's did, and vomit lunges up my oesophagus. I swallow it back down and glance at my hands. Blue with fear. The fear of hurting someone I care about. The fear I live with every day. I don't even have the heart to suck it into my siphon. It just scorches the floor beneath me.

"Think of the good we will do for humankind, Steven," Zachary continues, his voice nearing. He must be just the other side of the bench now. "All the children like you we could help."

Then I remember the list of children from Dysley – tortured out of pregnant women and given numbers instead of names. The Leeches made from those he kidnapped, experimented on, and drained of life. All the lives his experiments have ruined, all in the name of his sick curiosity. Who is to say I won't be next? Drugged, tortured, then kept as a human battery, so Dorian Gay can continue the cycle with another unsuspecting victim. I stand up. This ends now, one way or another.

"Just come with me, and this will all be over," he says, reaching out a hand.

"I'd rather shit in my hands and clap."

I let disgust flood my entire body, and I do exactly what he taught me two nights ago. I imagine I am the bench between us and pour the green energy into it. The effect is immediate. Every piece of lab equipment, every jar of pills, every chunk of unmelted ice zooms across the room to the bench like a super magnet is attracting it. Dent howls with pain as he's pinned by microscopes and cupboards.

But he wrestles his hand free, grabs me by the throat, and pulls me over the bench. The disgust is sucked out of me into his talon ring, and everything clangs to the floor. He sends a wave of green with his spare hand and pushes everything to the very edge of the room.

"I gave you a chance," he spits, pushing me down to my knees and grabbing the top of my head. "Such a shame."

A dark grey aura covers his entire arm as an incredible force hits me. My body isn't completely giving in to the apathy like the second time at the hotel. Guess this time I'm not helping him by pushing with my own apathy. I feel my energy being sucked from me, but like through a straw rather than a drainpipe.

"You see, Steven. I don't care about you. No one cares about you. You are alone."

The waves of grey intensify. It's getting harder to move. I can't push against him or even stand. What the hell am I going to do. I screw my eyes up tight and pray for a miracle.

"STEVEN!"

"STEVEN, DON'T GIVE UP!"

Freya . . . and Troy. I peel my eyes open, and they are huddled together by the dentist's chair. Holding each other up. They're okay. They're alive and rooting for me. Dent is wrong – they care about me. And I care about them. Memories swim through my vision: Troy carrying me from the hotel, Freya and I shooting werewolves at the arcade, Troy and I eating ice cream and cooking eggs, Freya telling me everything was going to be alright after I came out to her. Their faces fill me as fast as Dent can take them away. More so. I feel powerful.

I love those stupid idiots.

Light explodes out of me in every colour. I stand and throw my hands towards Dent, casting a rainbow at him. This is the coolest and gayest thing that has ever happened. The shimmering rainbow collides with his grey. He tries to push it back, but he can't. All he can do is halt it. We are at a stalemate.

"You can't beat me. I am the zenith of human evolution. You are just a glitch. A mistake. A mutation," he says, baring his teeth with the strain.

"Yeah, but you forgot one thing, Zachary. The most important thing you ever taught me."

"And what's that?"

"Finger guns."

The wide rainbow wave immediately shifts to two narrow beams as my hands move. Like a laser beam slicing through the fog, they penetrate the grey and strike Zachary in the chest.

I feel it, his energy flowing into me, and I see why he did it. It's intoxicating. Everything shifts into sharp focus, and I feel even stronger than before. Like a god. Like I could do anything.

But I feel hands on my arms: one smooth and small, and one rough and big. They gently push them down, and I stop. The manifestation slides back inside my siphon. I give one last look at the wretched young man squirming on the floor before turning and burying my head in a three-way hug.

Freya is the first to break away, tears pouring down her cheeks. Troy's crying too. So am I. Freya punches me hard on the arm and says with a blubbering wail, "Don't ever go off with strange men again."

"Don't worry. I won't," I say, grinning at Troy, who pulls my head down and kisses my hair.

Suddenly the floor begins to shake. An earthquake? No, we're out at sea. Maybe the manifestation is running out. Maybe I took too much from Dent.

Or maybe he's standing again and manifesting sadness to bring the whole place down on us.

"Give it up! You'll kill us all, you twat!" yells Freya.

"I'm not letting DEMA take more credit for my work. My research, much like you three, will die with me!" he shouts, his voice hoarse and his eyes unfocused.

The purple wrapped around his hands flares, and the ceiling starts to collapse. The floor rips in half, and huge chunks fall into the sea below.

Troy grabs Freya and me and summons yellow from his dog tags. A neat circle cracks around us, and the falling debris misses us entirely. Dent is standing still, his face immovable and unreadable.

"ZACHARY, TAKE MY HAND!" I yell, holding it out for him. Yes, he's an evil scientist who just brought a building down on us, but he doesn't deserve to die. Not like this.

But Dent doesn't move. He holds his arms up to the side like a crucifix, and I swear I hear him say, "Julian."

A second later, the rest of the ceiling falls, and I shield my eyes from the dust. By the time I open them again, he's gone.

In fact, the theatre has gone, along with what was left of the pier. All sunk to the bottom of Grunsby bay or swept out to sea.

Troy, Freya, and I are huddled on a circle of vinyl flooring suspended above the crashing waves by a single wooden support beam.

"Who's up for a morning swim back to town?" I ask.

39

I, Field Director Elizabeth Fareborn, am formally closing the above case and withdrawing my request for back-up. My full report on this matter will be dutifully filed by tomorrow, but I have spoken to Director Delphi, and he has assured me that I should, "Relax, for God's sake, woman!" I have, after all, spent the last ten hours suspended in a cage above Grunsby-on-Sea, and am in desperate need of rest.

A few things, however, cannot wait.

First, it is my resolute opinion that Junior Agent Wren should be commended and promoted to the rank of full agent, effective immediately. She not only showed outstanding courage, resourcefulness, and intellect in my rescue, but she has also proven herself to be a capable (if unorthodox) agent of DEMA. Thanks to her actions (and the actions of four sixth-form students), we have recovered Agent Fowler and the missing people of Grunsby-on-Sea. The reversal of their Leechification has yet to be tested, but reading over what notes remained in Dent's hotel suite indicates that a mixture of UV light and high EME dosing should do the trick. I believe this will be successful as a burst of EME was seemingly responsible for Agent Fowler's ability to phone HQ. In any case, upon Dent's demise, the missing are behaving a lot less feral and have been easy to round up. We have dosed them with mild sedatives and will transport them to DEMA's hospital in Leeds for treatment.

The Alpha has been neutralised, although no body was recovered from the wreckage. I suspect he may have drowned, as his hold over the town has seemingly lifted, and ambient EME levels have risen to expected parameters.

As for the four students, I will detail them in my full report, as well as appropriate actions for them. But first, I think we are all in desperate need of a good breakfast.

This case has been eye-opening. I have (quite literally) confronted the ugly past of which DEMA is still built upon today. It will take time to right the wrongs, to root out the remaining corruption, and to educate so that these things are never repeated nor forgotten.

I still believe in the work we do. And I know there is much work still to be done.

But I won't be silent anymore.

- End of Log -

40

Freya

It's been two hours, and Marcus is still all over me like a cheap suit. It was sweet, but now I'd just like to eat my bacon without him kissing my neck like I'm in a perfume advert. I guess there's nothing like a good kidnapping to make you truly appreciate your girlfriend.

We've gone back to the Happy Smiles Café on the high street, all six of us. Fareborn's treat. We've been chatting about school and how the weather's suddenly cheered up like we weren't just fighting a mad scientist and his army of zombified kidnap victims. Guess no one knows what else to say. Once Troy and Steven levitated us back to the beach, and we'd swapped stories with the others, the only thing left was to round up the Leeches and then have breakfast.

Steven keeps glancing out the window as he pushes his eggs around his plate – as though Zachary might rise up from the sea and smash through the window at any moment. Must be a lot to process for him. Ex-lovers, deception, betrayal – it's like a telenovela with telekinesis. When he's ready to talk about it all, I'll be ready to listen. I reach over and squeeze his hand under the table, which brings his attention back here. We share a quick smile, and I know he's going to be okay.

Wren's jabbering away about how she'd love to come visit us. She's never been to the South Coast before, so we make plans we probably won't keep. Still, it would be nice to see her again when she's not tasing us or tying us to chairs.

We eat our greasy breakfasts, and the waitress, a lot perkier than the last time we saw her, brings us another round of teas. That's when Fareborn looks at the time and announces that they need to get back to HQ soon.

"But before we go," she says, surveying us like a proud parent, "I'd just like to thank you all, one last time. I have been a director of field operations for a few years now, and never before have I faced a challenge quite like this. Yet the four of you rose to the occasion and helped us overcome one of the more dangerous Alphas I've seen. I'm proud to call you my allies. On behalf of DEMA, I extend our thanks, and I'd also like to extend an offer. A personal recommendation for each of you should you want to come work for us."

I look around, but everyone has their poker face on. Waiting for someone else to respond, no doubt. Fine, I'll do it . . . Men.

"That sounds really generous, but we've got school and—"

"Yes, I know you have your education, but this offer won't expire anytime soon. I'm sure we could work something out part-time during the summer or even an apprenticeship. You wouldn't necessarily have to do such dangerous assignments as this one was. In fact, Ms McCormac, I'd be very interested in having you join DEMA's research division. Your attention to detail in unravelling this case was stellar."

I mean, I had always had my heart set on forensic pathology, but this certainly sounds interesting.

"Mr Jordan," she continues, "given the speed at which you fashioned the ultraviolet weaponry, I'm sure we could use your engineering prowess in our R&D department. There is an internship going there if you are interested."

"Yeah, actually. I'll check it out," says Marcus, his ears pricking up at this.

"Excellent. And of course, Mr Anderson and Mr Percival, your abilities certainly make you suitable for fieldwork. You'd probably start with cataloguing Zeta-level EMTs, but you'd be helping people to control their manifestations."

The boys consider this, but Fareborn rises to her feet and throws a business card at each of us before they can respond.

"I don't need any definitive answers right now. Just think it over, and give me a call if you'd like to take me up on it. HQ will be in touch with you two in a couple of days to finish cataloguing your powers, etcetera. Given everything you've been through in the last twenty-four hours, there's no rush. Get some rest, all of you. And again, thank you. You were all exemplary."

And with that, she sweeps out of the café like a total badass. I would literally give my right tit to be her. Maybe I should start wearing power suits?

"I'll see you all later!" says Wren as she gets up to leave too. "Add me on Instagram, and we'll arrange that night out."

As she leaves, Steven suddenly gets to his feet and mumbles, "Be right back," and chases after Fareborn.

*

Steven

"Director Fareborn, could I have a quick word," I say, already out of breath. That's it – I'm getting a bloody gym membership the moment I get home!

"Of course. Wren, bring the car around," she says, throwing the keys to Wren like she's in an action movie. We make the short walk over the road and down to the beachfront. Already, I can see confused police officers patrolling the Grunsby Fun Zone, trying to figure out why the power is on. As my eyes travel along the sea, a jolt of fear grips me when I see the Grand Regalia, windows smashed and empty.

"What will happen to the hotel now that Dent's gone?" I ask.

"Once HQ has done a thorough sweep of it and cleared out anything he left, I imagine it'll get a new owner. Without his influence, this town should begin to get back to normality, though it'll no doubt take some time. For years, he pumped the whole of Grunsby-on-Sea with apathy. That doesn't just undo in a day."

"I still can't believe he got away with this for so long."

"Criminal, isn't it. But apathy is a powerful tool in making people compliant. Many a blind eye was turned here, and I'm not going to rest until I hold those responsible to account. At least everyone is safe now. HQ is also sending a fleet of coaches to take the Proto-Leeches to our hospital up in Leeds."

"Will you be able to get them back to normal?" I ask.

"We think so. Annoyingly, the one person who would know exactly what to do is Dent, but we do have a good idea of where to start. We are lucky. None seem to have transformed to the extent of the one from Dysley House. If they were, I fear euthanasia might have been our only option."

Jesus, just when I think DEMA are the good guys, she talks about putting them down like rabid dogs. Then again, if a whole bunch of Leeches got out, the country would be overrun pretty quickly. Good thing it hasn't come to that moral quagmire.

"Now, what was it you want to talk to me about?" she asks, leaning against the railing, her amber eyes looking fierce in the morning sunlight. Here goes.

"I don't . . . I don't really know who else to talk to. But before I came here, I . . . there was this party and erm—"

"Take a breath," she orders, and I do. "Try again. Slowly."

"The reason why I came here was because . . ." I breathe again and try to steady my heartbeat. Blue fear is glowing around my hands, so I push it into my ring before I set something on fire. Okay, you can do this, Percival. "I was at a party, and I accidentally used my powers on this guy and his head kind of exploded. And I didn't know what to do because I felt guilty, so I was glowing, and everyone kept looking at me. I just packed a bag and left. And Troy told us that a DEMA agent was asking about me. And I don't know what to do. I couldn't control my powers, but he's dead because of me. Harry is dead because of me."

Fareborn blinks slowly and places a hand on my shoulder. Her voice is low and barely above a whisper.

"When my sister died, the grief I felt caused the roof of my college to collapse and kill two of my classmates. That was how DEMA found me. It's often how we find Betas and Alphas: grief. In your case, it was the opposite. This happens. The DEMA agent assigned to your case will have stopped the police investigation and just wanted to help you control your powers. No one will blame you for what happened because you weren't in control. But that doesn't mean you'll ever stop blaming yourself. Not a day goes by that I don't think about them.

"But that is why I do what I do. To help people who have experienced what I have. To stop it from happening again. I can't

337

erase what I've done, nor can I ever make amends. But doing this makes bearing that guilt a little easier."

"Thank you," I say, my throat suddenly very dry, but my eyes very wet.

"If you ever need to talk, I'm just a phone call away."

∗

Troy

Steven and I walk back to his apartment while Marcus and Freya go pick up the rental. Something's definitely up with him. He's been quiet ever since he spoke to Fareborn. I want to hold his hand as we walk, but we've never discussed public displays of affection, nor have we really said what we are to each other – if we are anything. Maybe he was just trying something out before we walked into certain death? And now that we've survived, will he change his mind? Oh gosh, I really need to learn to calm my brain down – he might just have a stomach cramp.

We pack all of his possessions into two plastic bags, and he writes a quick note to his landlady to say he's going. And then we wait. We sit on the shrink-wrapped couch in silence and listen out for a car making its way up the hill.

"What's up?" I ask, and he chuckles to himself at this. "What? What is it?"

"I just never know how I'm supposed to respond to that."

"Tell me how you're feeling then, dingus."

"I don't know. I'm not glowing, so I'm probably feeling everything and nothing at once."

"Yeah, it's been a rough week."

"It's certainly been an experience."

"Do you think he's gone? Like for good?"

Steven pauses and chews the inside of his cheek. "I don't know. I didn't see him surface, so he probably drowned. Then again, he's pretty athletic for an octogenarian, so who knows. Maybe he's halfway across the Channel. Or maybe he's lying at the bottom of the sea, crushed by the debris from the theatre. Who knows?"

Another silence falls. Okay, no fear of looming death – time to be brave and direct.

"When we get back, what do you want to do about us? I mean, is there an us? I don't want to assume anything or put you on the spot. I just want some clarification about—"

"Troy, shut up," he says before pulling me in for a kiss. "I meant what I said. I like you and stuff."

"I like you and stuff too."

"Why don't we go for dinner after school sometime? I could take you for your first ever Nandos?"

"I have no idea what that is, but it sounds perfect."

We lean in for another kiss, but a car horn stops us.

"Time to go," he says. Gosh darn it, Marcus has terrible timing. We pick up the carrier bags and leave the ancient gaudy apartment for the last time. I can't wait to get back to the world of Wi-Fi.

As we peer over the balcony, our jaws drop. Marcus and Freya have just pulled up in a ruby-red convertible.

*

Marcus

"Nice wheels!" calls Troy as he and Stevie descend the metal staircase.

"Apparently, the paperwork got filed wrong, so we got this at no extra charge!" I say, patting the bonnet. It's honestly the most beautiful thing I've ever seen – even Freya is in love with it. I caught her posing in the mirror with her sunglasses like she's a movie star.

I pop the boot and stow their bags away next to the frog umbrella I bought Freya. While Troy heads round to gawk at the car, I grab Stevie by the arm and take him aside.

"Hey."

"Hey," he says back.

"Stevie . . . err Steven. Thanks. You saved Freya, and I know she's your best friend, but I also, you know, care about her. So yeah. You're alright."

"We're cool," he says, and I slap him on the back.

We pile into the car, and I'm about to drive off when Freya says, "Wait!" and I slam on the brakes again.

"What is it?" I ask, thinking someone's about to die, or Dent's back from the dead.

"Now that we've shown them how cool it is, can we put the hood up? I *will* freeze to death otherwise."

Of course, she will. I hit the button, and the soft-top slides over us like a Transformer.

Now, we drive off. Shame I have to give it back tomorrow. Freya's already been looking up cars in the area for me, so I shouldn't be without for too long. She wants me to name the next one Fareborn because she's got some woman crush on her, and to be honest, so have I. I reckon I might take the real Fareborn up on her offer. Not now, though – I've got an exam to revise for tomorrow.

I glance in the rear-view mirror and have to double-take. Steven is cuddled into Troy, and they are holding hands. Figures.

I always thought they had a thing for each other. I clear my throat and catch Freya's attention. As I jerk my head in their direction, her eyes light up like Christmas has come early. She does a secret fist pump in the air before sitting back with a smug look on her face.

She's going to be insufferable for the next week, isn't she?

*

Steven

Does Freya seriously think I didn't see that secret fist pump? She's going to be so bloody annoying now, isn't she? At least she's happy for us. I'm happy for us.

Just as we zoom past the high street, Freya turns round and chucks a bag of sweets at me.

"Saw these in M&S and thought of you."

Reversy Percys.

"Har-har very funny. How long have you been sat on that?"

"Thought of it the moment you told me your powers are reversed. Figured it could be your superhero name."

"She even made me drive to the petrol station halfway out of town, so we could get them," says Marcus.

"Commitment, McCormac. Real commitment."

"Is this yet another weird British thing I don't know about?" asks Troy, and we all fall about laughing. I open the bag and start distributing the gummy pig faces among the four of us.

We drive past the beach for one last look. I feel a weird sadness to be leaving in between the immense relief. Yeah, this is the town I was drugged and almost made into a human lab rat, but it's also the place I learned to control my powers and where I first kissed Troy. I snuggle back into him, and he kisses the top of my head. Freya tries her best to suppress a squeal of excitement, but it sounds like she has gas.

I think I'm going to call Fareborn sometime next week. I still have so many questions for her about my powers, about DEMA, and about this job offer. Troy and I haven't discussed it yet, but maybe it could be fun to do it together. Blue-sky thinking, of course. But I want to give back. I want to help those who haven't been helped yet, and being a professional emomancer sounds pretty cool. Perhaps it is just a selfish thing – wanting to absolve me of the guilt that still stabs my heart at least twice a day.

I'll tell Freya and Troy eventually. It's sort of a big bombshell to drop today, considering everything that's happened. I have no idea how they'll respond, but I hope they understand. They've seen what I'm capable of if I'm not in control. So, for now, I'll keep it to myself. What's one more secret between friends?

We pass the limits of Grunsby-on-Sea and zoom onto the motorway. I have no idea what the future holds for me or Freya or Troy or even Marcus.

All I know is that we'll face it together.

I'm not alone. It was silly of me to ever think I was.

Right now, I'm happy – the happiest I've ever been in my life – and there's not a single trick in sight.

Acknowledgements

OVEREMOTIONAL wouldn't be a book in your hands without the work of so many people. It really does take a village.

Firstly, thank you to my wonderful agent, Lina, for being my stalwart defender and shipping Steven and Troy from day one. To my fabulous editor, Clem, who made the daunting editorial process feel like a breeze. To Hannah, Thomas, Campbell, Alison, and the whole team at Ink Road for tirelessly working to make this book a reality, as well as Emma, Jess, and Nina for bringing this book into the hands of readers.

There are a lot of other awesome people I need to thank: Elliot, Michael, Lewis, Polly (whose name I lovingly pinched), William Hussey, Ann Sei Lin, the goons of Pinch Punch for keeping me sane and stupid in equal measure (Emma, Pete, Lottie, Eoin, Sam, Ange, and Sophie). My eternal love to Alwyn Hamilton and Jennifer Bell, who I celebrated with in Venice when my first offer came in. Chris and Glen for being the best downstairs neighbours and D&D adventurers I could ask for.

An enormous thank you to my mum and dad, who gave me life (literally), love, and so much laughter. I owe so much to their relentless support and frankly pathological belief in me.

My undying gratitude to Bethan Morgan. She was the second person to read this book and sent me a glowing four-page essay, a detailed line edit, and unparalleled advice throughout this journey. A very good owl indeeeeeeed.

To my husband, John, I owe the biggest thanks of all. He inspired Steven's magic, read it first, *and* has been my Pushy Stage Mom from the beginning. Without his unshakable faith, keen insight, and love, this book would not exist. I like him and stuff.

And finally, to you for reading this book and sharing Steven's world with me. Thank you.